Fate had been cruel

A silent tear fell down Marlee's cheek. Of all the people to come through her boardinghouse, fate had to bring Lucas. Every day it taunted her.

The peddler said the little raven carving she'd accepted from him was supposed to grant her one wish, if she wished hard enough. But what good would one wish be when the one person she wanted most in this world could never be hers?

Her love for Lucas was real and the kind that would last a lifetime. But sometimes the best way to love was to let go....

Marlee sensed his presence in the room before she ever heard his footsteps. She turned to face him, and yearning squeezed her heart as he strode up to her, shirtless, jeans slung low on his hips. He moved with grace and power, and stopped only inches away.

Let him go, her mind said. But she lifted her arms and walked into his embrace....

Dear Reader,

Welcome to Four Winds, New Mexico! It's one of those magical towns where no one is who they seem to be...and everyone has a secret. And the sexy Blackhorse brothers are just the perfect tour guides we need.

Harlequin Intrigue is proud to present the FOUR WINDS miniseries by bestselling author Aimée Thurlo. She's been called a "master of the desert country as well as adventure" by Tony Hillerman, and a favorite author by you, our readers.

Join Aimée for all the stories of the Blackhorse brothers and the town in which they live. If you've missed #427, *Her Destiny* or #441, *Her Hero*, you can order them through the Harlequin Reader Service. In the U.S.: 3010 Walden Ave., P.O. Box 1325, Buffalo, NY 14269. In Canada: P.O. Box 609, Fort Erie, Ontario L2A 5X3.

Happy Reading!

Sincerely,

Debra Matteucci
Senior Editor & Editorial Coordinator
Harlequin Books
300 East 42nd Street
New York, NY 10017

Aimée Thurlo
HER SHADOW

HER SHADOW

® are trademarks of the publisher. Trademarks indicated with
® are registered in the United States Patent and Trademark
Office, the Canadian Trade Marks Office and in other countries.

Harlequin Books

TORONTO • NEW YORK • LONDON
AMSTERDAM • PARIS • SYDNEY • HAMBURG
STOCKHOLM • ATHENS • TOKYO • MILAN
MADRID • WARSAW • BUDAPEST • AUCKLAND

Printed in U.S.A.

ACKNOWLEDGMENTS
With thanks to Jennifer West, who gave me such
wonderful insights into her profession.
And to our special friend, Dr. Curm, who took time to
share his knowledge.

ISBN 0-373-22457-5

HER SHADOW

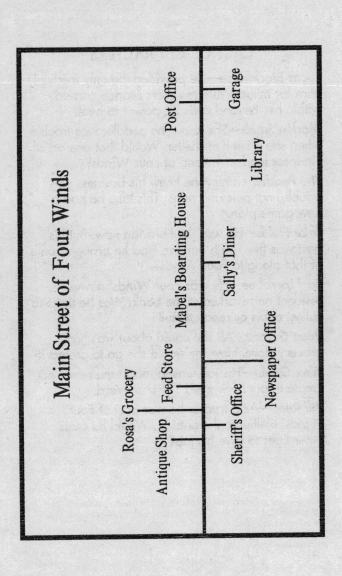

Main Street of Four Winds

Antique Shop

Rosa's Grocery

Feed Store

Mabel's Boarding House

Sheriff's Office

Newspaper Office

Sally's Diner

Library

Post Office

Garage

CAST OF CHARACTERS

Lucas Blackhorse—He provided the only medical care for miles. Were the scars Marlee carried within her beyond even his power to heal?

Marlee Smith—She knew the peddler was trouble when she gave him shelter. Would that one act of kindness lead to the end of Four Winds?

The Peddler—Everyone knew his business was trouble, not pots and pans. This time he had a new game plan.

Jake Fields—He was the librarian now. But his past was filled with danger. Had he brought some of that along to Four Winds?

Earl Larrabee—He was Four Winds' newest resident and worked at the bank. Was he there to collect debts or repay them?

Rosa Gomez—All she cared about was her grocery store. How far would she go to protect it?

Alex Green—His job was to report the news, not create it, but he wanted The Last Word.

Bill Riley—As a trucker he was part of Four Winds' lifeline to the outside. Would he cross other lines to save his job?

Prologue

Cloaked in the shroud of night, he crept forward, knowing the risks and not caring. The need for revenge pounded through him, pumping equal parts of courage and hatred with every beat of his heart.

She would pay, as she should have before, and justice would finally be served. It would go down as an accident. Then he'd move on and begin a new life, putting the past behind him. He was the only one who knew of her corruption and the fabric of lies that protected her.

As he approached his target, a vision flashed before him. He saw the accident and sudden flames engulfing the car. The vision thrilled and warmed him, protecting him from the icy cold wind that cleared the black skies above.

The purity of the flames would cleanse her soul. In that way, he'd be doing her a favor, which was more than she deserved. Acknowledging his own nobility filled him with a sense of purpose.

People around here insisted that Four Winds was a town of magic, where dreams came true. He was certain that his was about to. He slipped quietly underneath the old sedan, clenching a small penlight between his teeth. Wrench in hand, he located the brake line, then loosened the connection just enough to cause a drop of brake fluid to appear.

His work finished, he crawled out, moving back noiselessly into the shadows. Satisfied, he knew all he had to do now was wait. She'd been called an Angel of Mercy once, but now that Angel of Mercy was about to meet the Angel of Death.

Chapter One

Lucas Blackhorse enjoyed walking down the rough, time-worn sidewalk that bordered Main Street in Four Winds. He was on his way to meet his two brothers at the sheriff's office. Dressed in his denim jeans, a bright red Western shirt and a new pair of boots, he was ready to do his bit in today's parade and planning to enjoy it. The ladies in town always turned out in style for the event. It was going to be a great day.

He looked around at the old, Western-style storefronts, unable to suppress the smile on his face. He loved Four Winds. It was a part of him, though he had spent many years trying to deny that. Not that he regretted the time he'd been worlds away from New Mexico. He'd learned a great deal about himself and about life during his hitch as a Navy corpsman with a Marine recon unit in the Middle East. Being away from his older and younger brothers had given him a chance to get to know himself, learn his own strengths and his limitations and, most important of all, to accept himself just as he was.

Lucas smiled at Rosa Gomez, who was attaching the Stars and Stripes to the flagpole in front of her grocery store. A hundred years ago, it had been the Four Winds Emporium and it still fulfilled much the same purpose for the town's residents. A few doors down, Darren Wilson was sweeping the sidewalk in front of the feed store with a push broom that was more wood than bristles. Manuel Ortega, the town's only mail carrier, was up on a ladder with a squeegee, helping Postmaster Clyde Barkley clean the post-office windows in preparation for hanging the huge Harvest Festival banner. It would soon be displayed across the three storefronts.

The parade wasn't scheduled to begin for an hour, yet people were already gathering on the sidewalk, setting out folding chairs and buying soft drinks from the concession stand run by the high-school band.

As he turned the corner, Lucas practically tripped over Muzzy, Mrs. Burnham's terrier, trailing his leather leash. The small animal was the town's number-one escape artist.

Lucas snagged the leash and held the animal back so he couldn't run out into the cobblestone street.

Mrs. Burnham came running up a moment later, still trying to catch her breath. "There you are, you terrible little boy!" she said in a tone that the animal clearly interpreted as praise. He barked happily, his whiplike tail wagging.

Lucas handed the leash over to her. "There you go, Mrs. Burnham. You better keep a firm grip on that leash today. You don't want Muzzy running underneath a float once the parade starts."

"He's such a handful, but he's wonderful company," the elderly woman said, scooping up the little beast and hugging him to her chest. "He's going to be in the Pet Parade later on, dressed as a biker dog in his black leather vest. My niece Charlotte wants to show him."

The Pet Parade was an annual feature of the Harvest Festival. Kids of all ages would walk down the street with their favorite animal, everything from pigs on a leash to white rats on their owners' shoulders. Today everyone in town had the chance to be a celebrity.

Lucas checked his watch and picked up the pace, knowing Gabriel would be fuming by now because he was late.

His elder brother's adherence to schedules during the once-a-year parade was necessary, but it also made him hard to deal with for about a week beforehand. As sheriff, Gabriel was always on edge until the parade was over, but there was no denying that Lucas's older brother loved the town's yearly celebration as much as anyone.

Joshua, the youngest Blackhorse brother, held a different opinion. But then, that wasn't unusual. Although Joshua loved the parade, he hated anything that made him the focus of attention. Every year, Lucas and Gabriel had to pressure him into taking an active role.

As Lucas turned the corner and stepped into the alley behind the sheriff's office, he smelled the horses and heard the clicking of hooves against the cobblestone pavement. As arranged, Gabriel and Joshua were waiting with their mounts. Gabriel looked authoritative and impeccable in his sheriff's uniform. His giant of a younger brother looked formidable, too, wearing a bandanna around his forehead and a harvest gold shirt tucked into a leather-and-silver concha belt. His style, like him, spoke of the old ways while honoring the new.

"Where have *you* been, Shadow?" Gabriel snarled. "We don't have time to pick up your horse and you, too."

"Why don't you write me a ticket for loitering?" Lucas baited. The nickname "Shadow" had always gotten to him, especially back when it had seemed he'd had no identity at all, except when he'd been tagging along after his big brother.

"Don't start, guys," Joshua warned. "We have other things to do." A head taller than Lucas, and as strong as any horse, Lucas's younger brother reached into the bed of his pickup and lifted out his heavy Western saddle with one hand.

Lucas had to admit that his brothers had some cause to be angry. He was way behind schedule today. An emergency had come up at the clinic just as he'd been about to leave. Fortunately it hadn't taken him long to handle it, but he wasn't about to start whining to his brothers about how busy he'd been. He'd just buckle down and get ready. Joshua and Gabriel were working diligently, grooming the horses they'd be riding in the parade. Although Lucas was the only one who actually owned his mount, he was the furthest from being ready to ride.

"You two have become such sticklers for details you're starting to worry me," Lucas said good-naturedly. "Ease up a bit, will you? Where's your spirit of adventure?"

Gabriel stopped brushing the bay gelding he was going to ride and gave Lucas a narrow-eyed stare. His sense of humor was obviously out to lunch. "Right now, my spirit of adventure would like to pound your ugly face."

"Wishful thinking, Fuzz. You're getting soft and out of shape now that you have a wife to coddle you."

"After this is over," Joshua interrupted them, "I'd be more than happy to watch the two of you pound each other silly," he told his brothers, "but right now we owe it to the town to look sharp out there."

"Of course, that applies to me far more than you two. You guys don't have to look good anymore, being married and all," Lucas goaded playfully.

Gabriel slowly and deliberately placed the saddle blanket he was holding on his horse, then turned toward Lucas. "If there wasn't an ordinance against brawling, I'd make sure you'd have a real hard time impressing anyone today."

Joshua glared at Lucas. "Shadow, if you keep baiting Fuzz, he's likely to forget he's the sheriff and take a swing at you. I don't think you want to ride out today with a black eye."

"You're assuming Gabriel can land a punch," Lucas said casually, placing his saddle on his horse.

"It shouldn't be hard if I yank your head off and throw it right at his fist," Joshua said in a matter-of-fact voice that they both recognized as the last word in this discussion. The joke was definitely over.

"So I was a little late. What's the big deal?" Lucas shrugged, shaking his head and feigning innocence.

"Shadow, get a move on," Gabriel snapped. "We're already behind schedule. Remember that riding in this parade was your idea. You've been waiting for a chance to show off that mustang of yours."

Lucas patted the animal's neck, glad he'd taken the time to groom the magnificent beast this morning, before things got so busy. "Don't listen to them, Chief. They're just jealous because they know all the women will be looking at us today. Though why that should bother them when it's their own fault they both married, I sure don't know."

Joshua looked at Gabriel. "When the parade is over, I say we throw him into the nearest horse trough."

"Deal. But *after* the horses drink."

Lucas gave his brothers a smile filled with feigned sympathy as he finished adjusting Chief's bridle. "Remind me not ever to get married. It's made you both much too...sensitive," he said, and slipped easily onto the animal's back. "Not to mention *slow*."

Laughing, he rode to the end of the alley, stopped and waved for his brothers to join him.

MARLEE STOOD on the weathered old sidewalk, taking in all the sights. Four Winds was a special town. There was a kinship here between the citizens that really became apparent on a cool autumn day like today. She saw people stepping aside, giving Lanie Blackhorse all the room she needed to maneuver and a helping hand, as well. Lanie was so pregnant she had trouble sitting *or* standing for long, but nonetheless, she was here for the parade.

As Marlee watched the mother-to-be, a sad twist wrenched at her soul. Years ago, she'd given her heart and her life to helping expectant mothers. Walking away from

that career had torn her apart for a long time. Lost in
thought, she ran her fingers over the jagged scar that ran
from her left temple to her chin, a brutal reminder of days
long past.

A loud cheer from the crowd brought her thoughts back
to the present. Life went on, and so had she. Dwelling on
the past would accomplish nothing.

Marlee edged closer to the street as the Blackhorse brothers came into view, signaling the start of the parade. The
three Navajo brothers looked as different and as individual
as any men could be. Gabriel wore his sheriff's uniform
and cap. Joshua, the gentle *hataalii*, took a position between his two brothers, as he often did. Then Marlee's gaze
drifted to Lucas, and her heartbeat quickened.

His lean, muscular build made him look fabulously mas-
culine as he sat astride his horse. He exuded an easy confidence that made her breath catch in her throat. Then he
smiled, and Marlee heard her own soft sigh echoed by the
other women in the crowd.

In her opinion, and that of many others, Lucas was the
handsomest of the Blackhorse brothers. A yearning for
something she didn't dare define filled her as she watched
him ride down the street. Refusing to analyze her feelings
any further, she joined the others in the totally partisan
crowd and cheered as the three horsemen rode by. As they
passed, Lucas caught her eye and grinned. She smiled back,
suddenly glad she'd worn her new Western shirt with a red
yoke that exactly matched his.

The Harvest Festival float came next, a crepe-paper-
and-tissue-stuffed cornucopia fashioned of chicken wire.
Underneath, almost completely covered by the float deco-
rations, was someone's old pickup. The high-school band
followed, playing a loud and enthusiastic approximation of
a Sousa march.

Marlee hurried along the sidewalk, staying just behind
the Blackhorse brothers as they made their way to the high-

school football field, where the parade would end. There, booths were set up for folks selling crafts, candied apples and just about anything imaginable. There'd be games for the kids, and all kinds of contests. Harvest Festival was definitely the biggest day of the year in Four Winds.

As she approached the football field, Marlee's gaze kept returning to the Blackhorse brothers. They moved as a unit, their superficial differences nowhere near as important as the family ties that bound them. As she arrived on the field, she saw that Nydia, Joshua's wife, had given Lanie a ride in her Jeep so they could be there to meet their husbands at the end of the line.

Marlee was close enough to see the pride in Lanie's eyes as she greeted her husband. Gabriel smiled tenderly at his pregnant wife as he dismounted. When he went to give her a hug, Lanie tilted her head up and gave him a long kiss.

"Hey, if I'd have known I'd get this kind of welcome at the end of the ride, I'd have galloped the whole route," Gabriel teased.

Lanie smiled and playfully reached up to kiss him again.

Nydia helped Joshua unsaddle his mount. They complemented each other's efforts, working together beautifully as a team.

Marlee felt like a fifth wheel as she looked at her friends. Nydia and Lanie looked radiant, having found what they were searching for here in Four Winds, something Marlee knew she would never have. She sighed. She *had* found something valuable, however—peace from the false accusations that had followed her for so long. She had also found a way to feel useful, running the boardinghouse. And she had found friends, particularly the Blackhorse family.

Marlee walked past the pen holding Bradford the buffalo, the high-school team's mascot. Bradford was the last of the bison herd Mauro Martinez had owned when he'd attempted to raise and sell beefalos, a cross between cattle and buffalo. When the venture had not proved profitable, he'd sold off the herd, except for the placid Bradford.

Bradford had found a new home here at the high school, in the barns run by the agricultural club. The animal had lived up to expectations, remaining docile even through the rowdiness of high-school football games—just as long as the kids brought a few chocolate-chip cookies to bribe him with. This particular animal had developed a passion for chocolate-chip cookies when Mauro had used them as a training aid.

Marlee heard the buffalo stamping the ground as she walked past. "Sorry, Bradford. I don't have any cookies today."

Marlee heard something snap, then the animal grunted loudly. Surprised by the noise, she turned her head. As she did, Bradford butted his massive head against the gate, forcing it open.

She wanted to run, but fear and shock paralyzed her. In the time it took for her to draw her next breath, the beast turned in her direction and bellowed angrily.

Somewhere in the back of her mind, she became aware of the thunder of hoofbeats behind her. Then, the next instant, she felt herself being lifted off the ground and pulled up onto the rider's lap. Strong arms enveloped her as the horse brushed past the immense beast.

Marlee was aware of everything. The hard muscles of her rescuer's chest, the warmth of his breath against her cheek. Without turning to look, she knew the man holding her was Lucas. Her body knew his on an instinctive level she would never have been able to explain. As her hips pressed intimately against his thighs, a shudder traveled up her spine.

Lucas reined in his mount fast, turning to block the way between Bradford and the crowd as Gabriel and Joshua jumped into action, trying to herd the bison back into his pen. But Bradford was angry, and not in the mood for cooperation. He never quite charged at either Gabriel or Joshua, who were on foot, but instead tried to get around them, showing less patience after each foiled attempt.

"I think he's seen too many football games," Gabriel yelled. "He knows about head fakes and fancy footwork."

"They have to entice him, and for that they'll need cookies," Marlee told Lucas. Moving quickly, she slid off Lucas's horse, on the side away from the angry bison, and ran to Mrs. Tapia's booth. The woman made the best chocolate-chip cookies in the county. As she drew near, Mrs. Tapia held out a paper bag full of cookies.

"Here you go. If you can't bribe him with these, then it's hopeless."

Marlee thanked the woman, then circled around behind Gabriel. Taking a handful of cookies, she waved them in the air for Bradford to catch the scent. "These are hoofs-down the best you'll ever get, Bradford. Want a bite? Come on. Let's go back to your pen."

Marlee felt like a new kind of pied piper as the animal's focus shifted away from Gabriel and Joshua. He lifted his nose high, sniffing the air.

"Don't take your eyes off him," Lucas warned.

Marlee tossed one cookie on the ground before the animal, then moved toward the pen. Bradford snatched up the fallen cookie, ate it in one gulp, then happily trotted over to where Marlee had set down the open bag on the far side of the pen. As the animal discovered the cache, Marlee hurried out the gate.

"What happened to the latch?" she asked as Lucas swung the gate closed behind her and fastened it shut. "Did he break it?"

Lucas shook his head. "It works fine. Whoever fed him this morning must have been in a hurry and didn't close it properly."

Joshua gestured toward the animal. "Something aggravated him. Maybe it was a bee or wasp."

"Or some troublemaker looking for a little excitement," Gabriel said, bending down to pick up a large rubber band that was on the ground just inside the stall. "I'll ask around and see if anybody was watching Bradford just before he got out. I'd like to talk to the idiot responsible for this."

As more townspeople arrived at the school grounds, Lucas and Gabriel checked the latch again to be sure that the gate was securely fastened.

Lucas took Marlee's hand and gently pulled her aside. The warmth of his touch spread through her like fire.

"Great idea about the cookies," he murmured. "You deserve a reward."

His deep voice reverberated, dancing along her nerves like thunder from an approaching storm. "What did you have in mind?" she asked. She'd wanted to keep her voice steady, to act cool and collected, but as she heard her voice waver, she realized she'd failed miserably. She cleared her throat and hoped Lucas hadn't noticed.

"What do you say we skip the booths and take some time for ourselves? I've arranged for backup medical help here today, so I won't be missed for a few hours." He gestured toward his horse. "I understand you've been unable to get out to the spot in the mountains where you planted your camomile. Come with me now. Chief can carry double. Your car may not make it on that sorry excuse for a road, but Chief won't have any problems at all. We can put what we gather in the saddlebags."

The thought of riding with Lucas anywhere made Marlee's heart race, but she recognized it as a foolhardy and reckless temptation. She wouldn't torture herself with what could never be hers. She started to say no, but Lucas interrupted her.

"I know your herbal remedies help a lot of the senior citizens. The tea you make with that camomile is important to you and them. This is your chance. Are you game?"

She couldn't say no, not when he'd put it that way. "I

do need that camomile." Actually, she'd probably need tons of the soothing drink herself after she came back from that ride. Lucas's company was anything but calming.

"It's settled, then." Lucas turned Chief around, lifted her onto the saddle, then mounted behind her in one fluid motion. "Hang on to the horn and don't worry about a thing. I'll have my arms around you. You won't fall."

Marlee forced herself not to tremble as she felt Lucas's body against hers again. She was playing with fire, but surely even she deserved some carefree moments on this special day. His strong arms encircled her, imprisoning her in a tender trap as they trotted away. Having ridden as a teen, Marlee soon moved in rhythm with the animal and Lucas.

A melting warmth seeped through her. She was nestled securely between the horn, the saddle and Lucas. As she shifted, she felt his body tighten. Knowing she could affect him like that filled her with an intoxicating exhilaration.

They rode in silence to where she'd planted her herbs, and soon were on the way back, the saddlebags filled. As they crossed an old logging road on the way to town, she caught a glimpse of movement to her right. It was only for an instant, but Marlee saw the peddler clearly. He was walking slowly back to his van, which was parked just off the little-used track.

"Did you see him?" she gasped as they started up a nearby trail.

"See who?"

"The peddler. He was back there on the logging road," she said, cocking her head.

Lucas sucked in his breath with a hiss. "Let's go take a look." He reined the horse in, turned him around expertly on the narrow trail and trotted back to the spot in the road Marlee had indicated. There was nothing there now except a set of worn tire tracks and the faint impression of a pair of boots.

"Are you sure it was the peddler you saw?"

"He's not a person anyone from Four Winds would ever mistake," she said in a muted voice. "Good things happen whenever he comes, but the town always pays a price in blood and tears."

"From the tracks, I'd say he's on the way to town now. If we hurry, we may be able to cut him off before a new cycle of trouble begins."

Chapter Two

Lucas kept a sharp lookout for the peddler on the way back to Four Winds, but neither the man nor his distinctive old van was anywhere to be seen. "Are you sure it was the peddler?" he asked for the second time.

"Yes, but I just don't understand this. Where could he have gone? We should have spotted him by now, cutting cross-country like this."

Lucas urged Chief forward at a steady lope. "There's no telling what'll happen if he shows up in town today. He won't exactly be the guest of honor at the festival." Lucas remembered the peddler's last two visits. The gift he'd given Lanie before she'd become Gabriel's wife had almost destroyed the eldest Blackhorse brother and the woman he quickly came to love. Lucas's brother Joshua and his wife had fared no better when Nydia had accepted the peddler's gift to her.

The blackening clouds overhead suddenly flashed white, and an enormous clap of thunder shook the ground. Chief's ears went flat back, and he broke into a gallop.

"Easy boy," Lucas said, tightening his hold on Marlee as he eased the mustang back to a trot. "He hates thunder, but he'll settle down. Don't worry. I'll hang on to you," Lucas murmured, pulling Marlee back against his chest.

She was soft against him, trusting, though Chief's reac-

tion had scared her. Lucas felt a fierce sense of protective-
ness stealing over him, though he knew he had no right to
those feelings. His life, his loyalties, belonged to Four
Winds. They needed a medic here, and he was it. There
was no room for a woman in his life. But it was more than
that. Theirs was a town filled with secrets. Marlee had never
pried into his, and he'd returned the favor, though it was
obvious she'd had troubles in her past. The town's conven-
tion of privacy was a barrier that had kept them both safe.

Still, as she leaned back against him, desire knifed at his
gut. Her hair smelled of wildflowers. He felt her stir against
him, and knew that she was as acutely aware as he that the
desire burning between them did not require their consent
to exist.

Sometimes it felt as if some unnamed power in Four
Winds was trying to bring them closer, though neither of
them had given in to that attraction. Of course, if Marlee
had allowed it, and he could have been sure of not hurting
her, he would have been willing to see things through—to
explore his hunger for the sweet, gentle woman he now
held in his arms.

He let that dangerous thought die right there. Marlee deserved better than that. She didn't need halfway proposi-
tions any more than he did, and he wasn't able to go more
than halfway. He needed his independence. They were both
better off not taking things to a point neither was prepared
to handle.

As he slowed Chief to a fast walk, his forearm brushed
against her breast. That contact seared through him, and
instinct guided him to lower his head to press a kiss against
the soft column of Marlee's neck. As his mouth drew close,
the skies opened, and thick sheets of rain poured down on
them.

Marlee shivered. ''If the peddler is in town, it looks like
nature just found a way to cool off any hostility people
might be showing.''

It cooled off a few other things, too. Frustration ate at Lucas as he cradled Marlee against his body, knowing she was cold and hoping the fires within him would help warm her. He wished that it could have been different for them, that duty didn't demand that he continually suppress his feelings for her. It would have been so easy to just let go, to let passion rule. But that would have been a dangerous course for them both.

By the time they arrived at the end of Main Street, the roads and sidewalks were empty. The town's residents peered out from behind storefronts and doorways. As Lucas and Marlee approached the high-school campus, they saw that the water-soaked booths had been abandoned.

It took about a half hour to assure them both the peddler's van wasn't in town. Marlee was shivering by the time they approached the boardinghouse she operated. Although the rain had all but quit, the wind had risen and was cutting right through their damp clothing. Her house looked warm and welcoming.

"Why don't you come in with me? Chief can graze on the lawn while you dry off."

"You talked me into it," Lucas said, a shudder traveling over him.

"You're freezing, too, right?"

As Lucas dismounted and reached up to help her out of the saddle, he stopped suddenly, listening. Before she could move away, he reached for her hand, stopping her. "Wait. Stay still for a minute."

A stint with the Marines had taught him to trust his instincts, and something sure didn't feel right here. He waited for a long moment, listening, his body tense, poised for trouble.

"Do you hear that?" he asked at last.

"What?" she whispered, slipping down to the ground easily.

"It sounded like a car engine." He crouched down and

studied the imprint of tires evident in the sandy gravel of Marlee's driveway. "Someone came through here a very short time ago, and these tracks look familiar." He slipped the bridle off his horse so it could graze easily, then led the way down the narrow drive into the backyard.

An old VW van had been driven all the way around to the rear of the house, and was parked out of sight of the road. Marlee inhaled sharply. "It's the peddler's van. I'd know it anywhere."

"Yes, but where is the peddler?" Lucas turned around in a circle, trying to spot the old man. The van's engine was off now, but still ticking occasionally as it cooled.

"Let's go find him." Marlee walked around Lucas before he could stop her.

"Slow down. Something isn't right here," Lucas cautioned as they approached the vehicle.

As they drew near, the sliding door opened halfway. The peddler appeared at the opening, soaked to the skin, and looking pale and disoriented. He stepped down slowly, resting against the side of the vehicle. His breathing was labored. "I need help," he mumbled weakly.

Marlee didn't hesitate to offer him a hand. "Let's get you inside the house where it's warm. Lucas will take a look at you there."

"Wait," Lucas protested. "I'd rather take him to my clinic. I've got my equipment there, and some medical supplies. Besides, it may be dangerous for you to have him here, particularly if anyone sees his van."

The peddler turned, took a step, then suddenly collapsed.

Lucas reacted instantly, dropping the bridle he was carrying and catching the old man before he hit the ground.

"Looks like the choice is out of our hands," Marlee said, picking up Chief's tack. "You can't take him anywhere until you assess his condition, and to do that, we're going to have to get him out of this weather."

"I don't have my medical kit here," Lucas objected,

hurrying toward Marlee's house with the old man in his arms.

Marlee paused for a moment. "There's a doctor's bag in the house. It's been here a long time, but it should contain enough to get you started. It has a stethoscope, a BP cuff, a positive-pressure ventilator, sterile packs, sutures, all kinds of things."

Lucas was reminded once again that Marlee's past, like that of so many other Four Winds residents, was tucked away behind a closed door that hid many secrets. But something about her assessment of the situation, and her familiarity with medical terminology, attested to experience in the field. Wondering about her more than ever, he followed Marlee down the hall carrying the peddler.

By the time he stepped through the doorway of an empty guest room, Marlee had already pulled down the covers of the bed.

Lucas lowered the peddler onto the mattress, and was pulling off the man's wet boots when Marlee came in holding a towel and a dry change of clothes. "This shirt and pants aren't in the greatest condition, but they're clean and dry and about his size. They were here in an old trunk when I moved in. While you change his clothes, I'll go find the medical bag."

Marlee left the room, and returned a few minutes later holding a black medical bag.

Lucas met her gaze as he took the bag from her, not asking but hoping she'd offer some explanation.

"Use whatever you need from it. It's been sitting around gathering dust for years."

Lucas started to ask, unable to suppress his curiosity, but a soft moan from the peddler brought his thoughts back to the business at hand.

As she left him alone again with the patient, Lucas opened the bag. Everything looked used, but in good condition. Taking out the BP cuff and the stethoscope, he began to work.

Lucas checked the man over thoroughly, verifying there were no signs of trauma, but the peddler's skin was hot and feverish. Using a digital ear thermometer from the bag, he verified that the peddler's temperature was elevated, but not dangerously so. Finding such a modern piece of equipment in the old medical bag, however, disturbed him. It didn't fit with Marlee's story that the bag had been sitting unused in the house for a long time. Of course, she might have added that item recently herself, but he had a feeling there was more of a story behind the bag than she was telling him.

Lucas continued his examination. He knew nothing about the peddler, except that he appeared to be Navajo. There were lots of crazy stories linking the peddler to Four Winds, some connecting him all the way back to the time when the town was founded. But those were nonsense. The man would have had to be a century old. Of course, it was possible that the business had been handed down in the peddler's family. Unfortunately the man was in no condition at the moment to be questioned.

The only thing Lucas could say with any certainty was that the peddler was over fifty, though he exuded an agelessness that was not uncommon among the Dineh, the Navajo people.

The peddler's faded gray eyes slowly blinked open, and he tried to pull himself up onto his elbows to look around.

"Easy there. You're safe here," Lucas said, gently pushing the man back onto the bed. Lucas silently noted that his patient's pupils were not dilated. He seemed alert and aware of what was happening. That, in itself, was a good sign. "How are you feeling?"

The man brushed a lock of salt-and-pepper hair from his eyes, and tried to moisten his parched lips with the tip of his tongue. "Thirsty."

Lucas went to the bathroom, returning with a glass of water. "I'm going to need to get some medical information from you before I can help much. Do you have any idea what's making you so weak?"

The peddler closed his eyes, then nodded slowly. "It is the flu, nothing more. Many years ago I would have shrugged this off, but I am an old man now, and my body complains at the slightest problem."

"Okay, let's start there. How old are you?"

His eyebrows furrowed. "I don't really know. Nobody's ever asked, and it was never important to me."

The answer didn't sound as odd to Lucas as it might have seemed to an Anglo. He'd heard similar explanations from others of his tribe. "Can you approximate?"

He exhaled softly. "I remember buying gas at twenty cents a gallon, if that helps. Years are just memories of the seasons to me. Time passes, that's all I know."

Hearing those words from this peddler, particularly because of all the crazy stories, made the hairs on the back of Lucas's neck stand on end. That was the problem, he concluded. An undeniable mystique followed this man. The legend had grown from a grain of truth, like a misshapen pearl. "Your name?"

"I was called 'Gray Eyes' when I was a boy. Now I'm just the peddler. No one asks my name anymore. It isn't necessary for buying and trading. I don't take checks."

Frustration tugged at Lucas, but he knew the futility of giving in to it. He decided to concentrate on the present. "How long have you been sick?"

"Two or three days. I was on my way here to Four Winds when my body began to hurt. My skin burned. I had some herbs, and I used them, but they weren't enough. Not this time. That's why I came into town. I knew I could find a place to rest here at the boardinghouse and, once I found you, I was also certain you'd help."

"Have you ever been to a doctor?"

"No. It hasn't been necessary."

"But you came to find me. Why?"

The eyes that held Lucas's seemed to gleam with an inner fire that spoke of power barely contained. Lucas saw himself reflected in the silver pools and, for a brief instant, he felt a sense of recognition, an acknowledgment that fate was demanding its say.

"You and I are alike in many ways, nephew," he said, using the traditional Navajo term to denote respect or friendship between an old man and a young one. "When others come to us for help, we are honor bound to find ways to meet their needs. That's why I know I can count on you. You've walked that difficult road between the old and the new. I knew you would help me while still respecting my ways."

The words disturbed Lucas more than they had a right to. "You and I are not the same. I try to make things better for people, but every time you come into town, trouble is close behind."

"I've heard those rumors. But what of the blessings? You should learn from your brothers and stop seeing only the darkness in the world. The gifts I gave their wives brought good, too, not just evil. Remember what you were taught. Everything has two sides, and only by seeing and accepting that reality can you find harmony and peace."

Lucas studied his features carefully. "You sound like a Navajo, Uncle."

"I come from no tribe and all tribes," the peddler said, and closed his eyes again.

"You're speaking in riddles."

"I'm tired now. If you can, find something that will ease the ache in my body so I can rest. I won't be staying any longer than I have to."

"As always," Lucas muttered, stepping toward the door.

"Yes, as always."

Lucas heard the whispered words. They touched him like

an ill wind, and left him feeling more unsettled than ever. He quickly uttered a Navajo blessing, one Joshua had taught him.

As Lucas stepped out into the hall, he saw Marlee there, waiting. Compassion and determination were etched in her features. He had no doubt that, even if the entire town had stormed her front door demanding she run the peddler out, she would have refused. The peddler had chosen wisely all the way around.

"Our patient should recover. It appears he's got a mild case of the flu. What he needs is rest, and some aspirins to bring the fever down. He's unlikely to accept more than that."

"I'll bring him something warm to drink. He needs to build his strength up, even if he's not hungry."

"That'll be good, but my advice is for you to stay away from him as much as you can."

"Why? What are you worried about? I'm not afraid of the flu."

Lucas shrugged, hating the vague feeling he had that assured him something was wrong, without giving him the ability to define it in a more logical manner. "I don't believe in superstition. That means I don't believe all the crazy stories about the peddler. But I'd be a fool to discount the things that I *do* know about him. This man is the perpetual outsider, stirring up trouble, yet never really becoming part of it. I have a gut feeling a lot of what he does is premeditated."

"Maybe it's a skill he's had to acquire. He survives with very little," Marlee said quietly. "People learn to get by."

The empathy in her voice surprised Lucas. She had revealed much about her own life with that statement, which was something Marlee seldom did. He was about to explain why he was worried about leaving her with the peddler, a man who'd caused so many problems for his family, when the pager on his belt went off. "I have to use your phone," he said quickly.

Lucas hurried to the living room and dialed the number on the display. It took only a few minutes to learn that the Ayers boy had taken a bad fall off a haystack while rushing to get their last cutting under a tarp before the rain. His parents were worried. Lucas checked his watch and swore briefly under his breath. "Don't move your son at all, and keep him warm and dry. I'm on my way."

As he hung up the phone, Lucas saw Marlee watching him. "I have to go," he said, checking his watch. "By now my backup medical help has already left for Santa Fe. He only promised to give me a few hours, and there's an emergency I have to take care of. A boy's been hurt, and I need to go check him out."

"Do whatever you have to. I'll be fine. I'll heat some soup and give the peddler that and some aspirin, as you suggested. I'll also monitor his temperature, if he'll allow it."

"I'll be back as soon as I can. Hopefully there won't be any other calls, but with the storm and it being Harvest Festival, who knows?" He drew in a long, deep breath. "The peddler came here to find me. He's linked to my family, you know, not just to Four Winds, so do me a favor and be careful. I don't want you hurt in any way, not because of me."

Marlee smiled gently. "Stop worrying. I can handle it."

He stood there, sensing her fears, yet knowing that she would not welcome any comfort from him. Despite the friendship that had grown slowly between them in the past two years, to Marlee independence meant the right to her secrets. It was her lifeline. His, too, he had to admit. It was in freedom that he'd found his purpose. He didn't want to tie himself down to any responsibility that could interfere with his duty to Four Winds.

Lucas opened the door to the occupied guest room for a

last quick look. The peddler's even breathing told him that the man was dozing. Lucas walked to the bed and studied his patient. Had he really been in pain, in the throes of a high fever, would he have been able to sleep so quickly, without even having taken one aspirin?

Lucas sensed a change in the sleeping man, and the atmosphere in the sick room suddenly became charged, as if the air itself had been sparked with a burst of electricity.

"You have no need to worry. All is as it should be," the peddler mumbled, his eyes still closed.

Lucas knew the old man's response shouldn't have unsettled him. His brother Joshua had that same ability to sense another's presence without having to rely on his vision. Still, his body grew tense again in readiness for trouble. "See to it that you repay in kind for the help you've been given here today. I want no harm to come to the woman in whose house you've taken shelter."

The light in the hallway dimmed as a loud clap of thunder echoed outside. Inside the guest room, lightning illuminated the walls and bed in strobe-light flashes.

"Go. You have a patient who needs you now," the peddler whispered.

Lucas looked down at the old man, aware of how little he knew about his new patient. The peddler's face was hidden in shadows, only a memory in the reduced light. "I'll be back," Lucas said.

The peddler's breathing became slow and even again.

Lucas met Marlee in the living room and reached out to take Chief's bridle from her. "If you need me for anything at all, call my cell-phone number. I won't be far."

"Would you like to take my car? I'll make sure Chief's okay."

He shook his head. "I can take a shortcut if I ride, and be there in half the time. It's a good thing you had that medical bag or I'd have to go over to the clinic first."

Their hands touched as he took Chief's bridle. Marlee

laid her hand over his gently and held it there for a second. "Call me if there's anything else you need. I can drive out to the clinic for it. And be careful out there. The rain's picked up again, and it's one heck of a night for a ride."

Her touch sent a rush of desire through him like lightning. He wondered if she'd pull away if he leaned to kiss her, and hated that it mattered to him. Either way, there was no time to find out now.

As another peal of thunder shook the house, he heard Chief whinny.

Marlee stepped back. "Call me when you can. I'll be worried until I hear you're back at home—or at least the clinic."

The words filled him with pleasure.

"Friends are important to me," Marlee added, her voice husky with emotion. "Take care."

Lucas hurried through the rain to where Chief was standing, pawing the ground. He quickly replaced the bridle, adjusting it deftly. Marlee's explanation hadn't fooled him. Whether she was willing to admit it or not didn't change the fact that they were more than just friends. The attraction between them had been too strong from the day they'd met. He'd made sure Marlee had thought he wasn't interested in her. That had given her the illusion of safety around him, something he'd felt she'd needed, particularly when she'd been his patient. But there was no safety for either of them whenever they were together now.

"I envy you, horse. Everything you need to be happy is out here at your feet." Lucas climbed lightly into the saddle and rode off, ignoring his wet clothes and the cold, driving rain. As he left the boardinghouse behind him, his thoughts remained on the woman he'd wanted to kiss, and the peddler who'd appeared out of nowhere and stepped into their lives.

Chapter Three

Marlee went into the guest room, feeling a bit apprehensive though she couldn't explain why. The truth was she wasn't scared of the peddler. She wasn't even afraid of what the townspeople would say if they learned he was here. She'd met opposition before and knew exactly how to handle it. She also knew she'd done the right thing by giving the old man shelter.

The memory of Lucas's concern still warmed her, and maybe that was part of what was troubling her. Sometimes it felt as if destiny was determined to bring them together. Yet she knew she could never allow that to happen. She was a woman with an unforgiving past, and an uncertain future. A man like Lucas could never be a part of her life.

As she stepped inside the room with a tray of soothing herbal tea and some aspirins, she saw the peddler was sitting up.

"You look better," she said cheerfully. Hiding her thoughts was something she'd learned to do well around everyone, except maybe Lucas.

The lines of weariness on the peddler's face eased, and he smiled. His eyes gentled, and as they captured hers, she saw compassion mirrored in them. For a brief instant, another emotion flickered there, but it was hard to identify.

Resignation, perhaps? In the time it took her to consider it, his expression became inscrutable again.

"I brought you some camomile tea, and these are the aspirins Lucas said to give you. Is there anything else you'd like? Maybe something to eat? I have some soup warming on the stove."

"If it isn't too much trouble," he said. "It's been a while since I've been able to eat."

Marlee nodded, then returned to the kitchen. She dished up some of the homemade soup she'd made earlier that day. Placing a hot bowl and two slices of oatmeal bread on a tray, she returned to the room and placed the tray on the bed before the peddler.

As she watched the old man eat, she realized just how hungry he was. She turned away to the window and looked out, hoping she hadn't been staring. Protecting a person's pride was important. She knew how hard it was to be on the road all the time, making just enough money to keep body and soul together. It must have been particularly hard for a man the peddler's age. Remembering the lean times she'd experienced before she came to Four Winds, and the loneliness of that life-style, she felt a pang of sorrow and sympathy for the peddler.

Hearing the phone ring, Marlee excused herself and went out to the living room to answer it. As always, the sound of Lucas's rich, deep voice sent a thrill through her. For one heart-wrenching moment, longing for what she knew she could never have filled her.

"How are things going?" he asked.

"Everything's fine." She knew her voice sounded too soft, and she cleared her throat to mask it. There was no way she was going to burden Lucas by allowing him to think that he owed her anything or was responsible for her safety.

"The Ayers boy will be okay, but I have two more patients coming by the aid station. I won't be able to get back to your place for a while.''

"You don't have to come back tonight. Your patient's doing just fine," she explained, wondering why she'd hesitated to mention the peddler specifically. Was it a touch of paranoia about conversations held via the phone? She shook free of the thought, and tried to concentrate on the present. "If there's a problem, I can always call you."

Marlee heard someone start speaking quickly on Lucas's end of the line, and he put the phone down. When he picked up again, he said, "I have to go. But I'll stay in touch."

Marlee hung up the phone slowly. Something undefinable always shimmered in the air between her and Lucas. Denying that was as useless as trying to ignore the way the scar on her face tingled whenever she grew aware of her appearance, which happened often when she thought of the handsomest Blackhorse brother.

Regret clung to her spirit, chilling her like a winter storm. Lucas was free, and it was in that freedom that his love for life shone through. He made the most out of each minute. That was what she loved best about him. Capturing Lucas would be like trying to still the breeze or stop the river from flowing. She wouldn't do it if she could, and she doubted anyone else could. That thought comforted her.

When she went back into the guest room, Marlee was surprised to find the peddler sitting at the desk. He was leaning over something he was working on, holding something small and dark in his hands.

"Are you okay?"

He looked over at her and smiled. "I'm not used to all the luxury you have here in your home. The roughness of this wood I'm whittling helps me relax."

"That's beautiful," she said, peering over the table to take a closer look. The delicate carving of a bird captured her attention immediately. Scarcely aware of what she was doing, she ran her index finger over the carved feathers. It looked so lifelike.

"It's a raven. Raven is said to carry magic, and give a person the courage to face all the mysteries about themselves and the world around them. It brings awakening."

"That's a beautiful thought," Marlee said, letting him know gently that, while she appreciated that beauty, she did not believe in such things. She looked at the empty bowl and cup. "Shall I bring you some more food?"

"You have been very kind to me, and at some risk to yourself. I don't forget a kindness. It's not something I encounter very often."

Once again her heart constricted. She, too, knew a little about the cruelties of life.

Marlee picked up the bare tray. "If you feel up to it, I'll just bring you a bit of dessert. I hope you like apple pie."

He nodded. "I will continue to work on this."

Marlee went back to the kitchen. As she started to cut the pie, a soft rustling sound outside caught her attention. She froze in midmotion, listening, and heard the sound again, followed by the faint rumble of a car engine. Wondering if Lucas had returned, she walked to the front door and stepped out onto her porch. She looked up and down the street, but there were no vehicles anywhere in sight.

Disappointed, she decided to go back inside. That's when she heard a scraping noise nearby. Marlee turned her head just as a blur of white fur came crashing down on her.

She yelled and staggered back, but the bundle in her arms attached itself to her, digging its claws into her shirt. "Winston, you dumb cat!" she said, recognizing the trespasser as her neighbor's pet. "Don't you know enough to stay off rooftops on a blustery night like this?"

The cat began to purr, completely undisturbed by her reprimand.

"Oh, never mind. Come on in. It's cold out here. Mrs. Sanchez must have locked you out again. I'll give you

something to eat, then let her know where you are." She
put the cat down, and he shot through the doorway, making
a dash for the sofa in the living room.

Marlee walked over, picked him up and carried him into
the kitchen, where she placed a small dish of tuna on the
floor before him. "You stay here while I take care of my
other guest."

When Marlee returned to the guest room with the peddler's dessert, she found him leaning back in the chair, his
eyes closed. For a moment, she thought he'd fallen asleep
again, but then his eyes opened and she realized he'd only
been resting. She placed the tray on the table, and he eagerly took a forkful of pie. While he was eating, Marlee
reminded herself again not to watch or hover like an an-
noying waiter.

Finally, after he'd taken his last bite, he picked up the
carving of the raven from the table and held it out to her.
"I want you to have this. It isn't much, but it's all I've got
to pay you for your kindness."

She started to reach for it, but then drew back her hand.
He had few enough things, and this he could sell for food
or gas. She wouldn't take what little he had. "You don't
have to repay me. I was glad to be able to help."

"Don't deny an old man the dignity of repaying a debt,"
he said softly.

Marlee knew all about the sentiment he was voicing.
Pride was sometimes the only thing left to a person. She
could not turn down the gift he offered. After all, this
wasn't like the artifacts he had carried. It was a new carving, not something with a history or curse attached. Surely
there was no harm in accepting it.

"If you think of it as magic, it may not seem quite so
ordinary," he said eagerly as she took it from his hands.
"Let's say it will give you one wish, if you wish *really*
hard," he added with a gentle smile.

"Oh, but this isn't ordinary at all," Marlee protested. "It's really a beautiful carving."

"Just remember that true magic always reaches an open heart."

His insistence on weaving a fairy tale just for her was touching. "I'll treasure the gift always. Thank you."

"A debt has been paid," he declared somberly.

As Marlee walked out of the room, the raven carving grew warm in her palm. She studied it carefully, entranced by its lifelike quality. The bird's eyes were so beautifully carved and hand rubbed that they appeared to glow with their own natural light. She placed the raven on the bookshelf in the living room, then as she walked toward the kitchen, she felt a gust of wind and heard a loud bang.

Marlee hurried, knowing that the back door must have blown open. The catch was worn, and it sometimes came open when the front window wasn't completely shut and the back door wasn't locked. As she stepped into the kitchen, she saw she'd been right about the door. Marlee shut it and made sure it latched securely, then looked around for the cat. Winston was gone. So was the tuna and most of the pie that she'd left on the counter. The rest was on the floor.

As she began to clean up the mess, she saw vehicle lights flashing through the window. Wondering if she was about to have company, she went out for a closer look and saw the peddler's van backing out of her drive.

Horrified, she stared at it for a stunned moment. Someone had stolen the old man's vehicle; that was the only explanation. Marlee ran out into the street, but by the time she got there, the only vehicle within sight was the tail end of a pickup rounding the corner.

Worried about how the old man would take the news, Marlee hurried back to the guest room, trying to think of a way to break it to him gently.

She stood by the closed door for a minute gathering her

composure, then knocked. There was no answer. Opening the door slightly, she looked inside. The bed had been made, and the peddler was gone. On top of the desk was a scrawled note with a one-word message, "Remember."

LUCAS SLAMMED HIS HAND down hard on the steering wheel as he headed back into town. His last call had been a wild-goose chase. Someone's idiotic idea of a prank. He thought of Marlee, picked up the cellular phone, then set it back down on the seat beside him. She wouldn't appreciate another call. She'd see it either as meddling, or maybe as proof that he didn't trust her to take care of things on her own.

He really liked Marlee, but her pride could be like an impregnable wall. Sometimes he just wanted to push past that, to force her into his arms, feel her softness against him, to know the taste of her. So far sanity had always prevailed and he'd reined in those urges, knowing the danger of indulging those crazy thoughts and feelings. He knew himself too well. The attraction he felt for Marlee was too strong to ignore, but hormones had a way of scrambling a man's brain. The fact was he had his life exactly the way he wanted it. It had taken him years to get this point. He was finally satisfied to be himself, not Gabriel's shadow. And he had stopped feeling guilty every time he lost his temper. Who cared if he couldn't match his little brother's self-control, either?

As far as he was concerned, the middle kid had the worst of it. Fuzz had always known he'd follow in their dad's footsteps, and Joshua had always known his heart was in the old ways. Lucas, on the other hand, hadn't had a clue as to who he was or how he'd live his life until just a few years back, when he'd joined the military. He'd been a good warrior, but an even better medic. It was while serving as a corpsman that he'd discovered his talent. He was an excellent diagnostician, with an unerring gift for getting to the root of what was ailing a person physically or emotionally.

After completing his enlistment, honing those skills, he'd returned to Four Winds, where he'd become a valuable asset to the town as the only full-time medical professional. At long last, he'd earned his place here alongside his brothers. He was an integral part of Four Winds by his own right now, and he had no intention of letting anyone or anything interfere with the duty he'd accepted.

As Lucas pulled up in front of Marlee's house, his truck backfired loudly. He cursed. One of these days, he was going to buy a truck that didn't announce his presence with fireworks.

Marlee pulled back the curtain, then came to the door. She wasn't smiling, and as he left the truck, he wondered if she was going to read him the riot act for waking her and the neighborhood up at midnight. He had to admit she'd have a right to be mad. As he drew closer, stepping up to the front porch, he noted that she wasn't dressed for bed. The expression on her face wasn't anger or even annoyance. It was concern.

"What happened?" he asked quickly.

"The peddler left. I gave him something to eat, and he said he felt better so I left him alone to rest. But when I went to check on him later, he was gone."

Lucas wasn't sure whether to be relieved or angry. "His temperature was above normal. I hope that he didn't mistake the relief the aspirin gave him for actual health. His symptoms will undoubtedly persist for a few more days, if it *was* the flu."

"I wish he'd stayed, but I expect he'll be okay. He's used to taking care of himself. When you're on the road, you get really good at that after a while," Marlee said quietly.

Lucas followed her inside, and dropped down on the living-room couch, surprised by the weariness he felt all of a sudden. "Were you, like Lanie, on the road awhile before you ended up here in Four Winds?"

The question hadn't been one he'd meant to pose out loud. He knew better. It was a violation of the code of Four Winds. Everyone's past was his or her own.

She shrugged. "Let's just say I know that life-style very well. You've got to be tough to make it."

Her proud strength felt like a challenge to him. He stood, walked across the room and looked out the window, putting some physical distance between them. He needed to keep his thinking clear around Marlee. As he stared outside, he saw that only one star was visible at the moment. It peeked through a break in the cloud layer, bright against the gloom of night, but utterly alone.

"Believe me when I tell you that I can't imagine anyone freely choosing that peddler's solitary life-style," she said. "I wonder what he's running from."

"Interesting choice of words," Lucas commented, regarding Marlee intently as he returned to the couch. Marlee was physically close to him now, yet she couldn't have been further out of his reach if she'd been in a separate galaxy.

"Don't get me wrong. I don't think the peddler's all bad. He honors his debts, and he cares about people in his own way. He knew I wouldn't accept any of his wares, but he still insisted on repaying me, though he had no money."

Lucas sat up abruptly. "What did he give you?"

She scowled at him. "Relax. I told you I wasn't going to accept any of his antiques. Those always come with a history. This was just something he was making. It's a little bird. A raven. It's about the size of my thumb, but it's very pretty. And it's brand-new. He finished carving it here." She went to the bookshelf and took it down.

Lucas stared at the little carving suspiciously. It looked new; Marlee was right about that. Maybe the gift *had* been an act of kindness from the peddler, and the object wasn't cursed.

"It's okay. He really was just trying to repay me, not create more problems."

"Yeah, well, I've heard similar stories before. It seems he's always trying to repay someone's kindness when he gives them a gift that throws their lives into chaos."

"Ease up. This is just something he was whittling. It's perfectly harmless, unless you're ready to believe that he's some kind of supernatural being. And near as I can figure, supernatural beings don't get the flu, do they?"

"I still don't trust him. There's too much history between that man and Four Winds."

She held the fetish out to Lucas. "See for yourself. It's harmless."

He took it from her hand, half expecting it to burn him the way the skinwalker bowl had done to Gabriel. Instead, the fetish felt completely ordinary, just a piece of wood.

As he returned the carving to her, their fingers touched. He felt the shock of *that* contact all through him. There may not have been any heat coming from the fetish, but there was plenty of warmth in her touch. He forced himself to look at something other than Marlee as he put his thoughts back in order.

Marlee moved away, replacing the carving on the shelf. "You look really tired. Since I don't have any boarders right now, why don't you just sleep here?" she asked. "I've got plenty of rooms." A restless breeze blew through the half-opened front window, tossing a curl of her hair onto her cheek where the scar lay. She tugged her hair down, trying to cover the scar, and turned away from him.

Lucas longed to touch her, to kiss away that aching self-consciousness. The scar did nothing to hide her beauty, though she couldn't seem to recognize that, and would never have believed him had he told her. His gut knotted with the effort it was taking for him to stay away from her.

Slowly one thought formed and became crystal clear in his mind. He couldn't stay here tonight. To be separated from her by only one thin wall…he wouldn't get any rest.

Lucas came up with the first convincing excuse he could think of. "I need to get back and work on my grant requests. The first-aid station depends on the town and the state for funds, and I've got to make sure the paperwork is completed in time. If it's not ready, I may not be able to get the funds to keep the place supplied." It was the truth, though he certainly didn't intend on working on all of those tonight. Still, though he'd given it his best shot, he knew he hadn't sounded very convincing. He hoped Marlee would understand.

She nodded, her neutral expression making it impossible for him to say if she was disappointed or not. It didn't matter. He had to leave now, before he said or did something they'd both regret. He was tired, and that always made him less cautious.

As he walked to the door, she picked up a feather duster she'd left on the end table. "You're going to clean house now?" he asked, surprised.

"I can't sleep, so I might as well clean." One of the feathers of the duster got stuck in the crack of a drawer that was slightly ajar. As she tugged it loose, something fell with a thump onto the floor.

Marlee picked the object up and stared at it, eyebrows furrowed. "What the—?" Recognition flooded over her features, and she suddenly held a finger to her lips as she showed it to him.

It took him a moment to realize that what she was showing him was a small microphone. Before he could stop her, she dropped it back onto the floor and stepped on it hard.

He expelled his breath in a hiss. "I wish you hadn't done that. My brother Gabriel might have been able to track the bug back to its owner."

She stared at the pieces on the floor. "You're right.

Sorry. My temper got the best of me. This is *my* home, and having someone do this to me…"

Lucas rubbed his eyes, wishing he could will away the cobwebs around his brain. "Who do you think wanted to listen in on your conversations?"

"Nobody's been here recently except the peddler, and somehow I have real trouble believing he left that behind. I think we can rule you out, too," she said with a thin smile, "and I certainly wouldn't bug myself." As she looked at him, her expression suddenly gentled. "Look at you, you're practically dead on your feet. You really shouldn't be driving anywhere right now. Take one of my guest rooms before you fall on your face."

Lucas hesitated. If someone had placed a listening device in her house, it was possible she was in danger. The way he felt right now, he expected he wouldn't be much protection even if he stayed. He was so exhausted, a two-year-old's punch would have probably knocked him out cold. Still, whoever had left that bug here wouldn't know that, and he'd feel better knowing Marlee wouldn't be alone in the house.

"I *do* need some rest—you're right about that. I have several calls to make tomorrow, and unless I get some sleep I'm going to be worse than useless."

"Then that's that—you'll stay. I'll get a room ready and I'll even stop cleaning. It's time I got some rest, too."

"In the meantime, try to think back and pinpoint when someone could have left that little microphone here." As he followed her to a guest room down the hall, another thought struck him. "Assuming it wasn't the peddler's bug—and I, too, doubt that—whoever planted that bug knows by now that the peddler was here tonight. *That* may turn out to be a problem."

Marlee thought back to her last conversation with the peddler. No one would take that story about the wish seriously—if they'd even managed to overhear it in the first place. At least that was one thing she wouldn't have to worry about.

She placed fresh towels by the bed for Lucas and turned back the bedspread. "Get some sleep now. There's nothing pending that can't wait until tomorrow."

"Have you considered the possibility that wasn't the only mike?" he asked.

"Yes, but it still doesn't matter now. It's not like we're going to be chatting up a storm in our sleep," she answered.

As she left the room, Lucas dropped down onto the bed. The room smelled like Marlee, of the meadow flowers she loved. That special touch she gave everything around her imbued even the air itself with the gentle power of her femininity. It was like her, an undeniable comforting presence that made no overpowering demands.

He stood, unsnapped his jeans and stripped off his clothing. With one careless yank, he tossed back the covers and crawled into bed. As the gray mists welcomed him and he fell asleep, he felt Marlee's presence enfolding him, offering him peace.

Chapter Four

Marlee was fixing breakfast in the kitchen when she heard Lucas start moving about. His footsteps had been welcome this morning. These past few months had been especially lonely for her. It was rare for her not to have at least one boarder, but since the end of summer nobody had come to stay.

It was late fall now, and the house had begun to echo with a desolate emptiness that unsettled her. She really didn't like living alone. She needed to feel needed. These long stretches of silence made her feel as if everything in her life were standing still in preparation for something that had yet to be defined.

Marlee thought back to another lifetime, when her career had defined who and what she was. Her love for her work and her passion for life had been a circle she had thought could never be broken.

Those days were gone now, and the present was all she had. She stroked the scar on her face absently, reminding herself of something she could not ever possibly forget even without that physical reminder.

"Good morning," Lucas greeted, heading directly for the coffeepot.

The sight of him made a slow fire burn within her. His shirt was half-open, hanging loose over his jeans. He exuded an easy masculinity, a rumpled sexiness that only some men could carry off.

"We need to talk," he said, spooning some sugar into his mug.

She placed two strawberry waffles on a plate for Lucas and poured more batter into the waffle iron. "What about?"

"We have to search for other hidden microphones, and we have to go talk to my brother and see if he has any ideas who'd want to bug your home or, for that matter, who'd even own a bug like the one you found in the first place. It's not the sort of thing you can just pick up at Rosa's in case you ever need one."

"There are no other listening devices here. I've already searched the house—well, all except the room you were using, which I'll do while you eat."

"Let my brother and me help you look around some more. It can't hurt."

Marlee stiffened, then forced herself to relax. "It's not necessary." Now, more than ever, she needed to firm up the emotional barrier between them. The incidents of the past day seemed to be tearing down the defenses that had kept each of them safe from an involvement neither was prepared to handle. But the effort to resist him was tearing her apart. She felt as if something heavy were slowly collapsing inside her.

"You may be in danger. You can't ignore this," he insisted.

"I'm not planning to." She set down the waffles before him. "In fact, I've been thinking all night about who could have left that bug here, and why." She sat down across from Lucas. "I know it hasn't been here long. I clean the main rooms every day and I would have seen it. My guess is that it has been here less than twenty-four hours. I think someone must have seen the peddler arrive. They sneaked in and hid the bug to find out what was going on. I heard someone outside last night, and the back door flew open at one point. An intruder could have easily taken advantage of the high winds and the noise of the storm."

It was the only thing that made sense. Her past hadn't caught up to her here, at least not yet. If it had, the signs would have been clearer and as inescapable as the darkness that descended each night.

He poured honey on his waffles and started eating. "Did you see anyone?" he asked between bites.

"I saw a pickup going around the corner right after the peddler left, but it wasn't visible long enough for me to identify."

Lucas's fists clenched and unclenched on the table. "This peddler has targeted women my brothers have befriended in the past. I don't want his games to hurt you. Will you get rid of that carving he gave you?"

Lucas's hands were strong and supple. His restless energy teased her imagination. Those hands were meant for caresses that would add warmth to even the coldest winter night. The walls around her heart shuddered.

Aware suddenly of the direction her thoughts were taking, she turned around and got busy cleaning the counter. She had to pay attention to what he was saying, not to her own daydreams. "The raven is just a simple carving. I won't give it away out of fear of what some ignorant person might think about it. The day I start doing things because people are pressuring me to act in a certain way, I'll lose what I like most about myself—my ability to be my own person. Can you understand and accept that?"

"I'll have to, won't I, darlin'?"

"True." She smiled, pleased he'd used the endearing term, though she knew it was just a word and nothing more.

"You're too stubborn for your own good."

His deep voice, low and rough, danced over her skin, making her feel vibrantly alive. Even the air itself crackled with expectancy as they both stood their ground. For a breathless second, neither spoke.

Finally, with a smothered oath, Lucas stood. "If you won't let Gabriel and me search this place, I better get started on today's other jobs. I've got to stop by home, change clothes, then go on my rounds."

"I think I'll go up to the high school and check on Bradford. I like animals, even that crazy buffalo. I hope I didn't make him sick yesterday by giving him all those cookies."

"I doubt that," Lucas said with a smile. "Ask around and see if anyone's figured out whether somebody did shoot him with that big rubber band Gabriel found. That sure might have been the reason he got so riled up."

Her body tensed. "Are you thinking that what happened was more than just a kid's prank?"

He shrugged. "Maybe I just worry too much." His hand circled her wrist, and obeying an instinct that demanded it, he pulled her toward him. "I won't be far if you need me—for anything."

He brushed her hair away from her face so tenderly that a soft sigh escaped her lips. For that moment, the scar didn't matter to Marlee. Only Lucas's touch and the spiraling world of emotions it sent through her held any reality.

As if sensing her response, he drew her closer. A silver heat ribboned through her, making her tremble. There was no question of her pushing him away. An endless wanting overwhelmed any thoughts of resistance.

His kiss began slowly, with all the patient skill of a man experienced in the art of pleasuring a woman. He teased her mouth gently, insistently, showing her a need so primitive and so powerful it tore apart her caution and logic.

Danger, pleasure and longing combined, making her weak at the knees. It felt so right to be in his arms.

An eternity later, when he eased his hold reluctantly, she drew in a long, shaky breath.

"I've got to go now," he said, his eyes dark and smoldering. "Watch yourself."

Marlee shut the door behind Lucas, still tasting him on her lips. She'd wanted that kiss for such a long time. A silent tear spilled down her cheek as she forced herself to face her situation clearly. To Lucas it had only been a pleasant kiss, nothing more. To pretend differently was only to lie to herself. Lucas could have any woman he wanted. He was the most eligible bachelor in town. What had just happened between them changed nothing in the overall scheme of things. It had been nothing more than a bright flicker of light in the darkness of her soul.

Marlee took several deep breaths. At long last, when her hands stopped shaking, she went to the shelf and picked up the beautiful raven.

"One wish...wish upon a star," she said, smiling. She'd give anything to believe in magic, but real life wasn't so easy. "In this case, I guess it would be cravin' upon a raven," she continued, replacing the carving with a self-conscious laugh. "Nope, it just doesn't have the same ring to it."

After searching the room Lucas had slept in for any listening device, she came out empty-handed. Marlee considered everything that had happened, weighed her options and decided it would be a good idea to at least meet Lucas's request halfway. In light of her intruder, perhaps placing the carving in her safe-deposit box for now would be the wisest thing she could do. Marlee wrapped the tiny wooden bird carefully, tucked it inside her purse and walked out to her car. She'd had enough stolen from her in her life. Nobody was going to take anything else.

As the rickety old engine started up, Marlee caught a whiff of a peculiar scent. It reminded her of the odors inside Charley's garage. Her car had certainly spent a lot of time there in the past year. She eased out of the driveway in Reverse, but when she moved her foot to the brake to stop before she reached the street, the pedal went all the way to the floor. The sedan continued to roll backward, picking up speed as it rolled out into the street. The tires squealed as she turned sharply to stay in the road.

Marlee struggled to contain her rising panic. Driving backward down the hill was hard enough with working brakes, let alone without any means of slowing down. She pressed her foot down harder on the pedal, her mind rejecting the undeniable certainty that hope and force would not be enough this time.

Suddenly a small toddler ran out into the road, oblivious to danger. The tiny girl was busy chasing a bright red ball that was directly in the path of Marlee's car.

With a scream lodged in her throat, Marlee turned the wheel hard, catapulting the sedan over the low curb and into a field covered with scrub brush and weeds. The car bounded and squealed as it crashed into a waist-high thicket. Marlee pulled frantically on the emergency brake, and finally the car came to a jarring stop.

A young woman came running up a few seconds later as Marlee tested her limbs, verifying nothing was broken.

"Are you okay? What on earth happened?" Marlee's young neighbor, Jean, forced the driver's-side door open against the brush, then crouched by Marlee, looking for injuries.

"The brakes wouldn't work at all," Marlee managed to explain in a shaky voice. She took several deep breaths, assuring herself that she was fine and the danger was past. The problem was she knew better. The danger wasn't past. Not at all.

"Do you want me to call Lucas? He should check you out to make sure you really are okay."

Marlee gathered herself enough to shake her head. "I'm not hurt. Your daughter?" She managed to push the last two words past the formidable lump that had formed at her throat.

"She's back in the yard. You swerved so sharply you never even got close to her."

When she heard the news, Marlee's heart started beating again. "I saw her running out into the street, but there was no way for me to stop!"

"Come over to my house," Jean said. "I'll fix you something warm to drink, and you can try to relax."

Forcing her body to move, Marlee pulled herself out of the car. Jean's offer was tempting, but it was becoming clear that something was very wrong in her life right now, and the last thing she was about to do was get her neighbor any further involved. If there was one thing this last incident had brought home to her, it was that someone *was* after her. It was beginning to look as though she'd been wrong. The past had caught up to her. What frightened her most was the knowledge that as long as her enemy remained faceless, there was little she could do to fight him.

THAT AFTERNOON, Marlee stood in the repair bay at Charley's garage. He'd come by and towed her car, promising to fix whatever was wrong.

"You've got a loose connection in your brake line," Charley said, crawling out from beneath the car. "The fluid all drained out."

"I found that out this morning—the hard way. How did it happen?" she asked, forcing her voice to remain steady.

"Age, wear, take your pick. Your car is old, let's face it. There are probably more rebuilt parts on that chassis than original ones by now. But no matter how many things I replace, there'll always be something else wearing out. You've hit that point with this car."

"Can you fix the brakes for me just one more time?"

"Sure, but you better start thinking of getting yourself another vehicle soon. This one's on its last legs."

Depressed, Marlee slowly crossed the street to Sally's Diner, desperately wanting some company to cheer her up.

Marlee walked inside the door just as Sally stepped out of the kitchen, wiping her hands.

"Hey, I heard about your accident this morning," Sally began, concern evident in her voice. "Sounds to me like you were awfully lucky."

Hearing that her accident was already public knowledge in town didn't surprise Marlee in the slightest. She sat on one of the counter stools and forced a smile. "The price of having an old car keeps going up," she said, and explained.

"Well, just be glad that here in Four Winds nobody *really* needs a car except teenagers," Sally added with a chuckle. "I mean it's hard to go parking at Serenity Hill if you haven't got transportation." She placed a cup of coffee in front of Marlee. "This is on the house."

"Oh, you don't have to do that," Marlee said, reaching into her purse.

"It's just a friendly gesture, not charity," Sally answered with a tiny smile. "Don't get your feathers ruffled."

Marlee chuckled. Everyone knew she had a giant chip on her shoulder about accepting handouts. "Thanks. By the way, if anyone comes through town looking for a place to spend the night, send them my way."

"It's been a while since you had a boarder, hasn't it?" Sally noted with a thoughtful nod. "But don't sweat it. There's something really weird about the way things work around here. Your back is against the wall one minute, then your luck turns and everything's fine, again. That's the way it works here in Four Winds. You know that."

"Yes, it seems that way, doesn't it?" she observed, not really expecting an answer.

Marlee finished her coffee, said goodbye to Sally, then went outside. The air was crisp today, and the sky a beautiful shade of blue. She set out for home, determined to enjoy the walk as she came up with a plan. There was nothing better than action, the right kind, to restore her confidence. All her life, she'd prided herself on achievement, knowing that it was the greatest gift anyone could give to themselves. She'd found purpose through it, following her own course, setting her goals with single-minded determination. To her, few evils could have matched dreams without motion, without the power of direction only the dreamer could give them.

It was that philosophy that had given her the strength to go on when everything she loved had been taken from her. Now she was being challenged again. This time, however, she had much less left to lose and was in a far better position to fight. No one would ever force her into doing anything she didn't choose to do.

Hearing footsteps behind her, Marlee stopped and turned around. The street was empty, yet she knew someone was back there. She hadn't just imagined it.

A stab of fear shot through her. The suspicion that someone was stalking her made it difficult to think clearly. Her mind instinctively drifted back to another time when she'd known only too well the stark terror occasioned by helplessness.

Marlee struggled to gain control. She wasn't helpless now. Time had taught her how to survive. Marlee continued walking until she reached the alley that led to the library, then she ducked down it, out of sight. Hidden in the shadows, she held herself motionless, barely breathing.

She listened, keeping her body still until every single muscle in her body ached. Minutes passed, but no further sounds reached her. She peered out, but no one was near. Blaming it all on a case of nerves, she stepped out of the alley. Unfortunately Rosa came around the corner just then, and ran right into her.

Rosa yelped, dropping the case of pickles she'd been carrying. Startled, Marlee also jumped back, slamming into the wall.

Rosa crouched down, picking up the shattered glass jars

and placing the pieces into the cardboard box. "Oh, no! See what you made me do?"

"I'm so sorry!"

"What were you doing? Were you waiting to pounce on me, or did I just get lucky?"

"I ducked into the alley—" She stopped speaking abruptly. She couldn't tell Rosa what was going on. The woman would gossip about it to the entire town. "I discovered my blouse had come unbuttoned. I ducked into the alley to button it up again, out of view."

Rosa sighed loudly. "Every jar of pickles is broken."

"Let me pay you for it," Marlee said. "It was my fault."

"Well, yes, it was." Rosa considered the matter for a moment, then shook her head. "No, never mind. It was an accident. Let's just forget it."

As Rosa returned to her grocery store, Marlee resumed her trip home. Everything seemed to be unraveling for her now. In a way, it was almost as if every story she'd ever heard about the peddler was coming true, and the bad luck that preceded the good was just starting. Of course, that was utter nonsense. Curses and magic didn't exist.

Twice on her way home, she thought she heard faint footsteps, but invariably no one was there when she looked back. The incidents disturbed her despite efforts to brush her concerns aside. By the time she arrived at her boardinghouse, her hands wouldn't stop shaking. Marlee walked inside, and as she turned to lock the door, she felt a wave of relief wash over her. She'd be safe now.

Exhausted, she went to the sofa and dropped down unceremoniously onto it. Looking across the room, she began to wonder how much of what had happened had been nerves, and how much of it had been real. That's when she saw her face reflected in the mirror. Dark red lines had been drawn on the surface of the glass. As her face stared back at her, the crimson network of trails made her appear hideously disfigured—a portrait of pain and ugliness like noth-

Her Shadow

ing she'd ever seen. It made the scar she actually bore seem almost insignificant.

Her heart in her throat, she stood up, covering the scar on her cheek with her hand as she walked to the mirror. She was staring at her reflection in shocked silence when she saw a shadow flitter across the wall. The realization that someone was in the house with her made her blood turn to ice.

Terror swept over her. Forcing herself not to run, she headed for the door. To her surprise, no one tried to stop her.

She'd just reached the porch when she heard something fall onto the tiled kitchen floor with a crash. Without hesitation, she raced down the driveway toward Jean's house.

Chapter Five

Twenty minutes later, Marlee stood in her front yard, shivering and waiting for Gabriel to give her the all-clear. Time passed slowly. Finally he came out onto the porch, and waved for her to come in.

Marlee was walking up to the door when a loud backfire echoed all around her. The sound, though jarring, was familiar by now. She turned her head in time to see Lucas pulling up in his old pickup.

As he got out of his truck, Marlee could see the concern on his face. She wasn't sure how much he'd already heard about the accident or the break-in, but she was glad he was there.

As Lucas came toward her, that clean, pure strength he used to face the world emboldened her, supporting and bolstering her courage. There was no doubt that he'd seen the best and worst of human nature while he'd served his country in the military, but Lucas had the kind of nobility that belonged to a man who could not be compromised. He faced the world on his own terms. That bravery was the quality she admired most about him.

"Are you okay?"

She nodded. That those had been his first words meant the world to her, though she knew that she was probably giving them more weight than they merited.

"The house isn't in bad shape," Gabriel said, coming out the front door to join them, "but the damage was certainly calculated to hurt you."

"I already saw the mirror. Is it like that in the other rooms?"

He nodded. "All the mirrors, and any paintings or photos that had a woman's face, have been scratched up, too. But the intruder is gone. You can come in now."

Marlee followed Gabriel inside, and Lucas followed close behind.

"Whoever did this wants to remind you of your scar in a major way," Gabriel stated.

"As if I could forget?" she said, smiling mirthlessly. Then she noticed the magazines on the kitchen table. The face of each model had been ritually savaged with a red marker. "He's made them all ugly," she observed, forcing her voice to remain steady.

"My police experience tells me something like this is often the work of a jealous suitor. Have you been seeing someone, or have you broken up with anyone recently?" Gabriel asked.

"No, and let's face it, even if I'd tried to keep it a secret, if I had been dating someone, you and everyone else in town would have known. Four Winds is a very small place in that respect."

"Tell me about your scar," Gabriel said quietly. "How did you get it?"

She looked at him in surprise. "That happened a long time ago, before I came to Four Winds."

"I'm aware that no one in Four Winds is used to being asked about their private business. But if there's anything that might link that injury with what's going on now, I have to know about it."

"My scar is a result of a car accident. There's nothing mysterious about it. My guess is that someone's decided to remind me it's there just to hurt my feelings."

Gabriel held Marlee's gaze for several seconds, and she forced herself not to flinch.

"I'll accept that for now, but I don't think you should stay here alone until we find whoever is responsible for this. Lucas told me about the hidden microphone you uncovered, and I heard about the problem with your car from Jean. That's too many nasty surprises to be coincidental. Something's going on, and it's not good."

"I think Fuzz is right," Lucas added in a gentle, persuasive voice. "If you had boarders right now, it would be different, but it's not safe for you to be here alone."

"I'm not afraid, and I'm not about to allow anyone to run me out of my house."

Lucas expelled his breath in a rush. "Let me tell you something I learned while I was in the military. Young soldiers want to handle everything with a head-on assault. The ones with experience learn the value of an aggressive defense. They wait for their enemies to expose weaknesses, then they strike. That's how they live to keep fighting."

"I can't ask anyone to put me up. If someone is after me, I'd be endangering my host. That's not right."

"Then I'll stay here with you," Lucas said.

The thought sent a spiraling warmth all through her, but somehow she found the strength to say no. "I appreciate the offer, but I can stand on my own. I'll get out my shotgun and keep it handy. I'm perfectly capable of defending myself if it comes to that."

Lucas started to protest, but stopped when he saw the determined look on her face. Marlee knew he hadn't given up. He was just trying to find another suggestion she wouldn't object to.

Marlee walked them to the door, keeping her hands in her pockets so the men wouldn't see them shaking. "I appreciate your concern and your help, but I'll be just fine."

After saying goodbye, Marlee shut the door, and looked around the empty room. Though she'd put on a brave front

for the benefit of the Blackhorse brothers, the fact was she
was scared. She had no way of knowing for sure if her
enemy was part of her past or her present. But one thing
was clear. Whoever it was wanted to destroy her, body *and*
soul.

LUCAS FELL INTO STEP beside his brother as they walked to
their vehicles.

"There's more to this than she's saying," Gabriel said.

"So she's got secrets. That's no surprise in Four Winds,
and you know it."

"Yeah, but there's something way out of the ordinary
going on here, Shadow. That's why you've been hovering
over her since yesterday morning. You want to tell me
what's really going on?"

Lucas said nothing for a few moments, then finally broke
the silence. "Follow me to my clinic. We'll talk there."

When they arrived, Gabriel settled into the chair across
from his brother's desk, and put his feet up on the blotter.
"So tell me, Shadow, what the hell is this all about?"

Lucas pushed Gabriel's feet off his desk, then leaned
against the front of it, regarding his brother thoughtfully.
"I've got some news you're really going to hate. The peddler paid another visit to Four Winds." He filled his brother
in on the details of the events at Marlee's, then added, "He
was genuinely sick when I saw him, but he recovered too
quickly, and that bothers me. I wonder if it could have been
a trick." Lucas shook his head. "No, never mind. I'm just
being paranoid. That fever was real—I know my job."

"I'll keep an eye out for him," Gabriel said. "Maybe
this time I'll get to catch up to the son of a gun before he
disappears."

"I wish you luck," Lucas muttered.

"Meaning you don't think I'll catch him?"

"No one ever has. I think a new series of events is about

to unfold, like before, and there's not one damn thing you, me or anyone else can do to stop it.''

IT WAS MIDAFTERNOON. Marlee stood waiting for Earl Larrabee, the bank teller, to bring her the safe-deposit box. She'd intended to put the peddler's gift in the bank earlier that day, but she'd never quite managed it.

"Will you be long, or shall I wait?" Earl asked.

"This will just take me a moment." Marlee smiled at him.

Earl was always willing to help. He was also one of the best sources of information around. She'd heard from Sally and several other local women how much Earl loved gossiping with the ladies.

"Did you enjoy the Harvest Festival? The rain almost ruined it for everyone this year," Marlee prompted, hoping to get him started.

"Rain or not, it was sure exciting. That incident with Bradford was totally unexpected. Of course, right now everyone's more worried about the flu bug that's going around."

"Flu bug?"

"Haven't you heard? People have been coming down with it all day. Mrs. Torres and several of the high-school kids ended up having to go home. The feed store is short-staffed, and only Clyde is still at the post office."

"When did this all start?"

"Beginning this morning. It's hitting people hard and fast."

As they left the vault and stepped out into the lobby, Marlee saw the elderly Mrs. Murray standing by the teller's window. She seemed agitated and abnormally pale. Before Marlee could figure out what was going on, Mrs. Murray suddenly sagged against the counter, then crumpled to the floor.

Marlee rushed to her side immediately. The woman's

breathing was strong, but she was clearly feverish. Flu among the elderly wasn't something to fool with. "She's fainted. She'll need to be taken to the clinic now," she said quickly.

"Let me," Earl said. He tossed his safe-deposit key ring to the bank manager, then picked up Mrs. Murray as if she weighed no more than a child. "I'll take her over there in my car."

"I better ride with you and hold on to her," Marlee said. "If she regains consciousness, she may be frightened and need some reassurance."

As they drove over to Lucas's, Marlee's thoughts began to race. These symptoms were similar to those she'd seen affecting the peddler. Although his recovery had been fast, she doubted Mrs. Murray would be quite as lucky. The woman was in her eighties, and at her age, any illness carried a potentially high price.

"Looks like Lucas already has his hands full here," Earl said as he pulled up.

Several cars and pickups were in the small parking area. When they entered, half the people were milling around nervously, and more slumped in chairs waiting to be called. Just then, Lucas came out to call his next patient.

Seeing Mrs. Murray cradled in Earl's arms, Lucas threw open the door to the examining room. "Hurry. Bring her in," he urged, giving Marlee a concerned glance as he held open the door.

Earl stepped through the doorway, carrying Mrs. Murray. A moment later, the door swung closed behind them.

Marlee studied the people around her in the waiting room. The younger ones didn't look quite as ill as Mrs. Murray, but their flu symptoms were pronounced. Half were coughing, and all were pale as ghosts. Worry and exhaustion marred the expressions of the parents who had brought in their children for treatment.

Marlee took in the room at a glance, assessing the situation and suspecting that the worst was yet to come. Epidemics like these seemed relentless at first because of the explosive nature of an outbreak, and influenza was particularly contagious.

There was only one sure thing she could really count on now. She'd pay a high price if the news ever got out that she'd housed the peddler when he'd come into town sick with similar symptoms.

Deciding to make herself useful instead of worrying about things she couldn't change, Marlee helped the patients in the reception area as much as she could. Though an illness like whatever was striking down these people wasn't in her area of expertise, she knew she could at least help the moms by keeping their kids distracted.

She played with some toddlers, finding herself wishing that her life gave her more time with children. As she sat on the floor with a fussy two-year-old, entertaining him by playing with a hand puppet from the clinic's toy chest, she realized just how much she missed the life she'd left behind. But those days were gone. They were part of the price she'd paid to restore peace to her troubled soul.

THE HOURS PASSED QUICKLY. Mrs. Murray was transported to a hospital in Santa Fe by private ambulance service. The other patients were eventually attended to, and sent home with instructions. As stillness finally descended over the clinic, and a sense of hard-earned peace filled the rooms, Marlee stood by Lucas's office window watching the first snow of the year. It was late October, but still a bit early for snow. Tiny flakes fell silently, dancing in the beams of the front-porch lights.

"We're supposed to get several inches tonight, and the temperature is expected to keep falling," Lucas commented, looking outside and rubbing the back of his neck wearily. "That'll be a blessing. School will probably close, people will stay indoors and maybe that'll help slow down this flu outbreak.''

Compassion filled her as she studied his expression. A network of lines radiated from his eyes, and Marlee felt an uncontrollable urge to touch and smooth them. But aware of the temptation their slightest contact evoked, she remained still.

''I appreciated your help here today,'' Lucas added. ''I can't thank you enough for sticking around.''

''It felt good to be useful. If you ever need an extra pair of hands here, I hope you'll call me. I enjoyed it.''

''You may regret that offer, but I'll remember it,'' he said with a weary smile. ''By the way, you came here with Earl and he's long gone. Are you ready for me to take you home, or can I talk you into helping me bring in supplies from my storage building first? I've depleted almost everything I keep in here, and I'll need to have things accessible in case of a crisis later tonight or tomorrow.''

''No problem. I'll be glad to help you restock. Let's get to it.'' There was nothing waiting for her at the boarding-house anyway, except the howling loneliness of a stormy night.

They worked hard for the next hour. As they brought in the last of the boxes, Marlee stood by the door for a moment, kicking the snow off her boots. The wind raged like an angry god whose fury had just been awakened. Flecks of icy snow hit her face, numbing her cheeks.

''Looks like the heater's going to be working overtime tonight,'' Lucas said.

As she closed the door, a blast of warm air from the furnace enveloped her. The heat felt good. Though the first-aid station, a clinic only in the strictest of terms, was almost Spartan, there was a homeyness to it, particularly when viewed against the blizzard outside.

She moved back to the window. The world outside

looked like those paperweights one shook to produce a beautiful, self-contained snowstorm.

"Will you consider staying here tonight?" Lucas asked. "I'd rather not drive in that snow if I can help it."

The offer to stay was tempting, but she needed to justify it to herself. "Do you think you might have more patients? If you'll need my help…"

"I never know what's going to happen here. It can be peaceful one second, and chaotic the next. I like my work, don't get me wrong, but the best way for me to do my job is to take things as they come and never plan too far ahead."

"I can understand that." It had been that way in her work, too, she mused silently. "Four Winds is really lucky to have you. You're a wonderful medic. You've got an intuition for medical matters that's amazing. When you're with a patient, you see the whole person, not just the illness or the injury."

"That's part of Navajo teachings, as well as what I was taught as a medic. Being observant becomes second nature."

"It's more than that. It's a gift, a very useful one."

"It doesn't always guarantee answers, though," he murmured.

The way he was looking at her made her feel vibrant and wanted. She shivered, fighting the onslaught of feelings that swept over her. An excitement she didn't dare define, yet as wild as the wind howling outside, filled her.

"You have your own gifts," Lucas added gently. "The way you helped the kids and their moms here today was really something."

She smiled, pleased by his praise. It wasn't empty flattery. He wasn't a man to dole compliments out easily, and she knew it.

"I really would like you to stay at the clinic tonight. You'll be safest here, you know. Look at the storm as a

quirk of fate. Sometimes you just have to trust destiny.''
His voice was a husky murmur.

Her heart and her mind warred with each other, each
struggling for supremacy. *Do you know how tempting you
are? I want to stay, I want to lie with you, to feel your
touch and your tenderness. I need you.* She heard the words
in her mind, framing emotions she'd never before allowed
herself to dwell on, hoping that by the simple act of denying them, they would disappear.

Lucas touched her face gently, caressing her cheek.
"This is the best place for you tonight. I'll see to it that
you're okay. Nothing will disturb you here."

Could he be that innocent, thinking that the physical attraction between them could be tamed by sheer will? Or
was he that strong? His touch sent ribbons of warmth wind-
ing through her.

"I'll stay," Marlee whispered. "Let the storm rage outside. We have all we need in this station. If anybody in
Four Winds needs help, this is where they'll call."

As another gust of wind shook the rafters, she shuddered.
"I can't remember the last time the wind was this strong."

"It's this building. It's right at the mouth of the canyon,
and the wind always sounds worse than it is."

A branch hit the window hard, and Marlee jumped. "It
is bad out there."

He smiled teasingly. "Don't tell me that I've finally
found something that scares you!"

She looked out the window again and nodded, half-
ashamed because she knew it wasn't really the storm. It
was her feelings for Lucas as they stood here alone, isolated
by the storm, that frightened her.

He gathered her into his arms, enfolding her in a tender
embrace that left her weak at the knees. She should have
protested, but the temptation to enjoy their closeness while
it lasted was too strong to resist.

"Don't ever be afraid when you're with me," Lucas

whispered fiercely. He wrapped his hand around her hair, tugging gently so she tilted her head to meet his gaze.

The hunger and passion in his eyes stole her breath away. In a heartbeat, his tongue invaded her mouth, commanding, persuading. It was more than a kiss. It was a possession, a touching of souls that nothing in her previous experience had prepared her for.

When he finally eased his hold, she blinked slowly, like someone waking from a wonderful dream. Everything seemed wrapped in a smoky, warm haze that softened the colors and rounded all the edges in the room.

Lucas tore his gaze from hers and moved quickly to the window, looking out. Suddenly he urged her toward the front door. "We're in trouble," he said quickly.

Marlee started to take a deep breath, hoping to clear her thoughts, but immediately began coughing. "What's happening?" she managed.

"Keep your breathing shallow," he warned. "This building's on fire. Considering all the accidents lately, I think someone may be trying to kill us."

Chapter Six

The frigid air cut right through Marlee's clothing. She tugged the folds of her navy wool coat tighter against her as she stood outside the rudimentary clinic. The old pumper truck had showed up remarkably fast, considering the weather, but most of the fire-department volunteers had been in bed, either sick, sound asleep or both. Aided by the falling snow and two fire extinguishers, she and Lucas had been able to put out most of the fire by the time help had arrived, but extra hands had been welcome.

Her fingers ached from the cold. Making fists and jamming both hands into her pockets, she watched Gabriel and Lucas walking around, searching the hot spots for clues.

The possibility that the arsonist had come here because of her preyed on her mind. Confused, miserable and frightened, she stared at the charred outside wall of the clinic. The town needed this facility, particularly now, with the flu outbreak. She studied Gabriel's expression, hoping against hope that he'd be able to tell her that it had been an accident, faulty wiring or something like that. Yet in her heart, she knew not to expect that.

Gabriel came toward her as Lucas went inside the building with two of the firemen.

"You never saw or heard anything?" Gabriel asked without preamble.

She shook her head, not trusting her voice.

"You seem to be at the center of a lot of mishaps lately," he continued, his eyes boring holes into her. "I need your help to get to the bottom of things, and I have a feeling you're holding out on me."

"I honestly don't know anything. Was what happened here tonight really arson?"

"My guess is that someone poured charcoal-barbecue starter fluid against the side of the building, then put a match to it. It's a good thing the snow slowed the spread of the flames. You're both very lucky to have escaped injury."

She stared at the clinic, blinking back tears. The exterior was blackened by smoke and charred wood, and the door was burned half-away. Smoke and flames had penetrated to the front rooms, also, as if an evil wind had propelled the heat down the path where it could do the most damage. Water rested an inch or so deep in the waiting room.

The right exterior wall of the clinic looked slightly better, but not by much. It resembled a skull, with empty eye sockets where the windows had been broken.

As Lucas approached, she saw that worry and exhaustion lined his face. Her heart twisted inside her.

"The damage wasn't as bad as it might have been," Lucas said, trying to put a positive spin on things, as usual.

"I suppose," she answered, trying not to sound gloomy and failing miserably.

"How much help will you need to get this place up and running again, Shadow?" Gabriel asked.

"The medical equipment is mostly in the back and it wasn't damaged, but the front rooms are unusable at the moment. It'll be impossible for me to see patients here until we have the structure checked out completely. If it's safe, then we'll have to resurface the exterior and interior walls, put in new windows and a door and reshingle part of the roof. The wiring in this section of the building will need to be replaced, too.''

Lucas stroked his jaw pensively. ''All that will take time, and I've *got* to have a new base of operations here in town as soon as possible. Any suggestions?'' He glanced at Gabriel, then Marlee.

''Use the boardinghouse,'' Marlee suggested without hesitation. ''I'll clear out the rooms and do whatever it takes to make it workable for you there.''

''Bad idea,'' Gabriel said. ''The boardinghouse is right in the center of town. If the arsonist pulled something like this again, he could reduce the entire town to embers. I won't risk that.''

''You're not looking at the whole picture,'' Lucas argued. ''Marlee needs protection. If the clinic was being run from the boardinghouse, she'd be protected simply because of the volume of people around. There's only one of you, so you can't adequately protect her *and* the clinic if they're in separate places. This is the only solution.''

''No. The cons outweigh the pros, Shadow.'' Anger laced through Gabriel's words, adding a dangerous edge to them.

''This town needs a clinic right now. With the damage from the fire, I can't operate from here. You may not have the manpower to do your job, but I'm not going to let that keep me from doing mine.'' Lucas's voice cracked through the air like a whip.

The brothers' iron wills collided, and Marlee felt the force and determination that held each of the men as he stood firm. She wanted to do something to defuse what was happening, but she didn't know how. Frustration and sorrow tore at her as she accepted the knowledge that she was, at least partially, the cause of what was happening between them.

''Maybe there's an alternative,'' she offered.

"Like what?" Gabriel turned to Marlee, his gaze as ice-cold as the wind.

"The high school. Maybe they would let you use the gym or a classroom. You could take your equipment there and then set up room dividers of some kind," Marlee suggested.

Lucas shook his head. "I can't bring people who could be seriously ill into a school environment."

Gabriel pursed his lips. "What about the portable classrooms the county brought in? Those stand alone, and have separate heating units and their own water supply. They're not right next to the main building, either. They're on the other side of the track and playing fields."

"That might work," Lucas said thoughtfully. "But it still doesn't solve the problem for Marlee. She's the target of some lunatic now. How are you going to keep her safe?"

Marlee started to protest and assure them she'd watch out for herself, when Gabriel unclipped his cellular phone from his belt and handed it to her. "Here, take this," he said. "The recharger is built-in. I have a spare in my vehicle. Take the phone with you whenever you leave home. And avoid going anywhere where you'll be alone. If you even *think* something's wrong, call me. I won't be far. I wish there was more I could do, but there isn't, unless you'll allow me to put you in jail for your own protection."

Marlee grimaced. "Gee, thanks, but I think I'll pass on your kind offer."

Jake Fields, the town's librarian and one of the volunteer firemen, jogged up to them. "Boys, we have a problem. The snow's starting to come down heavy now. We've got to get the medical equipment and supplies out of there and put the stuff someplace where it'll stay warm and dry. We better do it quickly, too. In another thirty minutes, if the weather doesn't let up, this road's going to be impassable and we're going to be stuck out here."

"Get the pumper back to town now," Gabriel said. "We

can't risk it being snowbound here. But ask the men who came up in their vehicles to stick around. We're going to be packing up everything Lucas needs and taking it over to the high school. We're commandeering one of the portable classrooms on the north side.''

Marlee worked alongside the men carrying the medical equipment and supplies into waiting trucks. By the time the clinic had been emptied of all the necessary equipment, Marlee's entire body ached. The wind had picked up again, too, and snow was blowing into her eyes and stinging her cheeks.

She looked at the men around her and noted that they looked as weary and sore as she felt. Yet it was when she glanced at Lucas that her heart almost broke. He was beyond exhaustion now. The man needed rest, but it would take time to get beds set up in the high school's portable building, and if her guess was right, no amenities would be available there for at least another day or so.

Marlee approached Gabriel, who was sitting in his Jeep, talking on the radio. She waited a discreet distance away until he racked the mike.

''What's up?'' he asked.

''Your brother is going to need a place to stay, and I'm not sure your home is the best place for him now. Keep in mind that Lucas is going to be exposed to this flu that's going around, plus everything else that crops up. It may not be wise to have him around Lanie right now.''

He nodded slowly. ''Good point.''

''It's also not a good idea for him to be alone, either, in case either of you are considering having him stay at Joshua's home. Whoever did this tonight came after both of us, and there's no real proof that Lucas wasn't the real target.''

''You think this could have been the result of a grudge someone has against my brother or the clinic?'' Seeing her nod, Gabriel considered her point. ''That's possible. So what's on your mind? You know I'll do my best to protect both of you, but there are limits to what I can do," he said, biting off the words.

Marlee knew all about pride. Gabriel's had been stung badly, but he had integrity enough to admit his limitations, and that spoke well of him. "I wanted to get you started thinking of a safe place for him, because I'm afraid he'll want to stay with me at the boardinghouse. In my opinion, that could be dangerous. If it turns out that I'm the target after all, then being around me will increase the risk to him, and I don't want that. If I come right out and say that, though, nothing will dissuade him from staying with me. I was hoping you could think of something else. He's this town's only medic, and he needs to stay safe."

"I can't talk Shadow out of anything he wants to do," Gabriel said. "But I wouldn't worry about his safety. My brother is very good at handling trouble. All the Blackhorse brothers are," he added with a crooked smile.

Lucas strode up. "I'm going over to the high school to get everything set up, then I've got to get some sleep. I'm ready to drop."

"Let me take care of moving this equipment for you," Gabriel offered. "I'll see to it that everything's taken care of. In the meantime, I'd like you to go take a look at my wife. I just spoke to her a few minutes ago, and she's not feeling well. She says it's nothing, but I'd like you to take a look at her anyway."

"I'll go over there right now. I've been exposed to this flu, but I'm in good shape so she should be okay as long as I take a few basic precautions, like wearing a mask and gloves. Afterward I'm heading for the boardinghouse," Lucas added. "I'd rather get some sleep there than on the floor of the portable."

Marlee started to protest, then changed her mind and remained silent. It didn't seem likely that the arsonist would strike twice in one night, and she didn't have it in her to refuse Lucas, not when he looked as if his body would have slumped from sheer exhaustion if not for his raw, uncompromising will.

"I'll join you at my house as soon as I can, but if there's anything you think I should know before then, call me," Gabriel said.

Marlee walked with Lucas back to his truck. "Maybe I should go with you. New mothers have a way of getting jumpy when they're close to their due dates. I may be able to help."

After letting Gabriel know she'd be going with Lucas, they got under way. The ride to town took much longer than usual on the snow-packed road. The storm had turned into a blizzard that seemed as unrelenting as it was fierce. In the headlights, the curtain of snow glowed with an iridescence that made it appear as if a ghostly shroud were engulfing them.

"Your brother has a lot of responsibilities right now. The news of the peddler and these other incidents are added burdens. I think you may have been too hard on him," Marlee said, keeping her voice soft. She wanted to try to ease the tensions between the two brothers, not start an argument with Lucas.

Lucas said nothing for several long moments. "My brother has worries and concerns right now, but so do I. We all hoped we'd seen the last of that peddler, but it looks like the troubles he brings are already starting. You're caught in the middle of it, and so am I."

"We can't change anything, so we'd better find a way of dealing with it."

AN HOUR LATER, after Lucas had examined Lanie, Gabriel finally arrived home. Worry clouded his features. "Is my wife okay?" he asked, shutting the door behind him before another icy blast could invade the living room.

"Lanie's okay. She's in bed now. Don't worry. She's

bound to be sore and a little achy at this stage in her pregnancy. She could deliver safely any time now," Lucas said.

Gabriel leaned back against the wall. "I know. That's why I check on her often. I'm glad to hear things are okay here, though, because we have to go back to the school," he said, rubbing his eyes. "The portable doesn't have as much room as I'd thought, so a lot of the equipment is still in the middle of the floor. We had to stack the desks against one wall, and won't be able to get them moved out until morning. We need your guidance in setting up the equipment for maximum efficiency. I know you wanted to get some rest, Shadow, but I need you to supervise that part yourself."

Lucas took his jacket off the hook by the door and picked up his medical bag. "No problem. Let's go. I'll rest later."

Lanie came out of the bedroom just then, and smiled at Gabriel. "I'm glad you're home!"

"Not for long. I'm just on my way back out, at least until our medic has a place to work."

Marlee saw Lanie's expression change in the blink of an eye. Disappointment and a touch of loneliness shone there. "I'll be sticking around for a bit, though, if you don't mind," Marlee said. "I'd like to fix myself a cup of your coffee before I set out. I'll be walking home, and I still haven't warmed up again after being outside for so long."

"I'll be glad to get you something warm to drink. It is freezing tonight."

"If you'll point me in the right direction, I'll take care of it myself."

As the men left, Marlee stepped into the kitchen with Lanie. She could sense Lanie's concern for her husband, and for the child she carried. She remembered giving comfort to many young mothers in the past and, as the memory flickered alive in her mind, she grieved for the work she'd given up.

"They'll be okay," Marlee assured, putting the teakettle on. "It's not really as bad as it looks out there."

"But my family is in trouble again," Lanie said, and settled down in the nearest chair with a long sigh. "I've been hearing bits and pieces of conversations, even though Gabriel and I haven't had much time to talk lately. I know about the fire, and I know that you've seen the peddler. I also heard Gabriel's tone when he spoke about Shadow earlier. There was anger there."

"All families fight a little, or a lot. I heard that even the Blackhorse brothers get embroiled in a little rivalry from time to time."

Lanie smiled. "You're right about that. I guess I'll have to remember that they always work things out in the end."

"What binds them is stronger than anything that tries to split them apart." Marlee nodded. "Don't worry."

"I know," Lanie said softly. "But sometimes something evil strikes at people here, undermining them, turning friends into strangers. I became part of this town willingly, and I've grown to love the people here in Four Winds. But I've seen this town's other side, too. Things turned ugly here when Gabriel's father was killed, and it could be happening again. The peddler has come back. The troubles are starting and when that happens, Four Winds doesn't seem like such a safe place."

Marlee remembered the recent troubles, when Joshua and Nydia had almost been killed by people who had once been counted as friends. And her own life had acquainted her well with another kind of treachery. She knew how an enemy could come from nowhere.

"It won't last forever. Troubles never do," Marlee said, wondering if it would be better for everyone if she left. But would her enemy take revenge on Lucas and others here if she did? It was hard to predict her enemy's actions, especially when she knew nothing at all about him, or them.

"I know you're thinking of running as fast and as far as

you can from Four Winds. I've been in your shoes." Lanie raised her hand to interrupt Marlee's protests, then continued. "I don't know what secrets you're hiding, and the specifics really don't matter. You're part of Four Winds now, and whatever happens, you'll be better off facing it here."

It startled Marlee that Lanie had guessed her thoughts so accurately. "I just don't want anyone to be in danger because of me."

"I'm not talking to you as the sheriff's wife now, but as your friend. If someone *is* after you, then face them here on your own ground. Otherwise, the trouble will follow you for the rest of your life. You have friends here, Marlee, people who will stand by you. If you have to make a stand, Four Winds is the best possible place for you to be. I found that out myself because of people like Gabriel, Lucas and you."

Marlee weighed Lanie's words. If her enemy was someone from her past who'd tracked her here, he would continue to endanger her and others wherever she went. It was time to stand and fight. And if this trouble wasn't connected to her past, but was something to do with the peddler or linked to Lucas's own past or his work, then she was needed here, now more than ever, to help him in this fight. "I won't run away. I didn't start this fight, but I will see it through."

"I have a feeling that you're about to experience firsthand why everyone talks about the peddler with awe and a touch of fear. The path that lies ahead of you may not be an easy one. It wasn't for me or for Nydia, but remember that neither of us has ever had any reason to regret where it ultimately led us."

Those words warmed Marlee, and filled her with a strange sense of expectancy. She'd denied her own dreams for so long, she'd almost forgotten the blessing they could be in and of themselves. Marlee stood at the sink and rinsed out her coffee cup. The bright yellows and deep golds of her friend's kitchen spoke of a life filled with radiant possibilities and hopes for the future. But there could never be hope without courage.

Marlee knew that she'd allowed the past to chain her. If the trouble she was facing now was a result of who and what she'd been, the time had come to finish what she hadn't had the strength to fight so long ago. Lanie was right. It was time to take a stand.

BACK AT THE boardinghouse, Marlee sat in the stillness and warmth of her living room. It seemed more lonely than usual tonight. Outside, the storm raged. The snow was still falling beyond the porch. The light kept back the chaos of the storm, but she couldn't stop worrying and thinking about Lucas. He'd called her just a few minutes ago. He wouldn't be back till the early-morning hours, if then. Jake and Lucas planned to get some sleep in the camper of Jake's truck over in the school yard, using the former Ranger's down sleeping bags.

In a way, she was glad that Lucas was there, not here. Gabriel wouldn't be far away, and Jake and Lucas, though tired, would guard each other's backs.

She lay down on the sofa and closed her eyes, intending to rest only briefly. She knew she'd have to leave a key under the mat by the front door as she'd promised Lucas, but since he wouldn't be back before dawn, there was still plenty of time. Before she knew it, Marlee drifted off into the deep, dark cavern of sleep.

She wasn't sure how much time had elapsed when a sharp scraping noise at the rear of the house startled her awake. Marlee jumped up and hurried to the window. It was still dark outside, and she couldn't see far beyond the circle of light that escaped outward through the part in the curtain.

Marlee turned off the living-room lights and waited for

her eyes to adjust before trying to peer out again. The winds had died down, and everything was still. As her eyes adjusted to the darkness, she parted the curtain and looked out. A thick blanket of snow covered the backyard. As she studied the ground, she spotted fresh footprints leading toward the back of her house.

Fear stabbed through her as she heard a soft scrunching sound coming from outside, near the corner of the house. Marlee hurried to the phone, called Gabriel and breathed a sigh of relief when he answered on the first ring. In a soft voice, she told him about the intruder.

"Don't leave the house, and make sure the doors and windows are locked. I'll be there in minutes."

Marlee went to the closet and pulled out the shotgun she kept in there. She'd never be a victim again. After standing by the window a moment, she heard faint padding footsteps and caught a glimpse of a figure standing by the back door.

Her heart lodged at her throat. He was bent over the door handle, and from what she could hear, she was almost sure he was picking the lock. She stared at the shotgun, suddenly realizing there was no way she'd really use it unless she was being physically attacked.

Out of necessity, a new plan formed quickly in her head. She headed for the front door. If she could take the prowler by surprise, and use the shotgun to detain him until Gabriel arrived, then a lot of the mystery about her attacker could be solved.

After clipping the cellular phone to the belt loop of her jeans, Marlee slipped out the front door and crept around the side of the house. The cluster of trees and shrubs that bordered the back of her home would give her plenty of cover. Intent on her quarry, she kept the shotgun barrel up, not wanting it to become clogged with snow. As she ducked under an old pine tree, the barrel of the weapon suddenly struck a snow-laden branch. Wet, heavy snow pelted down on her, and a heartbeat later the branch struck the side of the house with a sharp *thwack.*

Marlee held her breath, knowing with certainty that the intruder had heard her. She inched forward and, as she peered out from behind the trees, saw that the man had vanished.

Icy fear shot through her. Marlee hurried around to the front door, intent on reaching the safety of her home. She was only a few steps from the porch when someone tackled her from behind, throwing her face-forward into the snow.

Chapter Seven

Marlee struggled to get free before the snow choked the air out of her lungs. In desperation, she shoved the stock of the shotgun into her attacker's middle as hard as she could. She heard him gasp and, as his grip loosened, she rolled away and scrambled to her feet.

As her assailant rose to his knees, she saw his face for the first time. For a moment, she couldn't speak. "Lucas!" she managed to say, helping him up. "What the heck are you doing out here?"

He brushed the snow off his body, wincing as he touched his stomach where she'd slammed him. "I was trying to protect you. I saw a figure creeping around the house, heading for the front door."

"I heard someone tampering with the back door, so I called Gabriel and then figured I'd try to detain whoever was out there. I had no idea it would be you," Marlee explained.

"You told me there'd be a key underneath the mat in the front, but there wasn't one. I figured I'd try the back door. The house was dark except for one small lamp in the living room, so I assumed you were fast asleep. I didn't want to wake you."

"You said you weren't coming until the early-morning hours! It's nowhere near dawn!" She brushed the snow off her wet clothes. Without a coat, she was freezing. "Let's not stand out here arguing. It's too cold, and now we're both wet. Let's get inside by the fireplace." She reached back for the cellular phone, intending to call Gabriel, then realized that it was gone. "Help me look. Gabriel's cell phone has to be here somewhere," she said.

Lucas stirred the snow with his boot, searching the place they'd fallen to the ground when he'd tackled her. "It shouldn't be that difficult to find it. It's not that small, and it'll be dark against the snow. When's the last time you remember having it?"

"I clipped it to my belt loop before coming out of the house. The loop is torn now."

"Trace back your steps. It probably fell in one of your tracks or close by."

Together they walked around the side of the house. "We're going to need flashlights," Lucas said. "It's too dark out here right now, in spite of the white surface."

"I've got a couple inside the house. Let's go get them, and I can call your brother at the same time and let him know that there's no danger."

"I'll keep looking while you're inside. I don't think it's something you should be without, and if it stays here in the snow for long it could short out."

Marlee went inside the house, called Gabriel, then returned outside with a pair of flashlights. The shotgun was now safely in the closet, and her wool coat was securely fastened around her, helping her stay warm. "Your brother was relieved to know it was you I'd heard, not an intruder, but he's coming over anyway. He wants to talk to both of us. I don't think he's thrilled I went on the offensive."

"Neither am I. I can see why you did it, but you shouldn't have taken the risk."

"Would *you* have waited?"

"No, but that's different."

"Is it? I wanted to see the face of my enemy. I knew

Gabriel was on his way over and I figured I could hold the person until he arrived. The shotgun was my way of getting his attention and keeping him at a safe distance. I knew the intruder was trying to get inside my house.''

Lucas shook his head. ''Would you really have shot him—or me, I should say?''

''I had no intention of shooting, and I certainly wouldn't have fired without identifying my target.''

''You should have left the house and just kept on going to the neighbors.''

''And bring the danger over to them?'' Marlee shook her head.

They followed Marlee's tracks all the way around the house, but failed to spot the phone. ''I thought about having Gabriel call me, then listening for the ring. But I didn't want him to know I'd lost it. And I don't know the number myself.''

''Let's go over your steps one more time, and if we haven't found it by then, then we'll go back inside. I know the number and you can call it from inside while I go back out and look.''

As they worked their way around the house, the beam of her flashlight fell on a gray metal-and-plastic object partially hidden under a rosebush beside the driveway.

''What is that?'' she said, reaching down and scooping it into her palm. ''Is it another listening device?''

''No, it doesn't look right, and besides, why stick one out here?'' Lucas took it from her hand and studied it. ''Wait a minute. Wasn't this about where the peddler's van was parked?''

She nodded. ''You think he left this and that microphone here?''

''No. This, I believe, is a tracking device that was placed on someone's vehicle, but it fell off and got run over.'' The flat plastic box had a magnetic surface on one side, and contained a small circuit board loaded with electronic parts.

"You don't usually park this far down your driveway, do you?" Lucas added.

She shook her head. "No. I park by the front, so that rules out my car as a candidate."

"I think someone discovered the peddler was in the area, and maybe even followed him here. They hid the bug in your house to find out what he was doing, and then decided to track him when he left. The peddler must have discovered the device and left it behind." Lucas paused. "It could have just fallen off, but that seems unlikely."

"Nobody's ever been able to follow the peddler when he leaves. Even the sheriff tried and failed, according to what I heard Lanie say once. I can see someone wanting to find out once and for all where he goes, but I wonder who was willing to go this far."

An undeniable sense of relief washed over her. All of a sudden, the incidents appeared to have less to do with her past than with that of Four Winds. The listening device she'd found in her home did make more sense now, when connected to the peddler.

"Here it is," she said, finally spotting and retrieving the cellular phone from where it had been caught on a pyracantha bush.

As headlights bathed the area where they stood, Lucas glanced around the side of the house. "That's my brother now. I bet he's going to be real interested in what we have to show him."

A SHORT TIME LATER, after changing out of their wet clothes, Lucas and Marlee were seated in the living room with Gabriel.

"I remember seeing similar tracking devices at a law-enforcement seminar," Gabriel said. "It's not a state-of-the-art device, but it does its job. I've got to tell you, though, it's just not the sort of thing I ever expected to see here in Four Winds. Then again, that's one thing about our town. Nothing is ever the way you expect.''

Though she avoided looking directly at him, Marlee felt Gabriel's gaze on her. He knew she was holding back, but for the first time, she didn't feel guilty. This time she was certain her past had nothing to do with what was happening.

''I can use my law-enforcement contacts to track down the manufacturer and that way maybe get a lead on who purchased it, but I want you two to leave this to me. Whoever bought this device and the bug already had them on hand, ready for the occasion, which means somebody in this town was a snoop even before the peddler showed up. We have no way of knowing who these devices were used on before.''

''I suppose I could ask around and see if there's anyone with a particular interest in electronics in town,'' Marlee said.

''No. I don't want you looking into this. You'll end up raising questions in people's minds, and folks are already tense enough with this illness that's going around.''

''Someone's coming after me,'' Marlee said. ''You can't expect me to sit tight and wait to see what he's going to do next.''

''If you start playing amateur detective, you may uncover more than you're capable of handling. Trust me to do my job.'' Gabriel stood. ''There's not much else I can do here tonight. Watch out for each other, and don't take matters into your own hands again. Think about what happened earlier tonight. You could have easily hurt each other out there.''

Marlee watched in silence as Gabriel left.

''He's wrong to think I might have hurt you. I knew it was you out there the minute I felt you in my arms,'' Lucas murmured, coming up from behind her and pulling her back against him.

Marlee had no armor against the husky promise of his

voice. Longing filled her until she ached. "We have to be careful," Marlee said, forcing herself to step away, though everything feminine in her begged to stay in his embrace. "The danger to both of us is real, and it seems to be coming from many directions."

Without turning to look back at Lucas, Marlee went to her room and closed the door. Hot tears spilled down her cheeks. She'd hoped never to care deeply about anyone or anything again. That was a road that led only to pain and heartache. But now, it was too late.

LUCAS WENT to the guest room she'd prepared for him earlier. The bed had been turned down, and a pitcher of water and a glass had been set on the nightstand.

He walked around the room restlessly. What was it about Marlee that affected him so much? With her, he felt whole, as if fate had brought her to him, and given her the power to rock his world. She filled him with a warmth he'd never known. Yet there was nothing he could do to change the situation between them. He closed his eyes for a moment, remembering the feel of her in his arms. So sweet, so soft, so tempting.

Muttering an oath, he walked to the window and opened it, hoping the sudden and icy blast of air would help clear his thoughts. As he stood there, staring at the dark emptiness outside, his thoughts drifted back to another time. He hadn't always known the high cost personal involvements could exact from someone in his profession. Yet back then, inexperience and circumstances had conspired against him. Now he had no excuse for repeating the same mistake he'd sworn to avoid for as long as he lived.

Wartime memories filled his mind. That one wounded man, his best friend. Loyalties were too easily divided when emotions took over. He shut the window and, with it, shut off the flow of his memories, then moved back into the room. He wouldn't let himself or Four Winds down by allowing anyone or anything to interfere with his duties here. Marlee tempted him with dreams he had no business indulging. A man who weighed his convictions against the cost they would exact wasn't much of a man.

Lucas stripped off his clothes. Despite everything, as the cool sheets touched his body, his thoughts returned to Marlee. He drifted into a restless sleep with images of Marlee, and what might have been, playing in his mind.

LUCAS REALIZED it was morning when the buzz of his cellular phone stirred his brain. He reached for the phone, forcing himself to come quickly awake and alert. Whenever calls began this early, he knew he was in for a long day.

He listened as the high school's journalism teacher spoke.

"They *all* look terrible this morning," Jennifer Sawyer said. "Yet all the kids were fine last night. We met to go over articles in the local paper and gather ideas for human-interest stories of our own. I'd like you to come over and take a look at them. I'm really worried."

"I'll be there in twenty minutes. My temporary clinic is in the portable building across from the track. If they can make it over there, that'll save us some time," Lucas said, dressing quickly.

A few minutes later, as he strode down the hall, Marlee stepped out of the kitchen. "More kids at the high school are ill," he explained. "I've got to get there right away."

"You should eat something. If you don't eat and get enough rest, you'll end up catching whatever this is that's going around."

Marlee quickly filled a plastic sandwich bag and held it out to him. "Here. It's just a couple of breakfast burritos, but they'll hold you until you get a chance to eat a decent meal."

Lucas took the food gratefully, aware all of a sudden of how hungry he was. "Thanks," he said, heading for the door. "You know, I just wish my brother Joshua hadn't left town with his family right after the Harvest Festival."

"I like Joshua, but I'm not sure he would be a help to you now. His kind of medicine is different from what folks around here rely on."

"That's true, but there's something about my little brother that puts people at ease. And he does know a great deal about herbs that can help relieve symptoms. The older ones here believe in the power of *remedios,* the herbal remedies that have been handed down for generations, as much as they do medical science."

"I may be able to help you with that. My knowledge isn't anywhere near as extensive as Joshua's, but I do know some local remedies."

"Good. I'm glad to hear it. That may yet come in handy. At this point, I think we have to be prepared for almost anything."

"If while you're making your rounds, you discover that you need an assistant to help you keep records or give you a hand whenever it's needed, give me a call. Just keep trying if you get a busy signal. I'll be using the phone a lot today."

Lucas's eyes narrowed slightly. "Are you planning to do some investigating on your own?"

"I'm going to do some *research,*" she corrected. "I want to find out if there are any companies in the Southwest that carry listening and tracking devices. Then I intend to call them and get some information as if I'm a potential customer."

"Be sure to pass any information you get along to my brother, but don't expect him to thank you," he added with a wry smile.

Lucas hurried out to his truck, then drove slowly down the snow-packed road. Four Winds was testing him, just as it had his brothers, but would learn soon enough that no

Blackhorse had ever backed away from a fight. And when a Blackhorse fought, he always came out the winner.

MARLEE WATCHED Lucas go, thinking how well his nickname fitted him. He moved with the fluidity of a shadow, controlled, never revealing the secrets he harbored within himself. There was much going on inside Lucas. He'd been at war with himself recently. That much she could sense with the certainty of someone who also battled inner demons.

Marlee dressed warmly, then, grabbing the cellular phone and her purse, headed for the library on foot. She'd start her search there, using their computers. Charley had dropped off her car earlier with the brakes fixed, but she'd just parked it in the driveway. The roads were bad, and most of the places in town she usually visited were within easy walking distance. She saw no use in risking a fender bender.

After saying good-morning to Jake, the librarian, who was reshelving returned books, she sat down by the terminal.

The computer search was more complicated than she'd expected, but she managed to get a list of ten electronics shops that seemed good possibilities. Though she was aware of Jake's questioning looks, she didn't stop to explain. It was better not to trust anyone.

"I've got the information I need," she told Jake. "Thanks for the use of the terminal." Ignoring the questioning look he gave her, Marlee quickly gathered her notes and left the library.

Contacting the companies whose phone numbers she'd gathered took another two hours, but at least she was home, where the calls she was making wouldn't raise questions in anyone's mind. Slowly a picture began to emerge. The items were not generally available except through mail order, but there were dozens of such catalogs in existence.

Trying to track down the exact source of the devices she'd found at the boardinghouse would take days, or longer.

Gathering the information she'd compiled, she placed the papers inside a file folder, bundled up warmly once again and walked to Gabriel's office. He was on the telephone as she walked inside, still scraping the snow off her boots.

Rosa, the grocery-store owner, was seated on one of the pine benches, waiting for him, too. She scowled at Marlee. "The sheriff is really busy this morning. Every time I start to talk to him, the phone rings."

"What's going on?"

"From the bits and pieces of conversation I've overheard, I think folks want him to call in some outside medical help from the state. This flu bug is going through town like wildfire. Did you know they could quarantine the whole town? Can you imagine what that would do to us? I couldn't get any of my stock in if they did, so I'm not sure what we'd do for food."

Marlee looked at Rosa in surprise. "Things aren't that bad, surely. I mean flu bugs come and go."

"Nobody's getting better, no matter what Lucas does, and that's scaring people. Who knows what could happen next?"

Gabriel set down the phone, then turned to Rosa, continuing where he'd left off. "You'll have to pay the fine. That's all there is to it. I've written you two warning citations already. You can't park in the red zone. That's the only access the fire truck has in case of an emergency."

Rosa scowled as she placed the ticket and two five-dollar bills on his desk. "You're as stubborn as an old burro, Sheriff," she said, then stormed out.

Marlee suppressed a laugh as Rosa slammed the door shut. "Looks like you're having a bad day."

"I've had better. Now, tell me what I can do for you. Is there a problem?"

"I came to give you some information I thought you

might find useful.'' As she placed the papers before him, he quickly closed the file on his desk. She'd only had a quick glimpse, but it had been enough. Her name had been at the top of the page. Gabriel Blackhorse was looking into her background.

Marlee said nothing and, as the phone on Gabriel's desk began to ring, she let herself out of his office. With the attacks on her, she should have expected it. She'd raised more questions in his mind than answers, and he was the sheriff, after all. The prospect saddened her. She'd tried very hard to leave the past behind her, but no matter how far she'd run, it still dogged her footsteps.

LUCAS PARKED HIS TRUCK in the snow-covered driveway beside old man Simmons's home, killing the engine before it could backfire. Arnold Simmons was the only current resident of Four Winds, *not* related to the Blackhorse family, who had experienced the peddler firsthand. Simmons's destiny had taken him from abject poverty to the fortune of a wealthy man.

Arnold was ill a lot nowadays, but not from the flu. His complaints were mostly those that came with old age. He had to be past ninety. Although Simmons could have easily afforded the hospital stay Lucas had recommended, even a private suite, he'd refused to leave his home and go among strangers. As a Navajo, Lucas understood that decision far better than most people could have.

Lucas knocked on the back door, then, knowing it was always left unlocked, entered. He called out to his patient, but only silence greeted him. This was unusual, because Simmons usually had the TV on, tuned to a news channel.

Uneasiness spread over Lucas as he walked toward Simmons's back bedroom. The house didn't feel right. He couldn't quite put his finger on it, but he knew something was very wrong.

Lucas reached the last door of the long hallway, and looked inside. Simmons appeared to be asleep.

"I'm here, Mr. Simmons," he called out, then stopped. The curtains hadn't been opened, though it was nearly noon, and the TV remote was on the nightstand. That wasn't at all like Arnold. He loved daylight, and felt the night with all its secrets was only one more enemy of the aged.

Lucas approached the bed, but Arnold didn't move at all. As he touched the old man's wrist to feel for a pulse, he had his answer. The body was cold. Arnold Simmons had passed away sometime during the night.

Lucas exhaled softly. He'd liked the old man, as most people had. Lucas admired the way Simmons had faced the world on his own terms. He'd bought one shovel from the peddler, and through a series of events, had come into a fortune. Yet, for him, nothing had essentially changed. He'd remained a man who took pleasure in little things, from a sunrise to his much loved potted marigolds sitting on the windowsill. It looked as though they needed water. Lucas poured a generous portion from the bottle on the nightstand.

Lucas left the bedroom, closing the door behind him, and sat down wearily on the living-room couch. As he filled out the form required by the state, he felt an oppressiveness settle over him. Navajo teachings taught that Death was not an enemy. Without it, old men wouldn't give way to the young. It was part of the balance and the harmony of things.

Yet, as it was with many of his tribe, he did not like being around the dead. Unlike Joshua, he didn't believe in the *chindi*, the evil in man that stayed earthbound and was said to pose a danger to the living. Still, he'd never quite been able to develop the ability to remain at ease around the dead like most of his colleagues who helped the ill or injured.

Lucas telephoned the Santa Fe funeral home that served

their community, but was told that because of highway conditions, it would be hours before the body could be taken away.

It was not natural for the living to remain with the dead.

Pushing such thoughts aside, he called his brother to report the death. Gabriel was at the high school, dealing with other issues. Two teens had decided to square off, and the administration hadn't been able to cool their tempers with threats other than jail. Lucas asked about the boys' physical condition, but they'd only inflicted bruises on each other, and he wasn't needed.

He called next to find out about repairs to the clinic. One of the local contractors, a friend of Joshua's, was making a written estimate now, but thanks to the weather, work couldn't begin for another day, at the earliest.

Lucas paced around the room, then stopped by the window to stare at the snow outside. The temperature had risen slightly throughout the morning, and the snow was starting to melt a bit. But that wouldn't last long. Once the sun went down, the temperature would drop by thirty degrees or more and the partially melted snow would, by morning, become a layer of ice, as treacherous as it was beautiful.

Beautiful things were often the most dangerous. He thought of Marlee. Her softness called out to him, offering him things he'd long denied himself. Lucas stared at the phone, thinking of calling her, yet knowing he wouldn't. Suddenly the cellular phone rang.

"It's me," Marlee said.

As he heard her voice, he wondered what link had formed between them that had compelled her to call at just that moment. "Is everything okay?" he asked.

"Yes. I was just wondering how things were going for you, and whether you had any more news on the flu epidemic. I'm going to be visiting the seniors' center this afternoon, and I know they'll have lots of questions."

"Reassure them as much as you can that there isn't anything to worry about."

There was a lengthy silence before she spoke again. "Then why do you sound so depressed? What's happened?"

He smiled. So she could sense his moods now, too. Maybe he'd become too easy to read. He told her about Arnold Simmons.

"I'm really sorry to hear that. Let me come over and keep you company. Duties like that are easier when they're shared."

"It's not necessary."

"No, probably not, but I'd like to."

"Okay. I'll see you shortly, then."

Marlee arrived fifteen minutes later, and Lucas couldn't deny he was glad to see her. Desire tugged at him, tormenting him even in this place that, until now, had been filled only with death.

Marlee handed him a thermos of coffee, and opened the sack she was carrying. "I know you're probably not hungry, but I brought you something to eat anyway. It's mostly snacks you can pick at through the afternoon."

"Thanks." Lucas took the thermos from her and, as their fingers touched, he forced himself to suppress a shudder. He wanted to hold her, to feel her softness and warmth against him. In this house of death, she was a light burning bright, beckoning to him.

He did his best to concentrate on her words as she told him about her meeting with Gabriel. "People are sure getting scared," she said. "Your brother has his hands full right now."

"There haven't been any more emergencies this morning so, with luck, maybe the flu outbreak has already started to level off."

She met his gaze and held it. "Do you really think so?" Her eyes, so pleading, so soft, almost destroyed him.

There was an intensity in their depths that spoke of hidden passions held in check. Lucas wanted to kiss her, to drive all the fears and concerns out of her mind and fill her only with a need for him.

"Do you?" she insisted.

He struggled to remember her question, but before he could answer, his cellular phone rang again. Lucas identified himself quickly, listened for a moment, then spoke. "I'll be there in ten minutes. Keep her warm. And don't worry. High temperatures aren't that unusual in children her age."

He concluded the call, clipped the phone to his belt and grabbed his jacket from the chair. "Mrs. Vega's baby is ill, and so's her husband. She's worried about the baby's temperature, but from what she's told me, I'm more worried about Bob. He's got another medical condition that makes anything like the flu much more complicated. He's not one to complain, so things usually get out of hand before I'm called in. I've got to go."

"I'll stay with Mr. Simmons's body until the mortuary people come by."

He looked at her in surprise, grateful that she'd offered but unwilling to force such a task on her. "You don't have to do that."

"I know, but I think somebody should be here. Mr. Simmons always treated me well. Just leave whatever papers I'll need to turn over to them to make it legal."

"I'll do that. And would you do another favor for me? Keep your ears open when you go to the seniors' center later. Senior citizens tend to speak their minds, and I'd like to know what they think this illness is. From what you told me about your conversation with Gabriel, there's a lot of speculation going around and I'd like to know what's on people's minds. Can you do that?"

"Is there something in particular that's worrying you?"

Lucas handed her the papers she needed. "When I'm

treating a patient, I usually know exactly what's needed to restore them to health. It's an instinct that has never steered me wrong. Yet lately all I get is the gut feeling that I'm missing a vital piece of the equation.'' He rested his hand on the door handle and looked back at her. ''I need answers, and unless I find them soon, superstition and fear may deal Four Winds a fatal blow.''

Chapter Eight

Marlee sat by the window, waiting. Two hours had passed, and no one had come by for the body. The snow had continued to slowly melt outside, but now a thick, blanketing fog had crept in, reducing visibility to a dozen feet or less. She'd never seen weather like this in Four Winds before.

She tried not to think of it as an ill omen, but it was difficult not to do so. First the flu epidemic, and now this crazy weather was forcing her to pay closer attention to the stories she'd heard about the peddler, and wonder if there'd been more truth to them than she'd thought.

She heard a sudden dull thud, then another. Gooseflesh dimpled her arms as she realized the sound had come from the back, from Mr. Simmons's room.

Wild images rushed into her mind. It didn't seem very likely, but perhaps Lucas had made a mistake and Mr. Simmons wasn't dead. She'd heard of cases where a patient's heart had started beating again without any medical intervention at all. The possibilities urged her forward, and she ran back to the bedroom. If he'd awakened suddenly, he'd probably need her help.

Marlee threw open the door, then stopped in midstride. The blanket still covered the body. She reached underneath, intending to check Mr. Simmons's pulse, but the cold temperature and pallor of his skin told her that the man was indeed dead.

She was standing next to the bed, trying to come up with an answer to what had happened, when something hit the windowpane hard, making it rattle loudly.

Marlee's hands began to shake. Someone was trying to scare her. Holding on to that knowledge, and determined not to give them the satisfaction, Marlee picked up the cellular phone Gabriel had given her. She dialed, but the call wouldn't go through. All she could hear was the sound of loud static. She tried Lucas's number next, but ended up with the same results. The weather was obviously playing havoc with cellular-phone communications. Once again thumps rattled the door, this time in the back.

Hoping that a land-line call to the sheriff's office would get through, Marlee used Simmons's phone and dialed the dispatcher. A young woman answered and quickly assured her that she'd radio Gabriel and he would respond.

While she was waiting, Marlee took another look out the living-room window. The fog was as thick as before, and whoever was out there was using it as a smoke screen. Marlee studied the snow on the ground just below the window and saw fragments of snowballs beside the house. She stared at them in muted anger. Someone had been pelting the house.

Suddenly a loud backfire cut through the gloom of the fog, and she saw the approaching headlights of Lucas's truck.

She walked out the front door, glad to see he was back. As Lucas stepped down from the vehicle, the strength and confidence he exuded with each step bolstered her own courage. Lucas's bearing sent out a challenge that few would have dared meet. With him around, she knew nothing would be allowed to harm her.

"Did they pick up the body?" he asked softly.

Marlee suspected that Lucas had avoided using Mr. Simmons's name out of respect for Navajo traditions. "No. He's still here."

Lucas's gaze was keen and thorough as it searched her face. "Something else is wrong. What's happened?"

She filled him in quickly, telling him about the snowballs. "It's probably just a kid who ditched school, but I'd still like to throttle him."

"Let's go take a look around," he said.

Gabriel arrived just as Lucas and Marlee found a trail of footprints leading to the road.

Marlee repeated her story to Gabriel. As she finished speaking, Lucas looked at his brother. "Normally I would have said that it was some teenager out messing around, but recent events put a whole new slant on this incident."

"It's not a young kid, either, not by the size of those tracks," Gabriel said, crouching down.

"This isn't a stunt I would associate with the same person who vandalized my home," Marlee commented thoughtfully. "I wonder if it's a high-school kid cutting class because he's angry that his friends are all out sick. Throwing snowballs at a house is an act of frustration more than anything else. And if it's a neighbor trying to pick on poor old Mr. Simmons, they're too late to bother him anymore."

"You may be right, either way," Gabriel said.

Lucas stood up slowly, hearing the sound of another vehicle approaching. "The funeral-home people are here," he announced, then walked out to meet them.

After the body was taken away, they locked up the house and took another look around outside. "Are you getting on top of this health problem our town is having?" Gabriel asked, photographing the imprints in the snow. "I'm getting a lot of pressure to pull in troops from Santa Fe's state labs."

Lucas shrugged. "They won't come, not unless we start having a string of deaths. Bad as it is, what we're facing here isn't a crisis, not by their definition. We'd be lucky to get the doctor I work with to make a special trip out here. I've got a feeling he'd be reluctant to stay even for a few days, because then he'd have to refer his patients to another doctor.'' Lucas lapsed into a thoughtful silence.

"What's bugging you?" Gabriel prodded. "There's more to this, right?"

Lucas nodded. "I've been keeping tabs on my patients, and by now, some of them should have shown improvement. But that's not the case. They're not worse, mind you, but they're certainly not getting better, either.''

"When exactly did this whole thing start up?" Gabriel asked.

"About the time of the peddler's visit. For a while, I thought maybe it was a virus that he'd brought with him to town, but I've looked into that. It just doesn't fit. The people I treated had not been in contact with the peddler, or with us, prior to their coming down with the flu. And it would have to be a real short incubation period. He was only here a few hours before the first cases were reported."

Gabriel nodded slowly. "Shadow, you're good at what you do. You'll find the answers."

Just then Lucas's cellular phone rang. It was such a bad connection Marlee could hear the static even from where she was standing. The transmission faded in and out, and Lucas had to repeat much of what he was hearing to confirm the caller's message.

As Lucas closed the handset, Gabriel gave his brother a worried look. "Did I hear that right? The girls' volleyball team has come down with this?"

"Yeah, and it all came about in just a matter of hours. They'd volunteered for a recycling project earlier today, gathering newspapers and cans, and all were fine then. But now they're in the locker room, most of them too sick to go back to class. Their coach is worried about even letting them go home."

"Let me ride over with you and see if I can help," Marlee said. "I can keep records, and help you interview the kids. Maybe we can come up with a theory as to how this started and why no one's getting better."

"I could use a hand," Lucas agreed with a nod. "Normally I can deal with this town's minor aches and pains, and there's a doctor I contact for advice, prescriptions and referrals. But as I'm sure you've noticed, times aren't normal."

Gabriel accompanied them to Lucas's truck. "Keep me apprised, Shadow."

TWENTY MINUTES LATER, Marlee and Lucas walked into the school gym. A woman wearing slacks, a school sweatshirt and a whistle on a rope around her neck jogged up to them. Marlee recognized Mrs. Peterson, the girls' head coach.

"These kids are really sick."

"Tell me everything you can about what led up to this, and how the symptoms started," Lucas said.

"I—" Mrs. Peterson stopped and looked at Marlee curiously. "I know you run the boardinghouse, but why are you here?"

"I'm helping our medic today. There are too many sick people for him to also have to handle the record keeping and all that."

"Oh, okay." She led them into the locker room.

The entire room had an eerie silence marred only by sporadic bursts of coughing. Kids were lying down on the benches or sitting on the floor, leaning back against the lockers. A couple of the girls, apparently untouched by the sudden illness, were off by themselves in a corner, talking quietly.

Marlee followed Lucas from one patient to the next, lending her support, asking pertinent questions and filling out the medical forms. As she listened to the descriptions of how each of the kids had become ill, and what they'd been doing before that time, a pattern began to form in her mind.

While Lucas spoke to the gym teacher, Marlee went to talk to one of the girls who seemed particularly unaffected by the symptoms that were plaguing her classmates. She listened closely to Tina, a sixteen-year-old with long brown hair and a hesitant smile.

"What have you been eating or drinking, and where?" Marlee asked, repeating the same questions she'd asked all the others.

"I've been on a really strict diet. But it's good for me. Heck, I'm not sick, and that's a big plus. I feel a little woozy from time to time, but that's because of the diet."

"How do you keep from getting really hungry? You must drink lots of liquids, like water and juice, or coffee?"

"No, just soft drinks. The carbonation fools my stomach into thinking it's full. If I were to drink all the water this diet calls for, my stomach would get really upset."

After Marlee finished talking to Tina, the coach took Marlee aside. "Don't let her kid you about what she's eating or drinking. At lunch I saw her wolf down a sandwich she'd mooched off one of the boys. And this morning, during the recycling effort, she kept going out to get a drink of water from the fountain."

It was late afternoon by the time the kids had been checked out and sent home. Marlee walked with Lucas to the portable building that had become his clinic. Together they fixed up cots and stowed blankets and supplies that they'd managed to salvage from the fire-damaged building. The radio equipment he used to contact the consulting physician in Santa Fe had been acting up before, but now, curiously enough, worked perfectly. Maybe the drop in humidity had done the trick.

Marlee told Lucas about her conversation with the dieter. "For a short time there, I actually thought I might have found an answer. When she told me she wasn't drinking much water, and I could see she wasn't sick, I figured I'd found the link. But unfortunately that didn't pan out.''

He said nothing for several long moments. ''But you know, that's the closest to a connection we've found. It's a long shot, and the illnesses are too random to attribute what's going on to bacterial or viral contamination of the water supply. But it's worth checking. Take water samples from the school and different locations around town,'' he said, handing her a tray of vials.

''What if someone sees me?'' Marlee said. She knew only too well what panic could do to people in a small town like Four Winds.

''I see where you're heading,'' Lucas said, considering the problem. ''We'll need to come up with a standard answer for people when they start asking why we're checking out the water.''

Hearing a knock at the door, Lucas turned and saw Gabriel and Lanie. Lucas hurried over and helped Lanie to a chair. ''Are you okay? Don't tell me you've got a touch of this flu bug, too?''

She shook her head. ''I'm okay. My husband worries too much, that's all.''

''You really shouldn't be working so hard,'' Lucas said. ''What's wrong with taking it easy until the baby arrives?''

''I only came in to help with the plans for an assembly, since the other teachers have their hands full today.''

''What she's not telling you,'' Gabriel added, ''is that she has been on her feet all day trying to do everything by herself. So now her back hurts, and her feet are swollen.''

''All par for the course at this stage,'' Lanie said with a gentle smile.

''Lanie's right, you know,'' Lucas answered, checking her vitals, then glancing at Gabriel. ''You're going to have to stop worrying about her so much or you'll be the one who ends up sick.''

"Yeah, yeah," Gabriel answered, then sat down in one of the metal-backed chairs. "What were you saying about the water when we came in?"

Lucas filled him in. "It's Marlee's lead, and one that's certainly worth checking out."

Gabriel looked over at his wife. "Until this question is cleared up, I want you to only drink water that's been bottled or boiled."

Lanie nodded. "But what about the rest of the town? Will this warning go out to everyone, even if there's only an off chance that it might be the reason people are getting sick?"

Gabriel nodded. "I'll have to make sure people know about this, but I'm going to explain it to them very carefully. I don't want a panic on my hands." He lapsed into a thoughtful silence for several seconds before continuing. "This is going to put a different slant on your situation," he added, looking at Marlee.

"I don't understand. What do you mean?"

"I'm the only law enforcement in town, and this business is going to make me busier than ever. You're going to have to stay alert and be very careful, because I may not be as available as I'd hoped."

"Which makes me real glad I decided to stay at the boardinghouse," Lucas finished, giving his brother a guarded look.

"Yeah, in retrospect, I think that was a good idea."

After Gabriel and Lanie left, Marlee picked up the vials from the tray and placed them in her handbag. "I think this will call less attention."

"Let's do that job together. I may be able to help my brother keep a lid on things if I take time to explain what's happening to people who see us collecting water samples. I also want to pay Rosa Gomez a visit. I need to tell her what's going on, and encourage her to start ordering a bigger supply of bottled water."

They made several stops, filling and carefully labeling the vials of water collected at each location, then finally they drove to Rosa's grocery store. It was open, though it was past closing time.

Marlee smiled. "You know, in her own way, Rosa is as dedicated to that grocery store as you are to your job as medic."

"Yes, I think you're right. She can always be counted on, which is a good thing because this town needs her."

"That's probably one of the reasons she operates that store and why she works so hard. Everyone needs to feel needed."

"You don't," Lucas said. "Not really."

"I don't allow myself that luxury," Marlee answered quietly. "But sometimes I do envy you. Your job is vital to this town. You're doing something that makes you indispensable."

"It exacts a price," he said quietly.

Marlee heard the tension in his voice, and glanced over at him. His jaw was clenched, and a muscle stretched taut across his cheek. On an instinctive level, she understood exactly what he was saying. Lucas loved his job, but its demands took a toll. Though the work took everything he had to give, it also left a void in his heart.

She observed the pride in his features. It defined his strength, but also his vulnerabilities. A new realization dawned over her. Lucas was afraid of needing anyone, just as she was. Questions filled her mind as she wondered what secrets the middle Blackhorse brother held safe within the iron walls of his heart.

Chapter Nine

While Lucas stood outside and spoke to Clyde Barkley, the postmaster, Marlee went inside Rosa's grocery store. The moment she stepped through the front door, Marlee felt the tension in the room.

"If you're here for bottled water, you're out of luck. I sold my last case about fifteen minutes ago," Rosa said. "Word got around about the sheriff's warning, and people rushed over. It's just too bad he didn't tell us about the water before now."

A murmur of assent went around the half-dozen customers there.

"It wasn't even suspected until a few hours ago. And it may not be the water anyway, remember that," Marlee cautioned, surprised by the harshness in Rosa's voice. As she studied the woman's expression, she saw something else there that chilled her. There was a haunted look on her face that spoke of fear barely kept in check.

Disturbed by the realization, Marlee walked over to the produce section and started to pick some apples from the bin.

"By the way, I'm not taking credit anymore," Rosa called out from behind the counter. "I'm going to have to pay plenty to get a delivery truck into this town. My regular wholesalers have started postponing shipments because they've heard people are getting sick left and right in Four Winds, and none of the drivers want to be exposed.''

Mrs. Tapia, whose famed chocolate-chip cookies had kept the bison from stampeding at the Harvest Festival, strode up to the counter. "The problem is that we need *real* medical care in this town. If our medic wasn't so proud, he would have already called the state for help. Then maybe we wouldn't all be trying to figure out who's going to get sick next.''

"You're all free to drive all the way to Santa Fe to see a doctor, if you can get an appointment. Meanwhile, Lucas is doing his best,'' Marlee argued. "Everyone knows he always consults with a doctor by radio. Stop jumping to conclusions and overreacting. This may not be anything more than a nasty outbreak of the flu.''

"Oh, sure, and that's why you're going around testing the water, right?'' Mrs. Tapia challenged.

"It's just a precaution, nothing more. He has to consider all the possibilities.''

Lucas caught the last of Marlee's words as he came inside. "She's right. I have no reason to suspect that this is anything other than a virus that's going around. People have become sick, but no one is dangerously ill.''

"That's exactly what I would have expected you to say,'' Mrs. Tapia said. "But the facts are plain enough. We have to watch out for ourselves now.''

"The real danger is what's happening to all of you. You're letting fear overrule your common sense, and that is going to be the biggest threat facing Four Winds,'' Marlee warned.

"Well, I, for one, have to say and do what I feel is right,'' Rosa said. "I'm going to need to take care of me and my family, too, so all accounts are cash-and-carry, and everything is on a first come, first served basis.'' Rosa glanced at Marlee. "And stop handling the fruit so much. Nobody wants your germs on it.''

Marlee settled her bill quickly and walked outside with
Lucas. "Did you see the shelves? They're almost half-
empty. Your brother didn't let out that information more
than a few hours ago, and it's already like a war zone in
there."

"And this is only the beginning."

THEY WERE HALFWAY to the boardinghouse when Lucas
suddenly slowed down and pulled to the side of the road.
"Do you have to go home right now? If not, there's one
stop I'd like to make."

"We can go wherever you like," she answered, glad for
the chance to extend her time with him. She glanced at the
way his strong hands gripped the wheel and remembered
their gentleness when he'd caressed her. As a delicious
warmth spread through her, she glanced away, afraid he'd
guess the direction her thoughts had taken. "Do you need
to see a patient?"

"Yes and no. Riley Sayers boards Chief for me out on
his farm, but he hasn't been feeling well. I thought I'd go
see if he needs a hand with the livestock. Would you
mind?"

"Not at all. I can certainly help clean stalls and feed the
animals." She found herself wishing it were summer. The
image of Lucas stripped to the waist, working hard with
the animals, almost made her shiver. Determined not to
dwell on that, she forced her thoughts onto the passing
scenery.

LUCAS DROVE SLOWLY up the snow-packed hill that led
away from town, making sure his snow tires didn't lose
traction. A flash of light to the right, somewhere uphill,
caught his attention, but before he had a chance to consider
it, he heard a loud pop and the wheel jerked out of his
hands.

The truck pulled sharply to the right, and he fought the natural impulse to swerve in the opposite direction.

He held on to the steering wheel tightly, letting off the gas and slowly straightening out the sliding truck, which had gone almost sideways in the road. "We just blew a tire. It's a good thing nobody was coming, or we'd have hit them for sure. This road's a disaster. I wish the county would get a snowplow out here every once in a while, or at least sand down the hills."

After they coasted to a stop, Lucas climbed out of the truck and reached behind the seat for the jack and lug wrench. Marlee got out, too, and picked up a big rock to block a rear tire. He smiled, noting that she wasn't interested in just watching from the sidelines and looking pretty, like a few other women he'd met. Maybe that was what he liked the most about her.

As he began to loosen the bolts holding the damaged tire in place, the crack of a rifle reverberated in the air. He dived to the ground, taking Marlee with him.

Lucas pushed her underneath the truck and followed her to a spot next to the driveshaft. "Keep your head down."

"No problem. What the heck's going on? A stray shot from a hunter?"

"It's not hunting season yet, though we do have poachers now and then. It also could be somebody's sighting in their rifle. Stay down until we find out."

He crawled toward the engine, hoping to get a better look. It was twilight, but his vision was excellent. Suddenly a bullet kicked up the snow just a few feet ahead of him, whining away in a ricochet off the asphalt.

Anger filled him as he thought of how close he'd just come. He'd been in a few tight spots before, in the military, carrying bandages instead of a rifle. But since he'd left the Middle East, no one had used him for target practice, let alone endangered a woman he cared about. At the moment, there was nothing he would have liked better than getting his hands on the gunman.

"What are we going to do? Even if you can get to your rifle, we can't shoot at a target we can't see," Marlee whispered, her voice taut.

"I've got news for you. We can't shoot—period. My rifle isn't in the truck."

The revelation surprised her. "I thought you always carried a gun of some kind in that rack behind the seat. A lot of men around here do, and a few women."

"I used to, but I gave it to my younger brother. He goes out to the mountains to gather different things for his medicine bundles and to visit the shrines. I figured he needed the protection more than I. The only thing I carry with me is a pocketknife."

Another bullet whined through the air, and she heard glass breaking overhead. "So we're sitting ducks, then," she said, crawling up beside the engine, trying to put more solid truck between her and the gunman.

"Not quite." He maneuvered over to the driver's side, then reached up into the cab of the truck and felt around for his cellular phone. "Overseas during a mission, we could usually call for a gunship or artillery. In this case, my brother will have to do. He'll be here, pronto." After a brief conversation, Lucas handed the phone to her. "Gabriel's on his way. In the meantime, I'm going hunting."

"With what, your pocketknife? He's got a rifle."

"Sweetheart, just because I'm not carrying a firearm doesn't mean I'm harmless." He gave her a lopsided grin as he moved back toward the tailgate of the truck. "Keep the engine compartment between you and the shooter, and stay low."

"If you think you're leaving me alone while you go off, you're crazy. If you want to sneak up on the shooter, you'll need someone else working with you to create a diversion. Otherwise you're going to get your head shot off." Another round impacted against the truck, striking the right side of the cab.

He hadn't considered the possibility that Marlee would insist on taking part. He was willing to put his own neck on the line, but not hers. "All I'm going to do is flank him and get close enough to have a look. I'm not going to confront him. It'll be better if you stay."

She shook her head as she crawled up beside him on the ground. "Not a chance. I'm getting to know you, Shadow. You'll be more careful if I'm along. Besides, there's no way I'm going to lie here on my stomach on the snow and sniff hot engine oil while you're out sneaking around the forest, hunting whoever is shooting at us. This concerns me, too."

She rolled out behind the tailgate, and scrambled into the brush beside the road before he could stop her.

Muttering a curse, Lucas followed, diving behind cover beside her. "Will you slow down?" he whispered softly. She could be the most exasperating female at times, but he couldn't help admiring her courage.

"I think I know where he's at." She pointed to a rocky outcropping halfway up the adjacent hillside. "He's behind those rocks. I saw the last muzzle-flash."

Another shot rang out, but this time it wasn't aimed for the truck. The round struck a fallen pine tree several feet away. "He's seen us," Marlee said.

"No, he couldn't have seen us. He *anticipated* us moving out from under the truck. Whoever is out there knows us. In another few seconds, I was planning to go over to that log," Lucas replied.

Lucas was certain he was right. It would have been difficult for anyone to have seen them in the underbrush. That meant their enemy had accurately predicted their next move. The realization filled him with a cold rage, but tempering that emotion was fear, not for himself, but for the woman who refused to allow him to protect her.

"So we won't follow the path he expects," he said quickly. "It's our best chance."

"What do you have in mind?" Marlee asked.

"He doesn't know for sure that we aren't armed, or he would have walked right down the hill and shot us at close range. He'll expect me to circle around, and you to either stay put or go with me. We can use that to our advantage. Let him see you go off to the side, like you're circling. He'll figure I'm with you. But I won't be. While he's keeping an eye out for us to the side, I'll go straight up the hill toward the shooter and maybe get close enough to identify him. If you're his primary target, we'll be keeping you further away," he said.

"In view of what we heard at Rosa's, it's just as likely he's after you. And you'll be going up right under his nose."

The point took him by surprise. "Why do you think that? I'm the only medical help in town."

"People are scared. If something happened to you, then the state would *have* to send a doctor—or at least a nurse practitioner—to take your place."

Lucas pursed his lips. There was a warped logic to what she was saying. "Yeah, I can see how that might occur to some."

"I still think your idea is too risky," Marlee warned.

He waited for a moment, thinking. "Hang tight a little longer. The shooter will fire another round soon. His shots have been about two to three minutes apart." As time ticked by, Lucas found that the silence bothered him more than the intermittent shots. "We can't know for certain where he is until he fires again, so until then he's got the advantage."

Another shot rang out, this one hitting some brush a little up slope of them. Lucas nodded, having spotted the shooter. He touched Marlee lightly on the shoulder to get her attention, then whispered, "Let's use this time to put some distance between us and the truck. Stick with me, but stay low.''

Lucas chose the densely wooded areas, though the snow-laden scrub brush grabbed at their clothing and made passage nearly impossible in spots.

Marlee stayed up with him, appreciating the trust he was placing in her as they worked together against their enemy.

As they reached an area close to the shooter's last known position, a place thick with scrub oaks and pine, Lucas slowed down. "We'll lay low here until we can pinpoint his new location. There's no way he can get a clear shot at us now," Lucas whispered.

"Comforting thought—I think."

He smiled at her. "Don't worry. Even if he comes after us, we'll see or hear him before he spots us. I'm good at escape and evasion, and there's more cover here than there was in the desert. Trust me on this. It's one of the things that I had to learn on the recon team." He saw the questions in her eyes, but shook his head. "Another time."

"I trust you."

His gut tightened. He wanted to know she trusted him as a man, not just because of the training he'd received, but because he was worthy of her trust in every way. He pushed the thought from his mind. This wasn't the time to dwell on that. She was relying on him, and for now, that was enough.

They remained perfectly still, listening. Soon Lucas heard the sound of a vehicle somewhere behind the hill driving away, then another one approaching along the highway.

He took her hand in his, and tried not to think about the softness of her skin or the way she held on to him tightly as he led her toward the road. He edged past the brambles, keeping them hidden in case there had been two men after them, and the vehicle leaving was a ruse. Sheltered behind a large rock, he caught a glimpse of the red flashing lights on top of his brother's Jeep.

"The shooter must have seen the sheriff's vehicle approaching and high-tailed it out of here."

Gabriel pulled up alongside Lucas's truck and jumped out quickly, taking shelter from possible attack from either side of the road by staying between the two trucks.

Lucas punched out Gabriel's cellular-phone number, and brought him up-to-date, telling him where they were, as well. He was frustrated but not surprised that the attacker had left the scene and no one had gotten a good look at either the shooter or the vehicle.

As they hurried to meet his brother, a coldness seeped through him. He didn't like the idea that, as it had been many times during his boyhood, Gabriel's presence had affected the fight and swung it in their favor. Lucas glanced back at Marlee. When he saw the relief in her eyes, the iciness coursing through his veins intensified. He would have given anything to have seen that look on her face because of something he'd done, rather than because of the arrival of the sheriff of Four Winds.

When Gabriel met his eyes, Lucas saw the flash of awareness there. The last thing he needed right now was a lecture from his older brother about calling for help sooner. If Gabriel said one word about this matter, he'd bury his brother's face in the nearest snowdrift, and worry about it later.

"What happened?" Gabriel asked, his tone crisp and businesslike as he continued to watch the hillside, rifle in hand.

Lucas filled him in succinctly. "We didn't ever see him. Did anyone pass you heading into town?"

"No, but maybe one of the rounds lodged in your truck will lead us somewhere." He found one flattened against the engine block and peeled it loose with his pocketknife. "This is a soft-point hunting round from a .30-.30 Winchester. It's too damaged to do a match, even if we found the rifle. Half the people in this county have one of these weapons anyway." He looked inside Shadow's truck, and saw the empty gun rack. "Start carrying a rifle, again. Your aim's lousy, but the noise might scare them away. Things are getting ugly in town, Shadow."

Lucas's hands balled into fists. "Don't forget my aim's gotten better since I was away, but if I ever get five minutes with whoever did this, I won't need a gun—just me and him…"

"I know how you feel," Gabriel said, "but let me take care of this. Don't you go hunting for trouble."

Lucas glanced at Marlee. "The truck's going to need some repairs, not just the tires, either. You'll have to ride back with my brother."

"And where the heck do you think you're going?" Gabriel challenged. "I'm going to need both of you back in town to sign statements about all this."

"I came out here to talk to Riley Sayers, and I'm going to do that first."

"You're going to need more than Chief to get around now," Gabriel said. "The town council should be able to provide you with a vehicle."

"Yeah, no doubt, but I don't want to get stuck with the one they'll undoubtedly come up with."

Gabriel gave him a puzzled look, then suddenly he nodded. "Yeah, you're right. You'd probably be offered the old man's truck," he said. Like Lucas, he avoided mentioning Simmons by name out of respect for Navajo tradition.

"I'm not worried about the *chindi,* but I'd just as soon not drive his van around. It might unnerve some of my patients to see me coming in a dead man's vehicle."

"You have a point," Gabriel said.

"I'm going to ask Riley if I can borrow his son's Blazer.

The boy's off going through basic training now, and left the thing at home.''

Gabriel took his brother aside, leaving Marlee standing by his Jeep. ''What's eating at you, Shadow? You had someone gunning for you and her, yet your mind doesn't seem to be focused on what just happened.''

''You're wrong. It is focused. It just occurred to me that our town is going crazy again, like it did with you and then Tree. Only this time it's my turn, and Marlee's, too.''

''Maybe you should keep your distance from her, then. It's easier to handle your own problems without combining them with hers. I bet Coach Jenkins over at the high school would keep an eye on Marlee. He's asked her out twice that I know of. I could speak to him about it.''

''I wouldn't do that if I were you. Marlee is my business, not yours or his.'' The words came out before he could stop them. He glared at his brother as he saw the smug grin on his face.

''Well, son of a gun! Looks like Lanie was right. You're really stuck on her. Well, it had to happen sooner or later.''

Lucas contented himself by giving his brother a stony glare. When Gabriel's grin got wider, Lucas fought hard to suppress the impulse to deck him.

''Stop by my office after you get through at Riley's place,'' Gabriel said. ''And here—'' Gabriel handed Lucas his rifle ''—take this. There are fights you can win with your fists, Shadow, but this isn't going to be one of them.''

Lucas turned his head and walked back over to Marlee, who had decided to get into the Jeep where it was warm. ''I'll catch up to you later.''

''Go take care of your patient,'' she said with a brief nod. ''Gabriel will get me home safely.''

He knew she'd meant to reassure him that he was free to go, but somehow the words irked him more than he'd thought possible. He didn't want to need Marlee, but for some reason he wasn't ready to define, he wanted Marlee to need him.

His grip on the rifle was tight as he strode down the road to the turnoff, then uphill in the snow. He'd always prided himself on being able to handle any situation. Yet right now his biggest battle was against himself—between logic and feelings that defied his attempts to ignore.

THE NEXT MORNING, after a disappointing shopping expedition, Marlee returned to the boardinghouse with only a few groceries. Her thoughts were more troubled than ever. Lucas had come in late and left early, and she'd heard while trying on boots at the feed store, that almost a third of the schoolkids were now at home with the flu, and the town council was thinking of suspending classes. Most of the businesses along Main Street were closed. Only the grocery store, the feed store and the post office had remained open.

She'd gone into Rosa's briefly, having no other place to buy food, and the treatment she'd received was more chilling than the icicles dangling off the roofs. She was used to having people's eyes stray to her scar when they spoke to her, but at least before now they'd tried to hide it. Today she'd even heard one woman whisper something about how difficult it must have been for Lucas not to stare when he was with her. The words had hurt, though she hadn't let anyone know.

The worst was that the feeling of danger hanging over the townspeople had changed everything she loved about Four Winds. All of the friendliness that she'd come to associate with the town had vanished.

Marlee kept busy in her own kitchen, finishing the pies she'd promised to take over to the senior citizens' center. Since her supplies were getting short, she'd considered not doing the baking. Yet, unwilling to disappoint anyone, she'd decided to go ahead anyway.

As she set the pies out on the front porch to cool, a vehicle pulled up.

Lucas stepped out of the borrowed Blazer and walked up her front steps. Something about his expression chilled her spirit.

"What's wrong?" she asked.

"I was just at my brother's office. The news that the peddler paid Four Winds a visit is out."

"Do they know he was here at the boardinghouse?"

"Fuzz isn't sure about that."

"I was afraid this might happen, but I was really hoping it wouldn't come out until the flu epidemic was under control. Now people will start trying to find out who the peddler met. The Blackhorse family and you, in particular, will be at the top of that suspect list."

"Which means you're going to have to watch your back more than ever, because you've been with me a lot lately," Lucas warned, coming inside with her and dropping down on the couch. "I've got to tell you, in all the time I've lived here, I've never seen people acting this badly toward each other. Folks who've known each other for years, ones I'd thought of as fast friends, barely look at each other."

Marlee had never harbored any illusions about the nobility of people. She was a realist, but Lucas's observations were filled with the pain of betrayal and it nearly snapped her heart in two. She wondered just how badly he'd been treated by the townspeople he served.

"When people are scared, they say and do things they don't really mean," she said.

"I learned something in the military about situations like these—where nothing seems to stop an enemy. People's fears erode their confidence, and they begin to lose hope. When that happens, a kind of dry rot of the soul takes over, and they lose the battle all that much faster."

Marlee nodded thoughtfully. She knew intimately the feeling he was describing. "When dreams die, when people think they have nothing to lose, that's when they're at their most dangerous.''

Lucas met her gaze. "That applies to all of us—the good guys and the bad.''

Marlee didn't look away. An alliance was forming between them. He was acknowledging that they each had secrets, and their pasts each held a share of darkness. Yet it was through the lessons they'd learned there that they would find the courage and the cunning to fight the battles that lay ahead.

Knowing she didn't stand alone, that she had an ally who would remain at her side, renewed her determination and courage. Yet at the same time, she desperately wished her feelings for Lucas could have given him comfort and provided a haven for him, instead of propelling him headlong into danger. A dark rush of sadness filled her, weighing her spirit down.

As Lucas's cellular phone rang, she left him alone, giving him some privacy. Remembering she hadn't checked for mail, Marlee went out to the box. It looked like the seeds she'd ordered for next spring had been shipped early. Maybe that was a good omen, a sign that, like spring and the new life it brought, the situation in Four Winds would undergo a regeneration soon, bringing new hopes and peace.

Feeling better, she returned inside and walked to the kitchen. As she tore the small box open, a handful of dead insects fell out. Marlee yelped and jumped back.

Lucas, who'd only got as far as the living room, rushed to her side in an instant. He stared at the insects, then scooped them into a paper towel and placed them in the trash.

"Throw the box out, too, will you?" Marlee asked, and shuddered. "I don't mind bugs so much when they're someplace you'd expect. But this was too much.''

He picked up the box by the edges and studied it.

"There's something else in here," he said, then shook it. A small, black plastic rose fell out with a note taped to the stem.

"'The fruits of corruption,'" Lucas read. "What's that mean to you?"

"Not a thing," she said, staring pensively at the block-lettered words written in pencil.

Lucas placed the box and plastic flower back on the table. "Leave these for my brother."

"They're not much use as clues. What can you tell from a cheap plastic flower that's been painted black? It's not even new."

"It's still revealing. Look at the way it's worn around the edges, as if the elements like the rain and sun have taken their toll on it. My guess is that it came from a grave-site, which means it's meant as a threat to you, and also to me as a Navajo."

Chapter Ten

Marlee stood to one side as Gabriel studied the box and plastic flower. When she'd first seen the seed package, she'd thought of it as a sign of things to come. She'd been right, though not in the way she'd hoped.

"I agree with you, Shadow. This probably came from a grave at the cemetery." Gabriel glanced at Marlee. "Still no ideas of who might have sent you this?"

"No, but I bet it was tampered with after it was put in my mailbox. The return address is genuine, and so is the box. I've placed plenty of orders from that catalog company before."

Gabriel looked at his brother. "If this had happened a little later today, I would have blamed the article in the paper. Now I'm thinking that whoever leaked that story also arranged for this, but his timing was off a bit."

"What article?" Marlee asked. "I haven't seen the paper yet."

"You didn't miss much. Alex wrote another long editorial pointing out that Shadow is the only member of the Blackhorse family who hasn't been involved with the peddler—until now. He hints that the illnesses are linked to the peddler and to you two."

Shadow grimaced. "He's always been a thorn in our side. He reacted the same way before, with you and Joshua.

What I really need now to fight these allegations are the test results on that water. I asked it be given priority because of the town's situation, and requested it be faxed to me at your office. Have you received anything yet?''

"Not that I know about, but I haven't been in for several hours. I do know your medical supplies came this morning. The truck wasn't sure where to deliver them, so they came to my office. My dispatcher signed for them."

"I'll go over there and get them right now." He glanced at Marlee. "Will you give me a hand?"

"Sure, but I'd like to drop off the pies I baked for the seniors at the center first."

"No problem."

After delivering the pies and taking a few moments to say hello to some of the regulars at the center, Marlee returned to the Blazer with Lucas. For what seemed to be an eternity, they rode in silence.

Desire ribboned through her, as unexpected as it was powerful. She, who'd always held to the belief that keeping secrets meant trusting no one, felt the desperate urge to trust this man.

"Do you think Gabriel will catch whoever shot at us?" she asked at long last.

"I really doubt it. That's one of the things that worries me most. The person will know he got away with it, and that'll just build up his confidence. Then he'll try again." He took a deep breath, then let it out slowly. "I really hate being the target of someone who doesn't have the guts to face me."

"Maybe we should hedge our bets. If we stay away from each other, we may deter the attacks, or at the very least force this person to target only one of us."

"If I thought you would be safer without my being around, I would have offered to do that, but until we know who and what we're up against, any action we take could turn out to be making things worse. There's also another factor to consider. Right now, with my caseload getting heavier by the hour, I need your help. I've read through the notes and records you took for me back at the high school, and they're excellent. They're concise yet thorough, like someone trained and experienced in medicine.''

Their eyes met as he probed her face for answers. She said nothing. He was fishing. Eventually, of course, he'd learn the whole story. Gabriel would dig into her past until he got to know her far better than she would have ever wanted. And, of course, he'd tell his brother. But until then, she would continue to guard her secrets. For now, she'd enjoy the closeness she shared with Lucas, and allow it to soothe the ache in her heart.

When they arrived at Gabriel's office, Lucas and Marlee began the process of checking the shipment of medical supplies that had arrived there. Several minutes later, Gabriel came in holding a fax. ''Here's the report on the town's water. I took the liberty of giving it a quick read. It's only a preliminary screening, but they've given the water the all-clear so far from viral or bacterial contaminants,'' he said.

Lucas studied the lab's findings. ''So it looks like it is the flu after all.''

''We can all use news like this.'' Gabriel looked at the contents of the two open cardboard boxes. ''That isn't much by way of supplies,'' Gabriel commented. ''Do you have enough medications?''

''This is my normal order, and it's usually more than enough, but it won't be now, not at the rate I'm using up my stock. I'm going to have to get the town council to okay more funds. If we still had a mayor, I'd go directly to him. Since we don't, I have to do things by committee. That's slow and usually a hassle.''

''We really *do* need to elect a new mayor,'' Gabriel said. ''But nobody wants the job.''

''That's no surprise,'' Shadow answered, ''and I can't

say I blame them. It's a truckload of paperwork, and very little by way of rewards.''

"The problem goes deeper than that. Our town operates on the legend that holds us together—Flinthawk's legacy. Most people believe there's no need for something as structured as a mayor, because, one way or another, things will work out for us here in Four Winds.''

"Yes, but even so, there's still day-to-day business that needs to be handled,'' Marlee said.

"Sure, but convincing anyone that it's worth their time is another matter. Our last mayor had money already, and needed the job to keep his own loneliness at bay. But there's no one here now who has a need the job can fill. Until that happens, the post will remain empty, and the town council will keep trying their hardest to avoid any real responsibility.''

Marlee had always driven herself mercilessly, focusing on achieving whatever goals she set for herself. The way of thinking Gabriel had just described was as alien to her as the moons of Neptune. She had no equivalent, and no response.

Gabriel's phone rang, and he grabbed it immediately.

"What's going on? Slow down, Mrs. White." He paused, then Marlee heard him add, "Yes, they're both here.''

Giving his brother a questioning look, Lucas waited, his back erect, his shoulders tense.

"Shadow, you're needed at the senior citizens' center,'' Gabriel said, hanging up. "Two of the people there became ill a short time after you left.''

Lucas glanced at Marlee. "Come on. You can help me document the onset of symptoms and gather information.''

"That may not be a good idea,'' Gabriel said.

"Why not?'' Marlee asked.

"Mrs. White also asked that you pick up the pies you'd dropped off. They think that somehow you're responsible, and now everyone's afraid to accept anything you've touched.''

The words cut Marlee to the quick. She'd visited these people once or twice a week for years, and looked on many of them as friends. ''They think *I* put something in the pies?''

''No, nobody's even touched them. Apparently after you left, Mrs. Gonzales got really sick and then Mr. Archuleta. What they're thinking is that maybe the peddler put some sort of curse on you.''

Marlee exhaled softly. ''Gabriel's right,'' she said to Lucas. ''Maybe I shouldn't go with you. It could make your job tougher, and these people are going to need treatment. The flu isn't something the elderly can afford to ignore.''

Lucas's eyes narrowed, and she saw the flash of something dark and dangerous there. ''You're going with me. I need an assistant, and nobody else has exactly jumped up and volunteered. It's my job to treat them, and I'll do just that, but I won't let superstition dictate my actions. If they want a sacrificial goat, let them pick on someone besides you. I won't stand for this nonsense.''

''It may be nonsense to you, Shadow, but it isn't to them,'' Gabriel warned. ''I heard Mrs. White's voice. That woman was really upset.''

''Then reason is the only thing that will change that,'' Lucas countered.

''Reason only works when the mind is open to it. Fear denies reason as near as I've been able to tell, and is immune to it,'' Marlee said.

''You can't back away from this,'' Lucas insisted, his eyes hard as they held Marlee's. ''In an attempt to be kind, you may be doing serious damage to your reputation—and to the people I'm trying to help. I need your help with the paperwork. There are times when a person should back off out of respect for another's beliefs, but this isn't one of them.''

Marlee knew that to Lucas, things were either right or wrong. There were no shades of gray. That was one of the qualities she admired most about him. He set a course for himself based on his highest sense of right, and followed it whatever the odds.

"Let's see how it goes," she said at last. "If their fear of the peddler and my connection to him prevents them from accepting the help you need to give them, then I'll leave. It's not worth the fight if it'll endanger people."

MARLEE AND LUCAS ARRIVED at the senior's center a short while later. The atmosphere there had always been pleasant and friendly, but it was far from that today. From the moment Marlee walked inside, she felt as if the temperature had suddenly dropped by fifty degrees. People refused to meet her gaze and moved back out of the way as she and Lucas strode down the hall, avoiding any chance of physical contact with Marlee.

As they reached the games room, Mrs. White took Lucas to Mr. Archuleta, the retired barber, who now lay on a cot against one wall. His breathing was shallow, and his eyes were almost closed.

As Lucas began questioning the patient while he took his vital signs, Marlee decided to collect information from those around him. She approached Sherry Stinson, a woman in her seventies who had knitted her a gorgeous set of slippers last Christmas.

The woman Marlee had always thought of as a friend backed away from her now.

"Wait. Don't do this, please," Marlee said quietly. "What happened here was not my fault."

"I'm not blaming you, but I *am* afraid of the peddler. I don't trust anyone or anything associated with him."

"He's just an elderly Indian man." She studied Mrs. Stinson's face. The rational woman she'd known had vanished, hidden under deeply seated prejudices and fears.

"If you really want to help those who are sick, like Mr. Archuleta over there, you have to get involved. Talk to me, please?" Marlee pressed gently.

The expression in Mrs. Stinson's dark gray eyes shifted slowly from wariness to acceptance. "I don't know how much help I can be, but I'll try. I was here when they both got sick. It started a few minutes after you left. Mr. Archuleta had just come in—he'd been with his grandson over at the high school watching him during basketball practice. We kept telling him to stay away, that too many kids were getting sick, but he wouldn't listen."

"What about Mrs. Gonzales? I didn't think she got out much, except to come here and visit."

"That's true. I have no idea at all why she got sick. She's the last person I figured would have a problem with this."

Hearing someone moan, Marlee turned her head and saw Mrs. White clutching the back of a chair, swaying unsteadily on her feet. Marlee hurried to her side, and helped the woman sit down on a sofa.

"I'm sorry. I thought I could handle this. I've been feeling queasy, but it wasn't bad, not until right now."

As Lucas worked, Marlee recorded the events leading up to the onset of symptoms. There was only one common denominator that every one who'd become sick shared— the water. The center had just recently switched from their own well to using town water.

An hour later, Lucas and Marlee finished their work and left the center. "I've arranged to send blood samples over to the county hospital," Lucas said. "I doubt I'll get anything more specific than an elevated white count, but we'll see. I just can't shake the feeling we're missing something extremely important, that the clue to what's making people so sick is right in front of me."

"You really don't think this is the flu, do you?"

Lucas shook his head. "No. The symptoms aren't quite right, and let's face it, the flu proceeds through several stages that most people have experienced in the past and recognize. What we're facing here comes on fast, then lingers on, without much change or development.''

As they pulled up in front of the boardinghouse, they saw Gabriel's Jeep. He was standing on the front porch, waiting.

Lucas climbed out of the Blazer quickly. ''Everything okay?''

Gabriel waited for them to join him on the porch. ''Let's go inside before talking. There's been a new turn of events you should know about.''

Gabriel was silent until they were all seated in the living room. ''We've got problems. The town council decided to call the governor, telling him that we didn't have adequate medical help here. They threatened to call a press conference, contact federal officials and do whatever it took to make the state pay attention. They insisted the governor send help before whatever is making people sick here spreads to other communities.''

''What happened then?'' Lucas asked.

''The governor ordered the state health department to send a doctor down, and they managed to get the same physician you've been consulting with, that doc from Santa Fe. He'll assess the situation. If, in his opinion, it's warranted, a doctor from the county hospital will be sent here until the crisis is over.''

''Fine. I can use the help.''

''So this doesn't bother you?'' Gabriel pressed.

''I didn't say that. I think the town council should have consulted with me first, out of courtesy if nothing else. But my first concern is for those who are sick.''

''You can expect the doc either tonight or tomorrow morning. He'll be staying here at the boardinghouse, of course.''

''I'll get a room ready,'' Marlee said, seeing Gabriel out.

Gabriel's phone rang as he reached the door. Marlee

watched his expression change from one of worry, to something much darker and infinitely more dangerous. "They're doing what? I'll be there shortly."

Marlee felt a chill pass over her. Everything about Gabriel's stance and expression told her a fight was brewing.

"We've got serious trouble, Shadow. I can use your help. There's a group of families trying to leave town. Only right at the city-limit sign, near that big road cut in the hillside, there's a bunch of men from the next town blocking the highway. They're stopping anyone coming from Four Winds who tries to go through, and turning them back. The mountain roads are impassable, so there's no getting in or out any other way. We've got two groups standing eye to eye, and half of them are women or children. Jake was coming back from his cabin and saw what was going on, so he called me. He's still there trying to keep the lid on this situation, but from what he said, some of the out-of-towners are armed, and it's getting nasty."

"Let's go, then," Lucas said, following his brother out the door.

Marlee started to go with them, but Lucas stopped her. "No, you need to stay here in case the doctor shows up."

"He won't be able to get past their roadblock, and if people are hurt, you're going to need an extra pair of hands—I'm it. Let's not waste any more time."

Lucas looked at Gabriel as Marlee strode to his vehicle. "If you don't want her to go, then you better be willing to arrest her."

"Women," Gabriel muttered.

Marlee sneaked a quick glance back and saw the hint of a smile on Lucas's face as he rushed to join her.

"IT COULD GET ROUGH, Shadow," Gabriel warned, slowing down as they approached the row of cars parked on the road ahead.

People were gathered on both sides of a crude sawhorse

barrier that ran across the narrow cut in the hillside. The roadblock effectively blocked the only way out of Four Winds during the winter.

"Jake's a great ally," Gabriel added, "but this isn't a fight we can win by just smashing a few heads."

"I know, and it's too bad, because that's just what I'm in the mood for."

"Yeah, that's why I figured I better say something now. I need you to stay cool, no matter what happens."

Gabriel pulled over into the left lane and drove down the line of cars, stopping about fifty feet from the barrier. On the other side of the barrier, half a dozen armed men blocked the way, their vehicles parked a few dozen feet across the highway.

Gabriel, Marlee and Lucas stepped out of the Jeep, spoke to Jake and learned nobody had been hurt or threatened directly yet.

"This is not the answer, folks," Gabriel said when he reached the barrier. "What's going on here is illegal, unnecessary and dangerous. You all should go home before you catch colds."

"Maybe unnecessary to you, Sheriff," a young mother clutching a bundled-up toddler argued. "But we have a right to take our families out of Four Winds to someplace where they'll be safe."

"Then you'll all have to fly or walk out through the mountains," a muscular dark-haired man standing behind the makeshift barrier yelled out. "Your township ends here, and we're establishing a county citizens' quarantine at this roadblock. We're not letting anyone from Four Winds come into the rest of the county. We've heard what's going on over there. People are getting sick, and you have no idea why. You're not spreading that over here."

Lucas stood to one side of Gabriel, and Jake was on the other. His brother had one hand over the butt of his revolver, though Lucas knew he would never use it in a situation like this. "Listen to me, and listen carefully," Lucas said loudly. "People are sick—a lot of them, I grant you that, but it's flu season, so it's to be expected. There's no reason for anyone to panic, either, on either side of this hill. Nobody's died—"

"Yes, they have," the big man behind the barrier shouted. "We heard that a corpse was taken out of Four Winds and is slated for an autopsy. I saw the hearse myself, or at least my wife did."

"What are you talking about?" Lucas demanded. "Nobody—oh, wait a minute. You're talking about a man close to ninety years old, who passed away because of a bad heart. Why should anybody be surprised about that? And there was no autopsy ordered, either. His body was simply taken away to a funeral home. You can verify that in Santa Fe."

"We don't believe you," the man answered. "And you're not passing through."

Lucas looked around him. Fear held all these people in a stranglehold. He captured the gazes of two women he'd known since high school. "Jenny, Lucinda, your kids are fine, and so are both of you. Why are you so frightened? Are you both willing to leave your homes and your husbands?"

"Our men have to stay and look after the livestock, but our kids need to be someplace where they're safe from whatever is going around. I'm willing to believe that Mr. Simmons died of a heart attack, but you can't deny that nobody's getting better. This *flu*," she said, almost spitting out the word, "if that's what it is, just wears you down, taking away your will to fight it. I don't want my kids exposed to this."

"That's real touching, but what about the rest of the citizens? You want your kid safe," the man by the barrier shouted, "but you're willing to risk spreading this illness to the rest of the county in the process."

Lucas glanced over the man. He was over six foot six and looked as if he could have taken on Gabriel despite his brother's police training. It might take two of them just to make an arrest, and that would leave only Jake to deal with the others. The odds weren't good. He wished Tree were with them now. He could make any man back up.

"Our quarantine stands. None of you are coming any further down this road, so you might as well all go home," the man said, a smug look on his face.

Gabriel muttered a curse. "I'm going to have to get county and state police to help clear the roadblock. We're outnumbered. Jake, Lucas, could you two try and get our people back into their cars?"

Marlee, who had been noticing how people backed away from her, smiled wryly. "It looks like I can help you there. They don't want to be anywhere near me. I can use that now to our advantage."

As Lucas watched, Marlee did as she'd promised. When she approached the families, the mothers would quickly gather their children and hurry back to the cars. His gut wrenched knowing how their reaction hurt her, though she showed no sign of it. She had too much pride for that.

Suddenly they heard the reverberating blast of a truck's air horn. The racket made everyone shift their attention to the road leading back to town.

"I'm coming through," Bill Riley shouted through the driver's-side window of his eighteen-wheeler. "Get out of my way."

The men behind the barrier stared at the truck, then most stepped closer to their own vehicles in the road. Marlee's job suddenly became easier. People hurried back to their cars without much prodding. Nobody wanted to be in the way of a semi.

The burly man who'd been giving the orders from across the barrier stood his ground, and laughed. "I expected this.'' He turned his head and waved to another man who stood halfway up the steep hillside.

Lucas's instinct for danger kicked into overdrive. He saw a second man up on the hill move out of the shadows of a big rock overhang, unwinding a cord from what looked like a small reel. Lucas's neck prickled, and an edgy feeling filled him as his senses became almost painfully alert.

"That looks familiar," Jake said. "You don't suppose they plan on doing something unbelievably stupid, do you?"

Lucas saw one man produce a small flame, probably from a lighter, and light the cord. "He's got explosives!"

"Get everyone back!" Gabriel shouted to Lucas, then turned and ran for the hillside.

"Clear the road unless you have a death wish," the man behind the barrier said.

The people who remained outside panicked, and scrambled for their cars. Lucas heard a little boy scream as he got separated from his mother. The next instant, Marlee grabbed him and, lifting him off the ground, ran toward the cars, locating his mother in seconds.

Lucas's chest swelled with pride and another feeling he didn't want to define as he watched Marlee risk herself to help the people who'd treated her so badly minutes before. He fought the desire to go to her side and pull her into his arms right there and then in front of everyone.

Hearing Jake call and realizing he was needed elsewhere immediately, Lucas ran back toward the barrier. Jake was trying to direct traffic as people started their cars at once.

"You'll never make it in time, Sheriff. If you don't want this place to become your grave, you'd better slide back down that hill and run for it. This whole area is going to be filled with rubble in thirty seconds," the burly man called out, and began to back his truck away rapidly.

Lucas saw Jake taking Marlee to his truck and silently thanked the former Ranger. Looking around, he searched

for his brother. Just as Gabriel reached the road, the dyna-
mite went off. The concussion knocked him halfway across
the road. Seeing his brother fall, Lucas rushed up to him.
Grabbing Gabriel's arm, Lucas pulled him diagonally toward a drainage culvert. He heard the ominous rumble, and
felt the ground shake as tons of rock started to slide down
the hill. Lucas pressed on, refusing to look back.

In less than five seconds, both men were off the road
and inside the culvert. Rocks and debris rained down just
outside. Lucas grinned at his brother. "Good thing for you
I was around."

Gabriel rubbed his knee. "You've been dying to say that
for years, I'll bet."

"And how."

Gabriel laughed.

"You okay?" Lucas asked, checking his brother over
for injuries.

"I'm fine. I smacked my knee when the concussion
threw me to the ground, but it's no big deal."

When the rumbling stopped, both men crawled out,
working together to remove a few boulders that had nearly
blocked the end of the pipe.

The cut in the hillside was piled high with car-sized
rocks, rubble and mud that had been produced from the
heat of the blast melting the snow. Turning back toward
Four Winds, Lucas could see Jake checking that people
were unhurt. A few were outside their cars already, staring
at the spectacle of a road completely obliterated by tons of
earth and rock.

"Well, we won't have to worry about the roadblock being a source of contention anymore. It'll take days to clear
this road now. Not even a bicycle could get over that mountain."

Gabriel brushed the dust and snow off his uniform and
called out to the stunned citizens standing by their cars.
"Go home. I think you've all done enough out here today."

"Sheriff, you better pray your brother finds an answer, and fast. Without that road, there's not going to be any food, gas or anything else coming into town except on foot. Between shortages and this sickness, we're going to be fighting for our lives," Lucinda said. She looked at the crowd, then threw her shoulders back in a gesture of defiance and got back into her car.

Lucas stared at the massive rock pile that now blocked the road. "You realize that I'm going to have to hike around this rubble and get to a car on the other side before I can send the samples I've collected to the county hospital," he said to Gabriel. "And we still have to get the doctor through."

"I'll find a bulldozer and get men to clear a lane or make a detour. We can't let the road stay blocked."

"They won't be safe. I have a feeling that group of charmers on the other side will do their best to make sure this road stays closed."

"I have options. I'll be calling in the state police to break up that little gathering and to protect the road crew."

Marlee and Jake approached a moment later. Lucas's gaze stayed on Marlee as she walked toward him. Her gentle smile touched him, stirring his blood. He needed her softness, her tenderness, her warmth. Desire clawed at his gut, overwhelming and fierce.

Unaware of his thoughts, she came to stand beside him. "They don't know the harm they've done," she said, her gaze on the blocked road. "We're going to be pretty isolated for a while."

"I wouldn't want to be in your shoes, Shadow," Jake commented, his voice weary.

"Yeah, I know," Lucas said. "If I don't offer Four Winds some answers fast, the threat our own people will pose to each other will rival that of the deadliest virus."

Chapter Eleven

The following morning, Lucas sat with Marlee in Gabriel's office. The doctor they'd been expecting hadn't managed to get through on the blocked road, but he'd managed to contact the police dispatcher, leaving word that he would complete his journey by helicopter.

Gabriel looked at his brother, then at Marlee. "He'll be landing in the field next to Riley's cow pasture. This Dr. Soto has already had an eyeful of our situation. Apparently he'd been held up by some of those county residents who set up the roadblock. He saw the explosion and rock slide, then was told to go home and forget all about it. So he turned back and made alternate plans."

"Any doctor who has worked in an emergency room or attended trauma patients has seen people at their best and worst. I'm sure he's aware that when panic sets in, anything can happen." Lucas rubbed his right shoulder, trying to work some kinks out. "But why is he landing so far out of town? There are other possible landing sites closer in."

"I'd rather people didn't know when or how he's arriving. I think that'll be safer for all concerned. Come to think of it, I'm going to have to find a vehicle I can place at his disposal. I suppose you-know-who's vehicle is still out of the question for a doctor."

"He won't need the old man's van, or any other vehicle,

for that matter. I can take him wherever he wants to go," Lucas volunteered.

Gabriel shook his head. "Sorry, Shadow, but as he pointed out, his business is to find out about this mysterious illness and see how much of a threat it poses. Daily medical emergencies are no concern of his while he's here. He'll still serve as your consultant and adviser, as he normally does from Santa Fe, but that's it."

"Oh, great. So I have to talk to him by radio? I thought he was here to help us, not study Four Winds."

"The man won't win any popularity contests with his superior attitude, but he's supposedly got a great reputation. The town council was told Dr. Soto used to work for the CDC in Atlanta."

"How did he end up in Santa Fe, then?" Marlee asked.

"Apparently he wanted a less stressful position." Gabriel leaned back in his seat. "I'll need to have someone deliver my wife's sedan to the doctor. I was hoping you'd take it out," he said, looking at Marlee, "then ride back into town with Shadow."

"No problem. Glad to do it," Marlee answered.

Lucas looked over at her. She was tired. It had been a while since she'd had a full night's sleep, yet she was always ready to help whenever she was needed. Sorrow and frustration knifed at his gut as he realized that no matter how badly he wanted to, he couldn't protect her from a town that had gone crazy. But it was the intensity of his desire to protect her that rocked him clear down to his boots.

As they walked outside, Marlee looked up and down the street. "The town looks deserted. I've never seen anything like this. It's nearly ten in the morning, but no businesses appear to be open at all. Did you know that Rosa's taken to keeping her door locked? She opens it only if you tell her specifically what you want and if she has it available in the store. She's also raised her prices by fifty percent."

"After seeing what happened out there at the roadblock yesterday, I'll believe anything." As his gaze traveled over Marlee, he wondered about the life they might have had if things had been different.

They'd just reached Lanie's car when Lucas's cellular phone rang. He spoke into it briefly, then turned his attention back to Marlee. "I have to go check out Mrs. Davenport. She hasn't been able to eat much of anything for three days now. She's young and strong, but she'll need to get some liquids down." He glanced at his watch. "Looks like the doc will have to wait."

"Let me deliver Lanie's car to Dr. Soto, then. I'll catch a ride back into town with him."

Lucas exhaled softly. "The roads are icy and treacherous on that stretch, so be careful." He gazed into her eyes and caressed her cheek with his palm. The way she leaned into him, like a cat being stroked, made a rush of desire fork through him like lightning.

He felt her shudder and nearly lost his control. Flames raced down to his groin. He had to let her go now, or they'd both be very late to their next destination. With effort, he stepped away from her. "Stay in touch."

Lucas held Marlee's gaze a moment longer than was necessary, hoping to convey with that one look all the emotions he couldn't put into words. As he drove off, he saw her nod as if she'd understood and had listened to the silent words his heart had spoken.

MARLEE DROVE Lanie's old sedan down the access road bordering Riley's snow-covered alfalfa field. The helicopter was scheduled to arrive soon, if the weather hadn't delayed it. As she waited, she glanced at the bare branches of a row of apple trees along the road. They jutted out toward the sky like skeletal limbs, imploring heaven for help.

She'd only been there for a few minutes when the unmistakable thump of rotor blades signaled a helicopter circling in from the south.

Marlee stepped out of the car and walked out into the field to greet the middle-aged, energetic-looking doctor who jumped down from the chopper. He was thin, too much so, but his strides were filled with purpose.

He came toward her, holding a medical bag in one hand, while pulling his wool coat closer around himself with the other. "Don't tell me. You're my escort, whether or not I want one, right?"

"I'm only here to deliver a car to you, and tell you you're staying at my boardinghouse, but I'd sure appreciate a ride back to town, too," Marlee said, introducing herself.

"I'm Dr. Soto," he said, shaking hands with her. "I saw what happened on the road leading out of town yesterday. Things are certainly tense in this little burg of yours. I sure hope people aren't thinking that I can work any miracles."

The abrupt statement took her by surprise. "I don't think so. They just want answers."

"It sounds to me like that medic Blackhorse is handling things fine. I probably won't have any new answers to give them, not for a while." He threw his bag in the back seat of Lanie's car, then got into the passenger's side. "Time's wasting. Let's go."

Marlee got behind the wheel and tried not to smile. She'd worked with doctors like him before. To them, there was purpose in motion, in pursuing a goal. Resting was purposeless, and had no place in the field. She'd shared that philosophy most of her adult life, too.

"I've checked the samples Blackhorse sent in to our lab for testing," he said. "Nothing's come back positive. What I'd like to do now is interview some of the people who've come down with this mysterious flu."

"All right, no problem."

He glanced over at her. "You haven't been infected with this, I gather. Do you have any theories as to why not?"

"I'm hardy?"

"In other words, you have no theory."

Poor Lucas would have his hands full with this one. "I can't come to any conclusions without more information, doctor. You, of all people, should know that."

They spent the next hour gathering data. Marlee stayed out of his way as Dr. Soto talked to Lucas's patients, asking the same questions over and over with the tenacity of a pit bull. She had to hand it to him; he didn't know the meaning of the word *no*. Whenever he was denied anything, he simply overrode it by refusing to accept any answer contrary to the one he wanted.

Two hours later, after a thorough look at the grocery and Sally's Diner, which included taking numerous samples for testing, Dr. Soto sat at one of the tables in the lunchroom at the seniors' center, entering data into a laptop computer and sipping coffee. Marlee didn't interrupt him.

"I have no answers, conclusions or even theories, so looking at me with a million questions in your eyes won't help," he clipped, not glancing up. "I can feel you staring at me, but you might as well stop wasting your time. Now, let's go take a look at your medic's records, those specific to this outbreak. I want the latest data he's got."

"I've been helping him gather information, so I can tell you with absolute certainty that transmission, host factor and cause still remain a mystery."

His eyebrows shot up, and this time he extended her the courtesy of actually looking at her. "You've worked in the medical profession. Were you a nurse or a tech?"

"I picked up the terminology along the way," Marlee hedged. "My job here is to run the boardinghouse."

He held her gaze for a second, unconvinced, then leaned back in his chair and rubbed his eyes. "I've entered all my data, and from what I see, what we're dealing with here doesn't appear to be an airborne virus. Otherwise, we would have had a greater incidence of cases, particularly among families and here where people are most susceptible. But, of course, that's only a guess at this stage. The good news is, that since you haven't had any deaths due to this illness, I don't think it's something to be overly concerned about."

As they traveled to the high-school portable, Marlee filled him in about the fire at the clinic that had forced the move.

"Pets," Soto mused after a pause, "and livestock. Do any of the people who are sick now also have pets or livestock who are, or were, sick?"

Marlee thought about it. "No, and I would have heard by now if that had been the case."

"What about wild animals turning up sick or dead around here?"

"None that I've heard about, and certainly not in the numbers you have in mind. Whatever's happening here is more understated than that."

As they headed out the highway, it started to snow heavily.

"Law-enforcement personnel and the medic all have separate food and water supplies now, correct?"

"No. Everyone buys from the same grocery store, and except for some outlying farms with their own wells, we share the municipal water. The water supply has been checked for viral and bacterial contamination, though."

Marlee glanced in her rearview mirror and saw a vehicle approaching rapidly down the snow-covered highway. She gripped the wheel even more tightly, wondering what idiot would speed under road conditions like these.

Hearing the cellular phone ring, she reached into her purse and brought it out. Her heart did a little dance as she heard Lucas's voice.

"How's it going?" he asked.

The rich, throaty timber of his voice sent a delicious shiver up her spine. Sensing Dr. Soto was looking at her curiously, though her eyes were on the road, she kept her voice businesslike as she gave him a rundown. After a moment, she handed the doctor the phone. "Lucas Blackhorse would like to speak to you, Dr. Soto."

Marlee continued driving, only half-tuned to the segments of the conversation she could hear. The truck behind them was too close, and getting closer. The driver's recklessness angered her. She studied the road ahead, peering through the blanket of windswept flurries, searching for a place to pull off to the side and let the other driver pass. She didn't want him tailgating all the way back to town.

"The symptoms vary in severity, but they're consistent with an intestinal flu, a virulent one to be sure," Dr. Soto said. "What's especially significant is that there doesn't seem to be any upper-respiratory involvement."

Marlee kept a close watch on the truck through her rearview mirror. It looked like Bill Riley's monster truck, not the semi he used for work, but the pickup with the oversize tires and spotlights above the cab. But she'd never known Bill, who regularly brought supplies into Four Winds, to drive so recklessly.

She heard the blast of the horn as the truck came up behind them. It wanted to pass, which was all right with her. Without a clear place to pull over, Marlee moved to the right, pumping her brakes to avoid skidding as she slowed down.

Suddenly the truck's grill filled her rearview mirror. Panic filled her as she guessed his intent. A heartbeat later, the truck slammed into the back of their sedan. The doctor cursed loudly, the phone dropping out of his hand. Marlee's mouth was dry. Panic burned through her. Fighting the wheel, she managed to keep the vehicle on the icy road, and sped up, trying to pull away from their pursuer. Dr. Soto didn't say anything; he was too busy looking for his seat belt.

Just as she thought that perhaps they would make it, the

truck caught up and slammed into them again. This time the force and weight of the larger vehicle sent them hurtling off the road.

The snow-covered field provided nothing for the wheels to use as traction, and the sedan rocketed down the hillside. Seeing a large pine ahead, Marlee tried desperately to force the wheel to the right. The wheel turned but the sedan continued on its course, slower but sideways. Fear twisted through her as she realized they were going to crash.

Chapter Twelve

Marlee knew her only chance was to try something desperate. She swung the wheel all the way to the right, hoping against hope that the car wouldn't roll. Something in the front grabbed, and the car straightened out. They slid backward, but missed the tree by three feet. Steering by the rearview mirror, she fought to keep the car from slewing to the left or right.

As they reached the bottom of the hill, the car slowed, and Marlee touched the brakes gently several times. Finally they came to a jolting halt against an old wooden rail fence.

She sat there for several moments, her gaze frozen in the rear view mirror. Eventually Marlee looked out the front windshield. For one terrifying second, as she squinted through the snow-smeared windshield, she wondered if her vision had been damaged.

"Are you all right?" Dr. Soto's voice brought her back to reality.

"I think so. You?"

"Well enough to move—which is a good thing. I detect the smell of gasoline. The fuel tank must have sprung a leak. Let's get out of here."

Marlee picked up the cellular phone from the floor. Lucas was still on the line, his voice frantic as he tried to find out what had happened.

She explained quickly as she unbuckled her seat belt with her left hand, an awkward move. "We're okay, but we'll need help." After she and the doctor climbed out of the vehicle, she gave Lucas a description of the vehicle that had run them off the road, and asked him to let Gabriel know.

Cold flakes of snow stung her face as she ended the call. The flurries were turning into a full-fledged blizzard. Snowflakes swarmed around her face, clinging to her hair and coat. Taking a good look at Dr. Soto for the first time, she noticed he was holding his left arm with his right, and he had a long cut down one finger that was dripping blood onto the snow.

"You're hurt. Are you sure you should be moving?"

"I'm positive my arm is broken, but the rest of me works, and I intend to see to it that it stays that way. This car could catch on fire, and if it does, I want to be as far away from it as possible."

They moved away from the vehicle, then Marlee wrapped Dr. Soto's handkerchief around his finger and tied it in place, stanching most of the bleeding there. Once done, they continued walking, Marlee carrying the doctor's bag and laptop.

Her body was sore, but she'd been lucky this time. Her mind went back to another accident, when no one had been there to ease her fears. She reached up and stroked the scar that remained on her cheek, a reminder of that lonely night on the highway.

"Here comes help now," the doctor said as they reached the road.

Lucas was the first to arrive on the scene, with Gabriel directly behind him.

Lucas jumped out of the Blazer and ran toward them. As he drew close, his gaze ran over Marlee with a thoroughness and a gentleness that tore her breath away. Assuring himself that she was okay, he stepped toward Dr. Soto.

"My temporary clinic isn't far from here. We'll stitch up your finger if it's necessary, and we're going to have to x-ray that arm."

"It's broken," he said. "I'll get the cut cleaned up and take the X ray, but I want an orthopedic surgeon to have a look at this before I have it placed in a cast." He turned to Gabriel. "Have the helicopter sent back here to pick me up as soon as possible."

Gabriel nodded, took out his phone and placed the call.

"It's your decision if you want to leave, Doctor," Lucas said. "In the meantime, I'll be glad to set the arm and put it in a sling so you won't damage it further en route."

"Let's go, then." Dr. Soto glanced back at Marlee. "Did you recognize the madman who did this?"

Marlee shook her head, then looked at Gabriel. "Like I told Lucas. It was someone in Bill Riley's pickup, the one with the big tires, but I doubt it was him. This was no accident. Whoever was driving was trying to kill us."

Gabriel's dark eyes flashed with anger. "I'll look into it, but it couldn't have been Riley. He's not in town. He parked his semi and decided to snowshoe up into the mountains and camp out. His off-road truck has been parked over at Charley's garage all week."

Lucas had bandaged Dr. Soto's finger and he and Marlee were helping him into the Blazer when the thump of an explosion shook the earth around them. They all jumped, and Lucas instinctively reached out and pulled Marlee protectively against him.

"It's not Lanie's car. It's over there." Gabriel pointed to a spot about two miles away from where they stood, where a column of orange flames was turning into thick black smoke. "You attend to the doctor. I'll go check it out. If you're needed, I'll let you know."

Lucas drove Marlee and the doctor back to his clinic. Dr. Soto's silence was stony, and Marlee told herself it was his ego that kept him from groaning in pain.

Once they arrived at the portable building, it didn't take long for Lucas to x-ray and set the doctor's arm. He was just placing it in a sling when Gabriel contacted them on the phone.

"The explosion came from Riley's truck," he said. "The fuel tank was torched, and it went off like a firecracker. But there was no sign of a driver, and the snow has already covered up any tracks. Riley, by the way, *is* up at his friend's cabin. I got him on the radio, and he has no idea who might have stolen his truck."

Lucas hung up and explained what he'd just heard to Marlee and the doctor.

"From what I've seen, whatever's making people sick here won't kill them," Dr. Soto said. "Your own people will do that themselves. That's your real threat, and I can't help you with that."

Marlee faced Lucas, and felt the power of feelings neither of them could acknowledge. An ineffable longing wrenched her heart. She could stand by him, assist him and even act as a sounding board when he needed it—but she didn't dare believe him hers to love.

HOURS LATER, after the snow stopped falling and the sky had begun to clear, the doctor was airlifted back to Santa Fe. Marlee left the boardinghouse and walked to Rosa's. Her cupboards were nearly bare. Gabriel had a crew of men with heavy equipment working to clear the road, but progress was slow. It would be some time before anyone could restock.

When Marlee arrived at the grocery store a short time later, she knocked and Rosa opened the door. "There is precious little on the shelves," Rosa said. "You might as well come in and see what you can find."

As Marlee walked inside, she felt the other customers staring at her. For a brief moment, she remembered how it had been for her years ago, before her face had been scarred. People had often said that she looked like the All-American girl, wholesome and pretty. Now she received stares, never appreciative glances, and when she caught people's eyes, they'd look away quickly, embarrassed.

As she wandered the aisles, she felt the weight of her neighbors' suspicions. Finally, with a burst of courage, she met their gazes, one by one. "Okay, what's the problem?"

Two women turned away quickly and pretended to look through the canned goods, but Rosa came out from behind the counter. "We heard about your latest accident. It seems you're in the middle of a lot of trouble lately."

"Which makes me a victim, not a perpetrator. And it wasn't an accident, it was intentional. So why are you treating me as if *I'm* responsible?"

"We know the peddler paid you a visit. It's all over town. Alex wrote an editorial about it, and what he had to say made a lot of sense."

"I hardly ever read anything Alex writes, so you'll have to enlighten me," Marlee said.

"The peddler always either gives a gift to the person he meets, or sells something to them. That cursed object brings trouble, and everyone pays."

"I've heard the stories," Marlee answered.

"Yet you insist he didn't give you anything and that doesn't make any sense. As far as we've been able to tell, you're the only one who has had any contact with him. Well, you and Lucas Blackhorse."

"How can you be sure of that?" Marlee challenged. "The way people around here like you react, who here would tell if they did meet up with him?"

"Well, you certainly didn't," Rosa said with a shrug. "The problem with people who keep secrets is that they always try to divert attention from themselves, no matter what the cost to someone else. I know you, that fancy doctor and Lucas have been trying to make everyone believe that people are sick because of something in the food I'm selling.''

''That's ridiculous. Nobody's accused you of anything.''

''That doctor you brought here earlier took samples of my flour, of the fruits, of anything that wasn't canned, even the soaps! How else do you explain that?''

''He was doing the job the town council brought him here to do. Ask any of them.''

Rosa glared at her. ''You don't fool me, not for one minute. You're trying to cover for the peddler, or for yourself. But you're not passing the blame on to me. It's not my food. I eat from what's here just like everyone else.''

Rosa stood by the door and held it open. ''I want you to leave. I don't want you in my store again.''

''You can't do that,'' Marlee protested. ''There is no other grocery store.''

Sally, who was just entering the store, cleared her throat. ''No, Rosa, she's right. The sheriff won't stand for it, either. She's well connected.''

Rosa put her hands on her waist. ''Then you get what you need, pay for it in cash and get out.'' She glanced at the others and, seeing them nod in approval, continued. ''Your lack of honesty is endangering our town. I want no part of you.''

Marlee paid for the few staples she could find, then walked out into the street. She felt cold all over, and it had nothing to do with the weather. She thought of the little carving the peddler had given her. Had she told them about it now, more fear would have spread, and it would have been impossible to predict the damage it could have done.

As she approached the feed store, the doors were quickly shut and the Closed sign hung on the door. So this was the way it was going to be.

Lucas drove by, and slowed down as she passed the post office. ''Where are you headed?'' His gaze seemed to look right into her soul. His eyes narrowed and he quickly added, "What's wrong?"

"Nothing," Marlee said, and looked away. It made no sense to drag him into the problem. Nothing could be done about it anyway.

"Why don't you get in? We can talk on the way back to the boardinghouse."

She didn't have the energy to argue, nor was she looking forward to another walk in the snow. The chill that held her already went all the way to her bones. As they got under way, she noticed Sally staring at her from the street corner.

Lucas followed her gaze. "Okay, level with me. What happened?"

She could tell from his tone that he was not going to give up. Reluctantly she told him about her encounter at Rosa's.

"I'll talk to her."

"No. This is my problem."

He exhaled slowly. "Then remind them that there are certain unwritten rules we all abide by here in Four Winds. Rosa has the only food store, and that carries certain responsibilities with it, just like being the only medic does. She's bound by the same rules I am. I can't refuse a patient, and she can't refuse service to a customer.

"It's a code that goes back to the days when Flinthawk blessed the town," he continued. "He had been persecuted and falsely accused, but in Four Winds, he found a haven. We've prided ourselves on that legacy. The way they're treating you now is the same as if they'd turned their backs on what Four Winds has always stood for."

"People aren't concerned with history right now. They're only worried about themselves and their families."

"Then they better wake up to other realities. Flinthawk was persecuted and almost lost his life because people were too quick to judge. If Four Winds adopts the lawlessness that almost claimed the life of my ancestor, it will destroy itself. The legacy that blessed Four Winds would become its curse.''

"You mean the part about the wicked never knowing peace here in Four Winds?"

"That's exactly what I mean." He pulled up by the boardinghouse to let her out. "I've got to go to the temporary clinic and check on things there. Although people know how to reach me, some will invariably just wait there until I show up."

"Do you think Dr. Soto was right to suspect some kind of food contamination?"

"It's possible, I suppose. Food poisoning can be either immediate or take several hours, depending on the toxin. But to have it be something that continues indefinitely like this has, even after the person stops eating...I think it's unlikely, to be honest." He glanced at her. "Do you have any ideas?"

"I keep thinking of a point Dr. Soto made. He kept asking me about the livestock and pets around town. If it was anything in the food or water, they would have been affected, too. I'm thinking in particular of Muzzy, Mrs. Burnham's terrier. He's always running away from her and getting into the neighbor's trash or digging up someone's garden. I tend to think that if a contaminant was the problem, he would have come across it by now."

Lucas considered it. "You're right, but come to think of it, I haven't seen either Mrs. Burnham or Muzzy in a while. Have you?"

"No, I haven't."

"Let's go pay her a visit."

"It may be better for you to go alone. I have no idea where she stands on the issue I encountered at Rosa's."

"I don't care where she stands. You're going with me. I need your help. You've been documenting everything for me. You could end up spotting something vital in our conversation."

"All right. I'll do my best."

"If she does give you any problems, keep at her. I need your help more than ever now. I can't do it all. That's the truth. I'm barely getting any sleep. With you taking over the office duties, like keeping up the charts and gathering patient information, there's a chance I may be able to keep the work from being completely overwhelming."

Four Winds needed her now, but most important of all, Lucas needed her, and she had no intention of letting him down. "You can count on me."

"Thanks." He reached for her hand and gave it a gentle squeeze.

Her heart was drumming fiercely against her sides. His hands were strong, yet so gentle, like the hands of a lover who could arouse a storm of passion, then soothe it with the magic of his touch.

She forced the thought away. Lucas needed her support now as a co-worker and a companion, but he needed nothing more than that. She brushed aside the despair that touched the edges of her mind. Someone else would win Lucas's heart someday, and that woman would have a lifetime of love and the most loyal of friends by her side. Refusing to yield to the sadness that realization left in its wake, she looked away from him and out the window.

"You've had some medical training. I know that already. But it would help me to know to what extent."

"I don't talk about my past, but because of what's happening, I think you should know I'm not a doctor or a nurse. I can help you only in a supporting role."

His jaw tightened, but he said nothing. Without the need for words, she knew how much her lack of trust hurt him, but there was nothing she could do. Her past formed a barrier between them that would always be there. The death of that young woman would haunt her for the rest of her life, and she cared too much for Lucas to allow him to share that nightmare.

"Four Winds isn't perfect," he said, watching a new storm building on the horizon, "but it's the kind of town where people can come to accept themselves, whatever their pasts hold. It could happen for you, too, if you gave yourself a chance."

"You left town for a long time while you served in the military. When you came back, did you see Four Winds in that light?"

"Experiences do change a person," he admitted. "In my case, I left Four Winds to get out of my two brothers' shadows and find myself. By the time I came back, I knew how I could make a place for myself here. My job as medic gave me a sense of self and purpose."

She watched him out of the corner of her eye, thinking about what his words meant. Lucas had already given his heart away—to Four Winds and to his work. Although she'd always suspected that, she'd never seen it as clearly as she did now. Many times she'd been filled with sadness, thinking of the day he'd fall in love and she'd lose him forever. This new revelation made her ache everywhere as she thought of the high cost he'd pay for his dedication to their town. She knew what it was like to go it alone. It was not what she would have wished for a vibrant man so full of life. She would have wanted far more for him, even if that meant her own heart broke in the process.

They arrived at Mrs. Burnham's and knocked on her door, but no one answered. From the window that faced the front, they could see Muzzy running around, trying to bark without dropping the sock he held in his mouth.

"Well, at least we know he's okay." Lucas laughed.

"Mrs. Burnham's car isn't here. She must be in town somewhere."

"Then let's head on over to the school portable," he said, returning to his vehicle. "You know, I just can't get comfortable in that place. It's either boiling hot or colder than a duck pond in winter. The heating unit is about as unreliable as the weather itself.''

"Do you have any idea how long it will be before the clinic is ready for use again? I saw men working there earlier.''

"I'm not holding out much hope that they'll get finished any time soon. Between illness and fear, manpower is at a new low, lately, and if any materials have to come from out of town, I can forget it until the road is reopened.''

As they started down the street that led to the high school, only one truck shared the newly snow-packed road with them. "That's Jake now—I recognize his new camper,'' Lucas said as the other truck approached. "I wonder what he's doing out in this weather. We're in for another wave of this storm soon.''

"He's weaving everywhere, like someone who has been drinking too much. But I've never known Jake to touch alcohol.''

As they drew near, Jake pulled over to the shoulder of the road and leaned hard on the horn.

Lucas slid to a stop beside the still-running truck and jumped out, medical bag in hand. Marlee was close behind him, ready to give a hand, but nothing prepared her for what she saw next. As Lucas threw open the door, she saw Jake's shirt was covered with blood. Two bullet holes were at the center of the crimson stain, near his heart.

Jake mouthed something neither Marlee nor Lucas could make out, then he tried to climb out of the truck.

"Easy there,'' Lucas said, stopping him.

"He has to know,'' Jake said, more clearly now, though the effort was obviously costing him a great deal of pain.

"You can tell us later,'' Lucas said firmly.

Jake started to say more, but his body went suddenly limp, and his eyes closed.

"Loss of blood,'' Lucas said. "He's going to need a hospital, and fast.''

"The road is impassable. We can't get him there," Marlee said. "And I doubt they'd fly another helicopter in here with the weather so bad."

"We can ask. But if they can't, Jake's got the best four-wheel-drive truck around. Help me put him in the camper. I'll do my best to stem the flow of blood while you telephone my brother. If he can't get a chopper or a bulldozer to make us a quick road, then you and I are going to make our own. If any truck can make it past that rock slide, it'll be this one."

Chapter Thirteen

Jake had a lot of friends in town. When it was learned how badly he was hurt, and that bad weather had grounded the helicopter, even people who were sick turned out to help. Lucas rallied them to work together, trying to clear a narrow lane in the road that would allow the truck to get through.

The spirit that had always held their town together in a crisis finally reappeared, if only momentarily. And thanks to the state police, who prevented any outside interference with their efforts, the people of Four Winds managed to move enough rubble to allow the truck to attempt passage within thirty minutes.

Rocks and boulders shifted unpredictably beneath them as the truck climbed through the narrow gap. Lucas encouraged Marlee to keep the acceleration rate steady, knowing that if she got stuck or had to stop, it would mean failure, and possibly Jake's death.

Every bump and slide to one side took a toll on his patient, but Lucas had seen worse. Jake would make it, and if he knew the former Ranger, Jake would be ready to take on whoever had ambushed him just as soon as he was back on his feet.

After five minutes of chaos, the ride suddenly became very smooth. They'd made it through the narrow pass. Lucas could finally do more than just keep his patient on the bed and the IV of plasma flowing.

As Lucas continued to work, he wondered what could have happened to Jake. The only thing he knew with certainty was that it had been an ambush. No one could have managed to get close enough to Jake to do this much damage otherwise.

AN HOUR LATER, Lucas came out of the emergency room of the county hospital to talk with Marlee and Gabriel, who had followed them in. "Jake regained consciousness just before they took him into surgery. He wanted to tell me something, but I couldn't make it out."

"I went through his truck while you three were in here," Gabriel answered. "The only odd thing I found was an empty thermos bottle, and I doubt anyone shot him for that. Any idea where he'd been before you found him?"

"No." Lucas glanced at Marlee, who shook her head in response.

"I have to figure out where he went, and why. You've been seeing a lot of people, Shadow. Ask around for me," Gabriel said, then dropped heavily into a chair.

"You look like you're not doing so well, Fuzz," Lucas commented, and reached for his brother's wrist to check his pulse.

Gabriel pulled his hand away. "It's just this weird flu. Don't worry about it. I'll be okay, and I'm going to be staying away from my wife. She's still healthy, and I intend to see to it that she stays that way. You two go on back to Four Winds. I'm going to stick around until after Jake comes out of surgery."

Lucas walked out of the hospital with Marlee ten minutes later. "In case I didn't tell you before, you did one heck of a good job getting us here."

The respect that shone in his eyes made her shiver, but she suppressed it quickly, not wanting him to see how deeply he affected her. "I wasn't at all sure we'd fit through that gap the people made for the truck. I just kept going and hoped it would be okay. Will Jake be all right, do you think?"

"He'll pull through, and when he does, the person who shot him is going to be in a world of trouble. I'm no wuss, and I could eventually take him, but I sure wouldn't want to go one-to-one with Jake."

"I hope the person who shot him does worry big time." Marlee paused, then continued. "Maybe he'll get careless and we can spot him. Will Jake have a guard at the hospital?"

Lucas nodded. "My brother hired one of the local cops to sit outside his door." Lucas flexed his hands on the wheel. "Something's been nagging at me about that thermos my brother found in the truck. Jake periodically checks the town water for minerals, and I know he uses a thermos to gather the sample directly from the pump house."

"So you're thinking that's where he was?" Marlee considered it. "It would make sense, but there's no way we can be sure."

"I'm going to call and find out if the lab ever checked the water sample I sent them for other than bacterial or viral contaminants. They've had it long enough."

The ride over the narrow pass dug through the roadblock was a little easier coming back, because even more rubble had been removed. Still, any vehicle that didn't have four-wheel drive and/or was low to the ground would have no chance of making it through.

When they arrived at the school-based clinic, Lucas went directly to his desk. Finding the lab's direct number, he dialed, then waited. The conversation didn't take long. After two minutes, Lucas set the phone down hard. "Every lead just turns into another question," he said. "There were no known poisons or heavy metals in the water, but they found minute traces of organic compounds and plant material—basically some kind of herbs. They haven't identified these yet, but the concentration was so slight that they assure me it's highly unlikely that it's the source of any existing problem.''

''That may not give us any answers, but at least it is some good news.''

He shrugged. ''Maybe. There are some herbs that have a strong initial effect, whose potency decreases quickly. I'm not saying that there's anything to worry about—I'm just not quite willing to dismiss this, not now after someone ambushed Jake. I'm going to recommend that the town stick to canned foods and bottled water, until we're positive we're not getting something like nightshade, for instance, added to our water supply.''

''I think you're right.''

''We also need to go up to the pump house to examine the source, but right now, there's no way anyone can get there, not in this weather.'' He gestured toward the window. Snow was coming down again, heavily, creating a ghostly landscape of white evergreens. Many were so snow laden they were starting to droop, like giant ice-cream cones.

''I can't imagine any resident of Four Winds doing something like tainting the water supply. Pure drinking water is such a scarce natural resource in New Mexico.''

He thought about it for a moment. ''Maybe that's the trail we need to follow. Let's find out who the newest resident is in Four Winds.''

''Let's see. There was Lanie, and after that, Nydia. Who else am I forgetting?''

''What about the new bank teller? He's been here less than three months,'' Lucas added thoughtfully. ''Do you know the one I mean? The guy with the beard, or is it a mustache?''

''Earl Larrabee? I've met him. He's harmless. He loves to gossip but he wouldn't hurt anyone.''

"It's too late to catch him at the bank, but I'd still like to talk to him."

"The custodian, Garry Johnson, works there until midnight, usually. He might know where Earl lives," Marlee offered. "Larrabee's so new he won't be in the latest phone book. If Garry doesn't know, we can always check with your brother when he is back in his office."

They arrived at the bank a little past seven. When Lucas knocked on the locked door to get Garry's attention, an attractive young teller, Mary Sandoval, came to the door and greeted him warmly. Her nod to Marlee was barely polite.

"Well, look who's here! The bank's been closed for hours, Lucas. Is there something I can help you with?"

Lucas gave Mary an apologetic grin. "I'm trying to find Earl Larrabee's address. He's not working late, too, is he?"

She scowled. "No, he's the reason I'm here now. Earl's been out all week, and I'm stuck with a lot of work that should have been his. I've got to say I'm surprised he hasn't called you. Earl's never been the type to suffer in silence. I've got his number if you want it, but not his address. That would be in the personnel cabinet, and I don't have a key to that. Let me go ask Garry if he knows."

With a wave, she rushed back across the lobby, and out of sight.

A minute later, Mary returned with a number on a notepad. "The best we can come up with is his phone number. Will that help?"

Lucas thanked Mary, then they both returned to his car. "We'll go to my brother's office, see if we can get Larrabee's address, then go check on him. That'll give me a chance to see Gabriel, too. I want to make sure he's okay."

When they arrived at Gabriel's office, they found him working on the reports of the day's events.

Lucas noted the pallor on his brother's face, but seeing the determined, challenging look Gabriel gave him, refrained from commenting on it. Gabriel told them Jake had come through the surgery fine, but wouldn't be able to answer any questions until tomorrow at the earliest. Lucas filled him in on their speculations about the thermos, telling him what they'd learned, and explaining his suspicions about the water.

"Soto's got a point, but so does Marlee. If it was the water, the pets would have also become sick," Gabriel said.

"Yeah, maybe. But animals don't always react the same as humans."

"Good point."

"There's something else that I want to follow up on," Lucas added, telling him about Larrabee.

"Be careful. You're starting to speculate now, and maybe going off on a wild-goose chase." Gabriel leaned back. "I appreciate the help, but you've got your own job to do."

"And I'm doing it. I'm going to see Larrabee in my position as the town's medic. Of course, while I'm there, I intend to do some digging."

"You do have the perfect reason to be there."

Lucas's muscles tensed as he looked at his brother. Between his pallor and the unsteadiness in his hands, he knew Gabriel was a lot sicker than he wanted anyone to know. "You'd better get home and to bed, Fuzz. You can't afford to push yourself now. This illness will push back, and then you'll be no good to anyone."

"I'm leaving soon, but I'll be sleeping in the spare room and not letting my wife get close." Gabriel reached for the loose-leaf telephone book that covered the entire county, including monthly updates from the phone company, and looked up Larrabee's address. He scribbled it on a piece of paper, then handed it to Lucas. "Let me know how it goes, Shadow."

"Before I leave, let me check your temperature and—"

"Go. I have enough problems without you hovering."

Lucas nodded once, understanding far more than his brother's words had said. As in his own case, frustration and uncertainty met Gabriel's investigation at every turn. People were counting on them, including the people they both loved, and their efforts were meeting with failure.

As they left the sheriff's office, Marlee reached for Lucas's hand almost as if she'd guessed his thoughts. For that brief instant, he felt a closeness to her that transcended touch. The need to make it a more intimate physical contact pounded through him, but he held back. Those feelings would lead only to one major heartache. That was the last thing he'd wish for her, or himself, though he had a feeling it was already too late for him.

"We *will* find answers. And don't worry about your brother. Lanie will call you if he gets worse. She'll take care of her husband, just as he takes care of her."

Lucas was close enough to Marlee to pull her into his arms, but he did not. He simply held her gaze, staring down at her with desire and the hunger that came from too many nights of wanting her.

She looked away, but he couldn't tell if it was because she didn't want to face what she read in his eyes or because she was afraid he might read the same feelings in hers.

LARRABEE LIVED at the end of a long driveway, in a cottage that bordered a wooded area. The snow was really deep out here, having accumulated in drifts.

As they reached the front door and knocked, Marlee glanced at the path going around the side of the house leading to the woodpile. "He's been up and around. There are fresh tracks out there." She pointed.

Before Lucas could answer, the door opened. Earl Larrabee looked surprised to see them, but politely invited them in.

Lucas glanced around, studying everything, though he tried to appear casual. "I heard you've been ill," he said, focusing back on Larrabee. "I was in the area, and thought I'd come over and check on you. How are you doing?"

"Oh, it's just this flu that's going around—I'm sure of it. Rather than spread it to everyone at the bank, I figured I'd stay home for a few days."

"Let me take your temperature and check your vitals, then. Maybe there's something I can give you that'll help."

Larrabee shook his head. "Thanks, but don't worry about me. It's nothing, really. My stomach's queasy, and my muscles ache a bit, but that's about it, except for the headaches." He picked up the can of cola on the table, finished it in one gulp, and then tossed the can into a paper bag next to his desk.

"I'm glad that you're drinking a lot of liquids," Lucas said. "Water, too, I hope."

"Nah, I prefer colas, always have."

"If you *do* switch to water, remember to only drink the bottled kind. I'm also recommending that people restrict their food intake to canned goods or prepackaged foods."

"You think it's food poisoning of some sort, then, from the water, or maybe ground beef or produce?"

"Not really, but we can't afford to leave any stone unturned."

Charts and paper in hand, Marlee began asking questions about Larrabee's food and water supplies, the same questions she'd asked others around town. Larrabee answered patiently until she was finished, then showed them to the door.

"If there is anything else I can do to help, all you have to do is ask," he said.

Lucas was quiet as they drove back to town. He had an instinct that had always served him well as a diagnostician. Right now, that instinct was telling him that Larrabee wasn't sick.

"I hate to say this, Lucas, but Earl looks healthier than any of the people I've seen in town. You know what I think? He wanted a few days off from work, and took the first opportunity that came his way.''

Lucas gave her a surprised look. ''That's exactly what I was thinking. His so-called symptoms seemed based more on what he's been hearing about the condition of the others who are sick than on fact. It sounded to me like he added that headache as an afterthought. Physically his color was good, and he didn't looked dehydrated or weakened by symptoms at all. But what bothered me most was his reliance on sodas.''

''I've known people who hardly ever drink plain water from the tap. It's not that unusual, especially if you come from a community where the water has a taste to it.''

''But it sends up a flag, particularly in view of the possibility of water contamination. I'm bringing this up with Gabriel first thing tomorrow morning. Right now—'' he yawned ''—I'm ready to get some sleep. It's been a long day.''

RIGHT AFTER BREAKFAST the next morning, they stopped by Gabriel's office. Lucas had used the pretext of reporting on his visit to Larrabee to check on his brother, and now he was glad he had. Brushing aside Gabriel's protests, he checked his brother's vitals and temperature. Gabriel accepted some pills for nausea, but quickly got back to the business of the day.

As Lucas filled him in, he could see the suspicion growing in Gabriel's eyes, and knew it matched his own take on Larrabee.

''I'm going to start a full background check on Earl Larrabee. I know very little about him.''

Lucas and Marlee were ready to leave when Gabriel stopped them. ''One more thing. I've been hearing some talk around town. I've tried to squelch it as much as I can, but it's going to continue—I'm sure of it,'' he said, then glanced at Marlee with a worried frown.

"It's about me, isn't it?" Marlee asked.

He nodded. "There's a rumor going around that herbs were found in the water."

"How did they get *that* information?" Lucas demanded.

"I checked it out. Apparently Alex has a source up at the lab in Santa Fe."

Lucas swore loudly. "I'm going to talk to the people at the lab. They're supposed to keep test results confidential."

"I've already taken care of that," Gabriel said, "but the damage has been done. I've heard there's an editorial coming out in this morning's edition of the paper."

Lucas paced around the room. "I hate that rag," he growled. "If Ralph was here, he'd keep Alex on a tighter leash, and that idiot sure needs somebody looking over his shoulder."

"I agree, but I can't interfere with what he's doing," Gabriel said. "Freedom of the press and all that."

"Looks like I better buy a copy," Marlee muttered.

Hearing a loud thunk at the front door, Gabriel stood up. "You may not have to. I think that's probably it."

He went to the door, and retrieved the paper from where it had bounced off the wood and into the snow. He opened the wet plastic wrapper, then reached for some paper towels.

Gabriel laid the paper on his desk and read the headline, which reported the attack on Jake. Then he opened to the editorial page. "That idiot."

Lucas skimmed the op-ed page, reading over Gabriel's shoulder and growing angrier by the minute. "Without actually saying so, he's connecting Marlee's herb garden and knowledge of herbs to the contamination of the water and the fact that people are getting sick."

Marlee read it over. "If I fight him on this, it'll just perpetuate the story. Since it's under the editorial banner, he'd claim he hasn't actually said anything libelous, and that he's entitled to state facts and print his opinion. I can't win either way.''

"He knows that, too," Lucas said. "This sentence about Mrs. Burnham's dog, Muzzy, really surprises me, though. He's the only pet that's become ill since this started, as far as I've seen or heard. Of course, this vague reference makes it impossible to tell what's wrong with Muzzy. He may have sprained a leg jumping, for all we know, and that would have nothing to do with the illness we're facing here.''

"This is going to terrify Rosa," Marlee said. "She's already afraid that people will hold her responsible. She's the only grocer in town, and we've been considering a food or water contaminant. That's why she's been giving me such a hard time. She needs to hold me up as a suspect, because without that, suspicion will turn in her direction. This news is going to make her really come after me now. She'll want people focusing on me as a suspect, because without that, she's the only other candidate.''

"I can see why she's worried. Rosa sells herbs at her store," Lucas said, "and has access to all the pickers and growers here. I think she also gathers a lot of herbs herself, and even has a small herb garden. She knows about home remedies, and carries some of the more common ones in her store.''

"I've heard something else recently that just didn't make sense to me," Gabriel added slowly. "I understand that she's having money problems. She applied for a loan recently, but her accounts were in such sorry shape the bank turned her down.''

"How did you—?" Lucas smiled. "It's Mary Sandoval, right? She's always had a thing for the Blackhorse brothers, but I always knew she liked you best of all. It's that trustworthy look in your eyes.''

"You're full of it, Shadow," Gabriel growled. "And nice try, but how I found out is none of your business.''

Marlee glanced at her watch. "It's too bad that editorial came out now. I really needed to stop by and get a few cans of beans and some vegetables. But going to Rosa's now will definitely create problems."

"Come on," Lucas said, almost eager for a confrontation that would force things out into the open. "I'll walk over with you. It'll be a way for me to show this town what I think of all the gossip."

"I'll stop by, too, but first I have a couple of things that need to be done here," Gabriel added.

"Neither of you have to do anything," Marlee protested.

"You're wrong. We do," Lucas said, then grabbed her hand and led her outside.

Lucas was aware of the way people they encountered watched as they went by. He could feel their fears and the weight of their suspicions as they stared at Marlee. Near as he could tell, they couldn't make up their minds whether he was a conspirator or a dupe. It hurt him to see this side of the townspeople he'd known for so long.

They'd just passed the bank, and were walking past the alleyway, when a flicker of movement caught his eye. Lucas glanced back, searching the shadows. "What's Larrabee doing meeting with Rosa in an alley? I thought he was supposed to be sick."

Making sure they both stayed out of view, Lucas and Marlee stood beside the entrance to the alley, but they were too far away to hear. Marlee sneaked a peek, then ducked back. "It looks like they're having an argument."

"Earl works at the bank," Lucas said, thinking out loud. "I wonder if Rosa's trying to convince him to help her get that loan."

"Maybe, or they could be arguing about an unpaid bill. Earl downs that soda by the case."

Lucas heard footsteps approaching and hurried Marlee away. For now, he'd rather Earl and Rosa didn't know he'd seen them. It could turn out to their advantage later on.

When they went inside Rosa's store this time, no one stared or made accusations. Lucas remained by Marlee's side, steadfast and undaunted by the situation. Marlee felt like a prisoner being escorted by a sympathetic guard. Resentment built up inside her, knowing that it was Lucas's presence that was making the difference. She shopped quickly, determined not to let it get to her. They were acting out of ignorance and fear, not maliciousness.

Because one van carrying foodstuffs had made it through the roadwork, the canned goods weren't completely depleted. Marlee managed to get enough to take care of her and Lucas for a few days. At the counter, she tried to meet Rosa's gaze, but the woman refused to look directly at her.

Aware of Lucas directly behind her, Marlee fought the shame that filled her. She felt dirty, and tainted by false accusations.

Marlee took a deep breath. She would not go through this again. "Rosa, I'm not guilty of anything and, deep down, I think you know that. I don't deserve to be treated this way."

Rosa's eyes narrowed. "If you're trying to shift the blame to me in front of everyone here, you're wasting your time."

"I'm not trying to do anything. I am willing to believe anyone is innocent until proven guilty, a luxury that you haven't extended to me."

"These are dangerous times," Rosa said, her eyes filled with anger. "We can't afford to give anyone the benefit of the doubt. But I know darn well that *I* had nothing to do with the herbs that tainted the water supply."

Lucas moved forward, stepping closer to the counter. "The test results said that there wasn't enough of anything in the water to harm anyone."

"Go tell Muzzy that," Rosa countered.

"That dog could be sick from just about anything, and you know it. The editorial wasn't specific."

"He was sick to his stomach, and wouldn't eat anything Mrs. Burnham gave him. That's enough for me."

"It shouldn't be," Marlee retorted, angrier than she'd wanted to become. "That little dog is always running away from Mrs. Burnham. He could have eaten something that was spoiled when he raided a neighbor's garbage, or maybe he dug something up. I understand he's big on tulip bulbs. Besides, there's another point you haven't considered. There are others around here besides you and me who know about herbs."

"All that's true," Rosa said slowly. "But the fact remains that you are the one who housed the peddler, and then tried to keep it a secret. That's enough in my book to make you an enemy of this town."

"I gave shelter to an old man who needed it," Marlee said. "If a bit of kindness makes me an enemy of the town in your book, then some of your pages must be missing!"

Marlee stormed out, then slowed down once she hit the sidewalk. She shouldn't have allowed herself to become so angry. She was reacting more to the injustices in her own past than she was to anything Rosa was doing. She should have handled it differently, but having Lucas hear and see all that had hurt. They were forcing him into the role of a protector, and that stung her pride and her feelings.

Lucas came out a moment later. "You shouldn't have lost your temper," he said. "That only made things worse."

"Yeah, I know. But I have to tell you, it's hard to stay calm when you know you're being used. The town desperately needs a scapegoat, and I happen to be convenient."

"I know, but you also have good friends here. Remember that."

The deep, level tone of his voice and the fire in his gaze made the harshness melt away from her heart. "Why can't they see that I would no more hurt them than I would hurt myself?"

"They will. Give it some time."

"You know, the peddler's said to bring bad luck and then good. I wonder when the good luck is going to start. I'm overdue, don't you think?" She managed a thin smile.

"Yes, you are," he said as they reached the Blazer. "But then again, maybe the good fortune he brings has already started, and you just haven't noticed it."

Marlee looked up at him quickly. She wanted to ask him to explain, to tell her what she already knew, but couldn't bring herself to do it. She knew her hesitation hurt him. She saw the brief flash in his eyes, though a second later it was gone. She knew he wanted her to need him, and not be afraid of that feeling. He wanted her trust.

"Some blessings are too dangerous to accept," she whispered.

Her words had been barely audible, but she knew he'd heard them. When he remained quiet, she knew it was because he couldn't argue against the truth.

THE DAY HADN'T IMPROVED as it passed, but finally it was close to midnight. Marlee stood in the darkened living room, staring thoughtfully out the window. Bathed in moonlight, the snow glistened like jewels against the black sky, and covered the ground in ice and shadows that swirled in the breeze. Though Lucas was in the boardinghouse, she felt more isolated and alone than she'd ever been. No matter how tempting it was, or how badly she yearned to reach out to him, she knew she could not. She wouldn't involve him in her problems any more than he already was.

She thought about the peddler and that little raven carving she'd accepted from him. He had claimed it would grant her one wish, if she wished hard enough. But what good would one wish be when the one person she wanted most in this world could never be hers?

A silent tear fell down her cheek. Fate had been cruel when it had brought Lucas here to her boardinghouse.

Every day it taunted her with her heart's most desperate wish. Her love for Lucas was real and the kind that would last a lifetime for her. But sometimes the best way to love was to let go, and that's what she had been trying to do. She would not have Lucas share the hell her past held. He stood for life, for freedom, and she would bring him neither.

Marlee sensed his presence in the room before she ever heard footsteps. She turned to face him, and yearning squeezed her heart as she watched him stride up to her, shirtless, jeans slung low on his hips. He moved with grace and power, and stopped only inches away.

He took her face in his hands and captured her gaze. "I know you, my heart, because I know myself. To you, being strong means standing alone. But standing with another, *with me,* will increase your strength. It won't take anything away," he said, his words a cracked whisper.

Desire smoked in his dark eyes. She felt the shudder that traveled over him as she placed her hands on his naked chest. He had come to offer the only comfort he could give her, the kind that would take the winter from her soul and replace it with the radiance of a new dawn. Longing pierced her. Every cell in her body wanted him to love her in all the ways a man could love a woman.

His gaze dropped to her mouth and remained there, caressing her without narrowing the gap between them. Her pulse was racing. Marlee shivered, yearnings ribboning through her until she couldn't think.

As if sensing her willingness, he lowered his mouth to hers and pressed her to him. Suddenly Marlee was overwhelmed with sensations that left her aching and exquisitely vulnerable. His needs burned through her, kindling her own. The roughness of his mouth, the hardness of his chest, the tenderness of his arms, wove a spell around her she didn't want to break. She surrendered to his kiss until only her connection to Lucas sustained her.

Instinct guiding her, she tightened her lips around his restless tongue and then loosened them, letting him taste her as she tasted him. She felt him shudder, and that violent need that he barely kept leashed fueled the fire within her.

Dark, heated images danced in her head as she pressed herself against him. She could barely breathe for the intensity of the feelings.

The phone rang four times before they parted, and Lucas picked up his cellular phone with a muttered oath.

"I hope I didn't wake you," Lucas heard Gabriel say. "But I've got some news that might interest you. I did a background check on Earl Larrabee, and found out something interesting. The reason I kept coming up against a brick wall was because he had his name legally changed."

"Why?"

"I haven't got a clue, but I will find out." Gabriel paused. "Were you asleep? You sound odd somehow."

"It's late, that's all. Are *you* okay? Why aren't you asleep?"

Gabriel didn't answer right away. "I was just up checking on my wife. She's fine and sound asleep."

Lucas closed up his cellular phone and smiled. "My brother misses his wife. He's lonely sleeping in the spare room, though that's not why he said he called at this hour."

"What happened?" Marlee moved away, needing to put some space between them. She could still taste Lucas on her lips.

"In a town like Four Winds, this shouldn't come as a big surprise, but it looks like we now have another wild card in the game. Earl Larrabee turns out to be a man very intent on keeping his own secrets. He changed his name before he came here."

"The people of Four Winds, for the most part, share one thing—pasts too dark to forget."

For a few precious moments, she'd almost forgotten all the logic and all the reasons why their relationship couldn't be. She'd never been reckless, yet in Lucas's arms she'd become a new person, someone she scarcely knew.

A million different kinds of wanting filled her. She welcomed the emotions. Despite the pain they caused, they proved that she was still alive. She moved to the window and stared at the emptiness outside, feeling as cold and as desolate as the moonless night.

"It's too late to turn the clock back," Lucas murmured. "You're not alone. I'm a part of you, my heart, as you are a part of me."

She started to answer, to protest, but when she turned around, he was gone. She walked to her room alone, undressed and slipped into bed. The cold sheets touched her, making her long for Lucas's warmth.

"Good night, my Shadow. Whether we're together or apart, you are and will always be the dearest part of me."

Chapter Fourteen

Marlee was in the living room with Lucas, going through and updating medical charts, when they heard a vehicle pull up. Lucas stood up and walked to the window. "Now, this is good news! *Both* my brothers are here," he said.

Gabriel and Joshua came to the door a moment later.

Lucas grinned at his youngest brother, who practically took up the whole doorway, but according to Navajo custom, Lucas refrained from giving him a hug. "Hey, Tree, when did you get back to town? Or better yet, *how* did you manage that feat?"

"The roads are icy and treacherous, but at least there's a lane, of sorts, cleared through that rock slide. When I heard what was going on here, I figured I was needed, so I came back as quickly as I could."

"He figured right, too," Gabriel said. "He planted a few prayer sticks in the snow, and already I'm feeling much better," he added.

"*Planted?*" Joshua glared at his brother. "I'll plant *you!*"

Gabriel smiled. "Lighten up, Tree. I was only joking. You know I'm grateful for your skills as a medicine man."

"Did your wife and son return with you?" Lucas asked his youngest brother.

"My wife came, but because of the illnesses here, we felt it best to leave our boy with his grandparents."

"Good choice."

"I understand our good friend the librarian was shot and nearly killed," Joshua added.

Lucas nodded. "I checked on him earlier." He followed his brother's example, knowing a traditionalist would not speak of Jake by name. It was said that names had power, and if that power was guarded, it could help that person in a time of crisis. "He's still in intensive care, but he's doing better."

"I've been keeping close tabs on him, too," Gabriel said. "I'd like to question him as soon as possible."

"Have you been up to the water tower yet?" Marlee asked Gabriel.

"I went out today, or should I say, I tried. Between the high winds and the road conditions, I couldn't make it. Even if I'd risked life and limb getting there, climbing to the top of the tower would have been impossible."

Lucas nodded. "Next time, don't go up there alone. I understand the need to check the town's main water source, but you'll need backup. Look at what happened to Jake."

"We're still not sure that he was shot there," Gabriel cautioned, "though admittedly, it does seem probable."

Marlee sat with them, but even working together and exploring different theories left them with no clear answers on how to proceed. As the howl of the wind grew stronger, Lucas went to the window. "You two may end up as boarders if you don't get going soon. It looks like we're in for even more snow."

"Part of the legacy the peddler left us this time, some would say," Joshua mused, pulling on his jacket.

"Or just rotten luck," Lucas answered. "Could we hire you to go out and do a sun dance?" Teasing his younger brother was always a fun game, one Lucas enjoyed even more than Gabriel. Joshua, despite his size, was too gentle to haul off and slug anyone.

Gabriel laughed. "Better make that your last jab, Shadow. Nydia said baby brother pushed his legendary patience to the limit while visiting with her relatives this past week."

"I'm disappointed in you, Tree," Lucas said, "you a married man, and all. Your ability to take abuse should be limitless by now."

Joshua just smiled. "You're lucky this town needs a medic. That's the only thing that saves you half the time."

Lucas laughed as his brothers walked off, then glanced at Marlee, who was standing with him on the porch, shivering. He put his arm around her. "Let's go back inside before you freeze. We need to catch up on those progress reports."

Two hours later, as they finally finished updating the patient records, Lucas's cellular phone rang. He answered it, and while he was speaking, picked up his medical bag.

"I've got to go," he announced after the call. "I'm headed up to Bill Riley's cabin. It's a long hike up there in this weather, but from the sound of it, he's sick and needs help."

"I'll get my warmest boots."

He shook his head. "No, I'm going to have to ride Chief up there. There's no way I'd want to walk that distance in this weather, and I'm not at all sure any vehicle could make it up the trail that leads there in all this snow. And I may need to bring Bill down with me, so I can't afford to be riding double going in."

Accepting the necessity, Marlee saw him off, then, after turning up the house heat, went to the kitchen to take inventory on her supplies. Suddenly a loud crash and the tinkling of broken glass made her jump, and set her heart pounding.

Marlee rushed into the living room. A blast of icy wind

brought her attention immediately to a gaping hole where most of her front window had been. A large rock lay against the far wall.

Anger ripped through her as she picked up the rock. A folded piece of paper had been attached to it with two rubber bands. She slipped the rubber bands off carefully, unfolded the paper, then read the message: "We don't forgive traitors."

Taking her jacket from the coat rack, she bundled up and tried to figure out how to cover the opening until the glass could be replaced. As the gusts whipped the curtains, and the room temperature plunged, the unfairness of it all filled her with outrage. She'd done nothing to deserve this. She crumpled the note and stuck it into her pocket. The town was set against her, just as it had been in another place, another time.

Marlee pushed back the sense of betrayal that nearly overwhelmed her. What she needed to concentrate on now was covering the gaping hole in her living-room window. Once that was done, she'd call Gabriel. He was the town's sheriff and would need to be told. She considered trying to call Lucas, but he was riding across country, and probably having to concentrate on staying warm and not losing his direction. The last thing he needed was a call on his cellular phone.

A half hour later, she'd sealed the window using duct tape and a piece of plywood she'd found in the garage and cut to the right size with a hand saw. She'd called Gabriel but had learned he wouldn't be back in the office until later. Figuring she'd have to go in and sign a statement, she decided to make sure the window patch was secure, then walk into town.

She was just adding more tape to hold the plywood in place when her phone began to ring. She picked up the receiver, and heard Alex on the other end. Her guard went up instantly. She didn't trust the little creep. His newspaper editorials had been the main reason the town had turned against her.

"I wanted you to know that I've only just found out how badly people are treating you. I never expected that here in Four Winds."

Marlee didn't believe him for a second. "Without using my name, you practically came out and told people I'm the one responsible for all the bad things that are happening here. Yet you're telling me now that you still expected everything to go on as usual?"

"I never slandered you. When you know folks here as well as I do, it's easy to think you can second-guess them. I expected a lot of gossip, but nothing like the persecution that's going on."

"Someone just threw a rock through my window on the coldest day of the year. My living room is freezing, and it'll get worse tonight. I should bill you for the expenses."

Alex paused. "I'll find someone to help you fix it, but this isn't my fault. You made a big mistake bringing that peddler into your house. And that's what's haunting you now. Give me a chance to help. Talk to me on the record. Right now people in town are worried that since the attempt to poison the water was discovered, the criminal will find another way to injure them. They'll be out gunning for you unless you do something to clear your name. Let me take a few photos of the vandalism and get your side of the story."

"First get your facts straight. There's still no definite proof the water was poisoned. And I don't want you coming here." The idea of having him at her home repulsed her. "If you want to see me, I'll stop by shortly. But first I've got to go by the sheriff's office," she declared, then hung up.

Hearing the wind outside and watching the thin plywood strain where it was taped in place, she shivered. She'd hoped to stay home today buried in a good book. Cursing her luck, she changed clothes, picking out her warmest outfit, then began the walk toward Main Street.

It took her twice the usual time, because of the cold and snow. At least the wind seemed to be slowing down a bit. But if that happened, and the sky cleared up, the temperature would go down even further. By the time she arrived at Gabriel's office, she was chilled to the bone. Gabriel saw her as she came in, and came to help her take off her coat. He still looked pale and a little shaky from the flu.

"I heard from my dispatcher that you were coming. I meant to tell you that I'd stop by and save you the walk, but I got sidetracked." As he finished saying that, his phone began to ring. "It's been like this ever since I stepped through the door this morning."

As he spoke on the telephone, Sally Jenkins, the owner of the diner, stepped into the office. She glared at Marlee, then moved to the other side of the office.

Marlee was about to ask Sally what was wrong, when Gabriel hung up. "What can I do for you, Sally?"

"You won't believe what's happened," she said, her voice breaking. "Someone poured powdered detergent into my flour bin." Sally glared at Marlee just as someone else came into the office.

Marlee stared back at her in shock. "Oh, Sally, surely you of all people know I would never do that!"

"Well, you have been in my diner recently...." She met Marlee's gaze then, after a second, sighed. "No, I don't think you did it. I apologize. You would never do that. I'm just so angry, and it would make things easier if I could blame someone." She glanced at Gabriel. "Now I'll have to close the diner, won't I? I can't guarantee other things weren't tainted."

"You should close until you can throw out any food containers that might have been tampered with. It's not worth taking a chance."

Sally's shoulders slumped. "I don't know how I'm going

to weather this financially. No customers, then I lose inventory…''

Marlee put a hand on her shoulder. "This craziness can't last much longer. Then you'll be able to open the diner again."

She nodded absently. "I guess."

Hearing footsteps behind her, Marlee turned, remembering that someone else had come in while Sally was so upset. It was Alex. Yet, from the spark in his eyes, she knew he'd heard enough about the incident at Sally's to know there was a story there.

Alex remained until Sally had finished giving her statement and signing it, then left with her instead of staying to talk with Marlee or Gabriel.

Gabriel glared at the doorway long after Alex had left. "I'm torn between wanting to come down hard on him, and the instinct that warns me I'll only be making things worse."

"He's asked me to talk to him on the record, but he must have not wanted to do that in front of you. In view of this latest incident, I think I will go by his office and do just that. At least I'll get my side of the story out, if he doesn't decide to edit the facts, that is."

"Good luck."

Five minutes later, after giving a complete account of the broken window to Gabriel, Marlee stepped into the newspaper office.

Alex came out of another room to greet her. "Looks like my theory was right. The culprit couldn't hurt anyone with the water now, so he picked on something else—Sally."

"I wish *someone* had good news for a change," Marlee said.

"I can help you there. Mrs. Burnham's Muzzy is going to be fine. The vet said it was a stomach upset, but he couldn't determine the cause." Alex offered her a chair. "But that doesn't let you off the hook. Unless you come clean publicly about the peddler's visit, people simply will not trust you.''

"What more is there for me to say? He came, but he didn't even spend the night. There was a storm that evening, and he wanted shelter. Driving that old van of his can't be a picnic in high winds.''

"What about the gift he gave you?''

"What gift?'' Marlee asked, fighting to keep her expression neutral.

Alex rolled his eyes. "Give me a break, okay? He *always* gives the person he targets a gift, or lets them buy something. Remember old man Simmons and the shovel? The medicine bowl Lanie got? And Nydia's blanket? Telling about whatever it was he left you will go a long ways in getting people's trust back. Right now, they know, just like I do, that you're covering something.''

"I've had my home vandalized, I've been the target of accusations that give new meaning to the word *unfair,* and now you're asking me to add fodder to the rumors. Nydia and Lanie both suffered at the hands of this town once word got out they'd had contact with the peddler, so your argument about trust just doesn't ring true. For the last time and for the record, I am not stupid enough to risk accepting any of that peddler's sale items, nor would I purchase anything from him.''

"If you believe he's harmless, why not?''

"Because people like you use him to create a problem for others.'' She stood up. "Instead of looking at the peddler so intently, people in this town should start taking a good look at themselves. That's where the real problem is. Think about how people behaved after each of his visits. Maybe the peddler does serve a purpose, when you look at it from that perspective—he shows all of us just how shallow and nasty ordinary people can become.''

"I will quote you, but I still say you're holding back— and it's going to cost you.''

Marlee left the office, and without turning back strode down the street. The weather was as bad as ever. The wind had eased, but the temperature had dropped. That made the walk just as miserable, but it was better than driving on the icy roads. She tucked her chin down into her coat, and continued at a brisk pace.

Snow was piled in thick drifts on the walkways, and in her heart, she felt as cold as the cobblestones that the wind had cleared of everything except the ice. No matter how hard she tried, nothing was working out for her. As she passed the feed store's loading dock, a big manila envelope lying on a clear sheet of ice caught her eye. It was between the delivery truck and the concrete platform. She drew near, and saw her name had been scrawled on it.

Marlee looked around suspiciously, but no one was in sight. She thought about the slippery surface, which sloped downhill toward the dock, then curiosity overcame her and she inched out onto the ice. As she bent over carefully and picked up the envelope, she heard a creak and the slam of a car door. She was aware of the sound of running footsteps, but her eyes and her attention were on the truck, which was suddenly rolling toward her.

It was silent, since the engine was off, but it was certainly going to crush her against the four-foot-high concrete barrier unless she got out of there fast. Marlee tried to dive out of the way, but her feet slipped out from under her and she fell facedown on the ice instead. By the time she got back up to her feet, it was too late to dodge or try to climb onto the dock. Someone had released the brake, allowing the dock area's incline to do the rest.

Marlee reached over and grabbed a heavy metal mop bucket from atop the dock, and held it beside her, lodging it against the dock wall and giving herself some clearance. The truck crunched against the bucket, but the container held, and the truck stopped. A second later, the bucket began to groan in protest.

With only the bucket maintaining a gap between the truck and the concrete dock, Marlee was trapped, almost compressed, in a space about a foot wide.

Marlee sucked her stomach in, and yelled for help at the top of her lungs. Surely someone inside the feed store would hear her.

Then she heard a familiar voice shouting her name and footsteps rushing from the street.

"Marlee, where are you?" Lucas shouted.

"I'm here, behind the truck, but I can't get out. A bucket's all that's keeping me from getting crushed, and it's not going to last much longer!"

She heard the sound of the truck door opening, then a loud curse from Lucas. It didn't sound promising. Then his face appeared in the narrow opening between the truck and the dock. "Hang on. I'm coming in there with you."

"Wedge something else in here, not your own body! We'll both be crushed." Marlee tried to push him back out with her arm, but she couldn't move him.

"If you work with me, we'll both get out of this in one piece," he said, scooting in closer beside her. "I've got a plan."

Chapter Fifteen

Despite the freezing cold, Marlee's sweater was clammy with perspiration. Her legs were weak from fear. She turned her head, no longer willing to face the truck that could crush them both to death in another moment.

Lucas suddenly grunted, and she saw him straining against the truck.

"I can move it back a little," he said. "Help me push. The brake lines were cut, so it'll roll the other way if we put some muscle into it. We just have to get the rear wheels past that little slope at this end. Put your feet against the dock, and don't slip on the ice."

Marlee used every last bit of her strength, pushing with Lucas, coordinating her efforts with his. She yelled once more at the top of her lungs, hoping someone inside the store would finally come out.

She felt the truck inch back, and realized that they were making headway. Before she could catch her breath to yell again, she heard help arriving on the loading dock. Darren Wilson and one of his clerks grabbed a two-wheel dolly, and Darren wedged it between the truck and the dock to keep the truck from rolling back toward them. Then the two men began to help Lucas and Marlee push the truck away.

In a few seconds, the truck had been pushed well away

from the dock and past the patch of ice. Darren placed a wooden block behind each rear tire to keep the truck from rolling again.

Darren rushed toward them, shaking his head in confusion. "What the heck happened? That's my truck, but I've been inside the store with customers. We only came out when we heard you yelling. How did you get yourselves in that fix and how did that sheet of ice get there?"

"I don't know," Marlee said, recapping the events as Gabriel came up.

"Did you see anyone?" Gabriel pressed.

"No," Marlee admitted, "but I heard someone. And if Lucas is right, those brake lines didn't cut themselves."

Lucas glanced at his brother. "Just take a look for yourself. The brake line was severed with something like a pair of tin snips, I bet."

Mrs. Burnham stood on the dock, Muzzy in her arms. "Trouble does follow you doesn't it, dear?" she asked.

Her tone was far from sympathetic. Marlee stared at her in stunned disbelief, then glanced at the others who'd arrived from the store. How would she ever be able to live here and treat these people as friends again, even after the truth came out? They'd turned on her as if she'd been a stranger or a criminal.

She tried to speak, but was shaking too much for words. Too close to tears, she remained silent.

Lucas's eyes were as cold as a frozen blade as he stared at the people gathered around them. "I've known most of you for years now. You've always seemed like decent people. But the way you're acting now is enough to make me ashamed that I've ever called any of you my friends. Consider this...will you be able to look at yourselves in the mirror when you finally find out that you've been victimizing an innocent person?"

A murmur went around the crowd, and as they dispersed, Marlee grieved for lost friendships.

Rather than yield to despair, Marlee chose to focus on action. She wasn't helpless as long as she could still act on her own behalf. It wasn't an assurance of victory, but it was a way to fight, and sometimes that was all that was left to a person.

"Let's talk with the people inside, and then walk up and down the street and see if anyone saw who was in the truck. It's a long shot, but it's worth a try."

"Good idea," Gabriel conceded. "You mentioned an envelope, Marlee. Do you have it?"

Marlee pulled it from her pocket. "It's empty," she said, handing it to him.

"I'm not surprised," Gabriel said.

Thirty minutes later, they still had no answers. Lucas walked with Marlee back to his truck. His presence calmed the fears she was trying so hard to keep locked tightly away inside herself. Though Lucas couldn't always be around, he did seem ready to stand up for her, to equalize the odds whenever they were together. He had the heart and courage of a lion.

Marlee glanced up at him, feeling the quiver of desire replacing the fear she'd experienced just an hour before. He'd touched her in a way no one ever had. She wanted to trust him, to give herself the freedom to experience the love that burned in his eyes whenever he gazed at her. He'd made her forget the scar that had not only marred her face, but cut her soul. For brief moments in time, Lucas had reminded her what it felt like to be whole and be admired.

"Looks like Alex printed a special evening edition," Lucas said, bringing her out of her musings. He gestured at the newsletter-sized papers stacked in the box near the bank.

Marlee placed a coin in the slot. "By the way, how's Bill Riley doing?"

"Miserable for now, but I think it's just a case of bronchitis. He should be okay soon."

Marlee picked up a copy of the newspaper. "Oh, yuck, they're all wet." She opened it carefully. "I hate to buy this rag, but I better see what he wrote about me. We had a rather—" she cleared her throat "—shall we say, substantial difference of opinion?"

She skimmed the lead story, not at all surprised by its contents.

"Do you realize what he's doing? He's blaming everything, including what happened at the diner, on the peddler's influence," Lucas said. "Then, after he documents his theory with half truths, he quotes you as insisting that you didn't receive anything from the peddler despite the fact that everyone knows otherwise. He makes it sound like you're pursuing your own agenda at everyone's expense."

"Alex has made a serious vocational error. He should be working for the tabloids."

"When Ralph comes back, I have a feeling Alex is going back to delivering papers and running the press, not writing," Lucas said. "I'd bet on it."

When his cellular phone rang, Lucas answered, spoke briefly, then closed the unit up. "I've got another patient I need to see. I won't be able to give you a ride back home. Will you be okay?"

"Sure. It takes more than a little thing like attempted murder to keep me down." She managed a reassuring smile.

His eyes were luminous and filled with purpose as he leaned down and covered her mouth with his own. His kiss was urgent, demanding and rough. Sparks travelled down her, bone by bone, leaving her shuddering helplessly. Her lips parted under his, and as she tasted him, the blinding power of emotions she'd tried to ignore took away her will to resist. She pressed herself into his kiss, longing for more of the white-hot pleasure she found there.

An eternity passed before he eased his hold. "Look after yourself, my heart."

Marlee watched Lucas continue down the street at a rapid pace. Heat swirled through her, an aftermath of the firestorm he'd created. With a sigh, she looked around the empty street. Since nobody had seen them, at least maybe she'd be spared an editorial in the next issue of the paper about how she was corrupting Lucas. She smiled ruefully.

Marlee glanced at her watch. She would have to hurry, but she could still make it to the bank before it closed. If she was going to be connected to the peddler and blamed for things that were not her fault, then the least she could do for herself was enjoy the carving the peddler had made for her. It was small enough for her to carry around in her pocket if she chose.

Earl was still at home faking illness, apparently. It was Mary Sandoval, the pretty young teller who'd flirted with Lucas not long ago, who accompanied her to the vault, then left her alone, giving her privacy. Marlee took out the carving, placed it in her purse and was on her way home a short time later.

As she recalled the look of suspicion on Mary's face, Marlee's heart sank. She'd never felt so utterly alone, so rejected.

Marlee was almost home when she suddenly began to feel ill. Despite the cold weather, she was burning up, and her body ached. She touched her cheek gingerly. Her scar ached like it had right after the accident three years ago.

By the time she reached the boardinghouse, her entire cheek was throbbing painfully. She wondered if perhaps the cold had triggered the pain somehow, but she couldn't remember ever having that happen before.

Sheltered in the privacy of her living room, she took out the small carving and held it in her hand so she could look at it. Marlee was sure it was her imagination, but a pleasant warmth enfolded her as she held the carving. Within a few minutes, her body quit aching and the scar stopped throbbing.

As she placed the raven on the coffee table to admire it, Marlee became aware again of the aches and pains that had bothered her only minutes before. Refusing to credit superstitions, she went to her medical bag, found the thermometer and took her temperature. It was a little elevated, but not enough to worry about.

Marlee crawled into bed. Maybe if she rested for a while... Placing the carving beneath her pillow, she drifted off to sleep. She never got up for dinner, sleeping all the way through the night. As she slept, jumbled images of Lucas, of the comfort of his love and the despair losing him would eventually bring, haunted her dreams.

LUCAS WOKE UP early the following morning. The sun was barely up, and though he was almost as exhausted as he'd been the evening before, it surprised him that he'd beaten the old alarm clock by his bed.

He'd been quiet when he'd come in last evening so as to not wake Marlee, who'd obviously gone to bed early. Though it had worried him, he'd decided to let her sleep. She'd been through a lot yesterday, and for several days before. If anyone deserved a little extra rest, it was Marlee.

As he walked into the kitchen, he was glad to see Marlee there preparing breakfast. Today it was oatmeal and toast with tea. Coffee had sold out at Rosa's quickly. He knew Marlee's supplies were dwindling, just like everyone else's in town. Even though the road had been cleared, only a few small truckloads had come in because of the weather. That was yet another factor adding to the tensions around town.

"What are your plans for today?" he asked.

"I'm going to have to see about getting the front window fixed," she said, then explained about the rock, leaving out the part about the note. He had enough to worry about.

Lucas's eyes blazed with anger. "I saw the damage when

I came in. You should have told me about it when it happened."

"You had a patient to see, and besides, it wouldn't have made any difference. As long as I keep the curtains closed and the tape secure, I can keep the weather out. The rest I can live with."

"Darren will probably have to order the glass, and it's going to take some time before he gets it in. Why don't you ride with me today while I make my rounds? I could use your help. Something strange is happening."

"What do you mean?"

"The flu symptoms are disappearing, but now we've got a rash of people sick to their stomachs, getting dizzy and complaining that they're sweating all the time, despite the cold. I'd like you to record all the details for me, so I can enter it into my database."

When she placed the bowl of oatmeal before him, Lucas saw that the scar on her face seemed darker. "Are you okay?"

He'd always been said to be a gifted diagnostician, but lately his instincts only told him when a patient was in serious trouble. Right now he couldn't shake the conviction that something was wrong with Marlee. With her, though, he couldn't trust his intuitions, because his personal feelings for her confused his perceptions, making even the simplest observations suspect.

"I got chilled on the way back home yesterday, and I felt really achy, so I decided to go to bed early."

"Are you running a fever?" he asked, searching for an answer that would explain the change in her scar.

"Not this morning. I feel fine. I haven't even needed an aspirin."

He stood and brushed the hair back from her face, studying her scar, though he knew she'd resent it. "This is getting darker. Any idea why?"

Marlee pulled away quickly. "I don't know, but there's no infection, so just leave it alone."

Lucas reached for her hand and held on to it. "Nobody in this town is perfect, including me. The only difference is that your scar is visible, and the ones most of us carry aren't."

He took her into his arms and held her. He wanted to love her, to feel her need for him become as great as his for her. Yet despite his own wishes, he struggled to keep himself under control. He would not betray her by pushing her to give him more than she was prepared to offer freely.

"You don't have to pity me," Marlee murmured, but she didn't struggle against him.

He pulled her roughly into the cradle of his thighs, feeling the shiver that went up her spine. "This isn't pity, my heart. What I'm feeling has nothing to do with that."

Lucas kissed her, driving his tongue deep into her mouth, searching out secrets and making the fire within his veins rage. He almost cried out in triumph as he heard her soft moan. Then, with a tenderness he hadn't known he possessed, he kissed her again, gently, patiently, drawing out the moment. He wanted her more than he ever dreamed possible. But this was not their time.

He released Marlee at long last when he'd reached his breaking point. He had to walk away now while he was still able to do it. "Do you have any idea what you do to me?" he asked, his breathing jagged.

"You've made me feel things I never dreamed were possible," Marlee whispered, "but we are not meant for each other. Deep down, you know that as well as I do." She tore her gaze from his, then started down the hall. "Let me change my clothes. I'll need to wear something warmer if I'm going to make rounds with you."

Lucas watched her walk away, his body shuddering with needs that would not be sated. He was playing with fire. It was reckless and dangerous, yet he couldn't force himself to stay away from her.

When Marlee returned to the living room, he noticed that she looked different. He studied her face for a second, wondering what had changed, and realized that the color of her scar was now back to normal. He couldn't decide if it was makeup skilfully applied, or just a change in the lighting.

"Let's go," she said, jamming her hands into her pockets and keeping them there.

"Don't you want gloves? I have an extra pair, if you've misplaced yours."

"I've got a pair in my pocket, but this jacket is fleece lined, so it keeps my hands warm anyway."

She was hiding something from him, but he couldn't figure out why. He decided to let it pass for now. He had other business to attend to right now.

Halfway to the home of his first scheduled patient, Lucas received a phone call. He heard the hurried words of a frightened parent, and felt his blood turn to ice. By the time he returned the phone to his pocket, Marlee was watching him intently.

"We have a full-blown emergency. Little Eric James fell down a mine shaft. His father hasn't been able to reach him. All they know is that he's hurt his leg, and may have additional injuries."

"I know Eric. He's a very active six-year-old. He always comes into town shopping with his mom. It's hard to get him to stand still long enough to listen."

"Yes, that's my recollection, too." Lucas increased his speed, going as fast as he dared on the snow-packed road. "Hang on. I have a feeling there's no time to lose."

They arrived at the James's farmhouse just outside town ten minutes later, and scrambled out of the vehicle. It didn't take long to see where the crisis was centered. Across a snow-covered pasture, Josiah James was standing at the base of the boulder-strewn hillside that bordered his land.

With a hammer, he was trying to pry loose a board blocking the entrance to an old mine shaft.

"Stop!" Lucas yelled out.

Before the man could react, a rock above the entrance came loose, triggering the collapse of one side of the opening and blocking even more of the tiny entrance to the mine. Delia James screamed, and tried to lift one of the massive stones blocking the way. Her husband pulled her away.

"Lucas, help us!" Delia cried out as she saw them approaching. The massive Great Dane beside her barked furiously, but she held on to him.

"Tell me what you know. Have you seen or been able to talk to Eric?" Lucas asked, pushing the dog away and peering into the darkness beyond the twelve-inch opening that remained.

"Yes, at first. But he hasn't said a word for the last ten minutes. His voice kept growing weaker," Delia explained, "but we couldn't reach him. Every time we try to get inside, more of the entrance caves in!"

Lucas pressed his face to the opening. "Eric!" he called out as loudly as he could, but there was no response. He stepped back, concerned about the air quality in the mine shaft. Whatever they did, they'd have to be careful not to attempt anything that would make the passageway any smaller.

"Have you called my brother?" Lucas asked.

"I left a message for him, and I've called the fire department, too, but they haven't responded yet. I think that they were having trouble getting their truck started, or maybe it had stalled, I'm not sure."

The town's emergency vehicles were old, and there was no telling when help would get there, though it would eventually arrive even if the volunteers had to walk.

One thing was clear. They couldn't afford to just sit

around and wait for help. The boy's probable injuries, and the uncertain air quality inside the mine, worried Lucas.

"We have to get in there ourselves. We can't wait," he stated.

Marlee stood by the hole. "I can squeeze through. I'm a lot smaller than any of you."

"No," Lucas answered. "We can't jeopardize anyone else, and you're not trained for this kind of thing."

"I'm the only chance you've got, unless you want to sit around and hope somebody shows up with a better idea."

Lucas knew she was right, but he had no idea what she'd be getting into, or even if the risk would be worth it. There'd been no recent sign that the boy was even still alive. He crouched and peered into the opening. "How far back does this mine go?"

"I have no idea," Josiah answered honestly. "I've looked inside with a flashlight, nothing more. It never looked safe enough to explore, because it slants downward at a pretty steep angle."

Delia began crying.

Marlee put her arms around the other woman. "It's okay. We'll get him out." Then she glared at the men. "Are we going to stand here debating this, or is somebody going to find me a rope and a flashlight? I figure I can carry Eric out if it's necessary, or tie him on to me. I've carried him before, but if I have to climb back out, I'll need at least one hand free to hold on to the rope."

Delia ran inside the house, and came back out with a coil of rope and a powerful flashlight.

It took several minutes before they had everything ready, including a two-way radio and emergency supplies Lucas brought from the Blazer.

Lucas tied the rope around Marlee's waist with a bowline. "This will keep your hands free, and the knot won't slip or tighten. Once you find Eric, check him for injuries and don't move him until I tell you."

"Got it."

Lucas's hands shook as he checked the knot one last time. He hadn't wanted her to see that, but it was too late. As he met her gaze, Marlee gave him a hesitant half smile. "It's okay. This is my choice, and my responsibility."

He would have given anything to stop her, but knew he could not. Even if he refused to allow it, the parents of the trapped boy would have been on her side. Marlee and the two of them would have proceeded without his approval or help. This was little Eric's only chance.

"Be careful," he said at last. He did his best to keep his voice steady.

"I'll be fine. Now, let's get started."

Lucas saw the fear in Marlee's eyes, and his gut clenched. "You don't have to go," he whispered fiercely.

"Yes, I do. This is not just for Eric—it's for me, too."

His heart slammed against his ribs while his brain screamed that Marlee was in danger. Anything could happen down in that damp, narrow passage. Drawing strength from within himself, Lucas forced his thoughts onto the situation facing him. Determination and fear held him steady, and he stood his ground. "Find your way back to me soon, my heart," he whispered.

THE MINE SHAFT WAS nothing more than a steep, narrow tunnel leading down into the bowels of the earth, as far as Marlee could tell. She closed her eyes for a moment, gathering courage, and remembered the way Lucas's hands had trembled. No words, no caresses, could have ever touched her more deeply than that evidence of his feelings for her. She'd never felt so loved and cared for, though at the moment only danger surrounded her.

"Eric, can you hear me?" she shouted down the shaft. There was no answer.

"How are things in there?" Lucas called on the two-way radio.

"The tunnel gets wider the farther I go, and it looks a little less unstable down here," she answered.

Stepping carefully down the steep slope, she saw a low side passage branching to the right. It was cluttered with fallen timbers and debris. Shining the flashlight down, she spotted what looked like a tiny footprint. Marlee crouched down and inched her way inside. After covering a dozen feet or so, she heard a soft whimpering noise.

"Eric?" She hurried forward, toward the sound, shining the beam of the flashlight ahead of her until she saw him. Eric lay huddled against the rock wall, holding his leg.

"He's here and he's alive," she called as she went toward him, stepping over fallen beams and around chunks of rock on the floor of the tunnel. "From what I can see, this section of the mine is partially collapsed. There are rocks and wooden supports lying all over the floor of the tunnel."

"Hey, Eric," she greeted, crouching down next to the little boy. "Remember me from your visits to town?" She'd mentally prepared herself for the worst, but he seemed more scared than injured.

Eric nodded. "My leg hurts," he said, pointing to his knee. "Really bad," he said, his voice shaking. "It won't bend."

"Okay, I'll take care of it."

There were several small cuts on his face, and his leg appeared broken, from the angle at which he held it.

Marlee tried the radio, but either it wasn't working, or the signal wasn't reaching the surface anymore. Since she knew what she should do, she went ahead and did what had to be done.

She winked at Eric. "You ready to go?"

He nodded.

Marlee stepped into the main tunnel, and found the radio worked out there. She quickly filled Lucas in on what she'd done, and announced she was on her way up.

It was a struggle up the incline, which was nearly as steep as a stairway. On that stretch, Eric seemed heavier than she'd thought. At least the rope gave her something to hang on to, and Lucas was pulling her along, as well.

As she got closer to the surface, she heard the earth and rocks above her shift as a wooden support cracked. The soft rumble continued as she hastened toward the entrance.

She was close enough to see daylight through the opening when the roof of the mine began collapsing. Fear paralyzed her for a second, but the weight of the boy in her arms gave her the courage she needed. She flattened against the rock wall and waited, protecting the boy with her body. Then, as abruptly as it had begun, the chaos stopped, replaced by silence as dust swirled in the narrow beam of her flashlight.

Lucas called out to her on the radio. Shaking, she set the boy gently down and directed the flashlight around the mine shaft before answering. "We're okay," she replied, "but the opening I used to come in is about half the size it was. I can still see light trickling through, though, so we're still getting air."

"The overhead supports out here have been sagging," Lucas radioed back. "We can remove rubble from the bottom, but we'll need to brace up the wooden beams before we can bring you out. That'll take us a few moments, so hang tight."

Marlee gave Eric a smile. "You know, I think you could make it through the crawl space that's left, even though it's too small for me." She pointed the flashlight into the opening leading to the outside.

"My leg won't bend, but I can pull myself along and make it. That's how I got in, by crawling," he said. "I just want to get out of here!"

Marlee called out to Lucas. "Eric says he can make it, and I believe him."

"His parents agree. Send him through. Two additional supports are in place."

Marlee watched Eric crawl and drag his way through the narrow opening in the rocks with the agility only children possessed, despite his injuries.

It wasn't long before she heard the happy shouts of Eric's mother as she was reunited with her son. A tear streamed down her face. Today she'd helped make a miracle unfold. She felt filled with a wonderful sense of accomplishment and wonder, something she hadn't felt in a very long time.

"Okay," Lucas's voice came over the two-way. "It's up to you now to clear your own path. We've got this side covered for you. But work slowly and carefully, and check before you start to shift things around."

Marlee crawled on her side, reaching ahead to find the large rocks in her way. Moving them one at a time, she inched forward. It was backbreaking work, far more difficult than she'd anticipated. She'd shredded her gloves long before she was halfway done. Finally, close to the outside, she radioed Lucas that she was moving the final big rock blocking her way.

"We'll be waiting. Watch yourself."

His voice, so filled with tenderness, gave her courage. She reached her hand around the boulder, pulling it along past her face and neck. The cold, crisp air brushed her face like a lover's caress, and she could suddenly see a lot more light ahead. She was only inches from emerging when she heard a loud creak directly above her.

She glanced up and saw that the support beam overhead was bending, and would snap any second. Marlee tried not to think about it. She looked up and saw Lucas ahead, right outside the entrance. One of the support beams above the opening had sagged, and Lucas was jamming a post beneath it, preventing the support from collapsing farther and closing up the mine.

"Lucas, no!" He couldn't let go now, or he could be crushed by the beam. He was trapped.

As she began to move toward Lucas, Josiah's arms clamped around her and pulled her clear of the entrance.

Marlee struggled to get free. As they tumbled out onto the snow, the entire structure collapsed behind them. Marlee screamed and tried to run back, but granite arms held her, making it impossible.

Choking back a sob, she stared at the dust that trailed upward in spiralling clouds, and the mountain of rubble that now covered the area where Lucas had stood only a few seconds ago.

Chapter Sixteen

Despair swept over Marlee until she couldn't even draw breath. A bitterness as corrosive as the most potent acid left her aching, then numb and utterly without hope. Her fingers curled around the carving she had in her pocket until it cut into her palm. As a shape began to rise from the rubble, her heart suddenly began pounding and her knees almost buckled.

Lucas stood up, coughing and shaking off dust and debris.

Marlee ran to Lucas and threw her arms around him, kissing his dusty face and lips. "I thought I'd lost you," she sobbed.

"I rolled away and managed to avoid most of what came down," Lucas managed to say, coughing from the dust. "Guess the ladies who've said I move fast were right."

"Not fast enough," Marlee whispered in his ear.

Lucas held her tightly against him. "My heart, watch what you say. I might misinterpret you, and think of all the trouble I'd be in then."

"Everyone needs to be a little reckless now and then. We've been too cautious." She felt his body respond to her whispered words, but before he could answer, Josiah came up and Lucas reluctantly released her.

"I won't forget what you two did for my boy—for my wife and for me, too." He shook Lucas's hand, then looked at Marlee, taking her hand in a gentle but firm grip. "I've heard the rumors going around about you, and I want you to know that I'll personally punch the lights out of anyone who dares say anything bad about you in my presence. Whatever you need, whatever we can do for either of you, all you have to do is name it."

Before Marlee or Lucas could answer, the sound of a siren echoed up the narrow valley. "Better late than never," he said, smiling ruefully.

IT WAS ANOTHER five minutes before the emergency airlift helicopter was dispatched, and another twenty before the boy was airlifted with his mother.

They said goodbye to Josiah, and filled Gabriel in on what had happened.

They entered the living room of Marlee's boardinghouse and stood inches away from each other, neither one breaking the silence. Marlee's gaze was filled with a gentleness that swept over him, stealing a piece of his heart. He felt her desire. Knowing she needed him made him ache. Soft and beautiful, Marlee stood close enough for him to feel the sweet warmth of her body.

"We came too close today," she managed to say in a strangled voice.

"I kept thinking that all our efforts to protect ourselves had come down to being nothing more than a waste." He reached for her hand and pressed a kiss to the hollow of her palm.

She drew in her breath as he traced a tiny circle on its center with the tip of his tongue.

The soft sound she made almost broke him. Desire clawed into him fiercely and suddenly. Tonight they'd know fires so hot that neither would ever be the same again. But he wanted all of her, not *just* her body. He cared too much to have it be otherwise.

"Can you finally bring yourself to trust me completely?

Will you stop holding back those secrets that keep you locked away from me even while you're in my arms?''

"What you ask…''

"Shouldn't frighten you, my heart.''

Lucas could have made love to her, fast and mindless, but he wanted so much more than that. He was offering her his love, but he would make no attempt to seduce her into overcoming any reluctance she might harbor. It had to be her choice. Then, when he slid into her sweet body and felt her encase him, he'd know that they were truly one.

"Everyone has a past, but some pasts hide more ugliness than others.'' Marlee stepped back, then faced him. "You want all of me, and that's what you'll get tonight, though you may regret it.''

"Never,'' he said in a fierce whisper.

"Everything about you stands for life, but my past is marred by a death that should have never happened.'' She dropped down onto the sofa cushions, then took a deep breath. "Before I came to Four Winds, I was a licensed midwife. I'd been attending a young mother-to-be. She was having a very difficult time with her husband, who had a tendency to be nothing short of dictatorial. I suggested she get away for a week and go someplace where she could relax, because she really needed to bring her blood pressure down. When the woman's husband found out, he called me up, fired me, then threatened to call the police if I ever came into their home again. He said I was trying to ruin his marriage by turning his wife against him.''

Marlee's voice was strangled as she continued. "She was only a few weeks from delivering her baby. I told the husband right then that they'd need to make arrangements for some kind of medical care, and I even offered to make those arrangements for them. Her husband was indignant, saying he'd take care of it himself. This was to be their first child, and he seemed very excited about it, so I never dreamed he wouldn't do as he said.''

Marlee took several deep breaths, then continued. "She

ended up having her baby at home, with the help of a neighbor who had no training. A week later, she called me. She was terrified because she couldn't breathe. I called an ambulance for her and rushed to her home." Marlee took a deep breath, then let it out slowly. "She died of a pulmonary embolism before we could get her to the hospital."

"You weren't to blame for that," Lucas said quietly. "You had no way of knowing that the husband wouldn't do as he said. The mother wasn't blameless, either. She could have called you at any time and told you she needed help."

Marlee shook her head. "I knew this woman would never go against her husband. He was a real control freak. I just never dreamed that he'd risk her health and that of the child in that way. I only met him once, when I first started caring for Ruthie. Yet from the way she spoke of him and their relationship, I really believed he loved her. What I didn't realize was that there's a big difference between love and possessiveness."

"What about the child?"

"The baby survived the delivery without complications, but that young woman died needlessly. Had I been less trusting and more alert, Ruthie might still be alive. Maybe that's why fate punished me." She ran a finger over her scar. It didn't hurt anymore. She kept one hand in her pocket, encircling the carving of the raven. "I had my car accident the same night she died."

"What happened was beyond your control. No amount of medical training will ever give you the ability to read minds."

"But there *is* something to intuition. We both know that. I shouldn't have ignored mine. I was uneasy about that situation, but because I had nothing to go on, I ignored it." She stopped and faced him. "When I got out of the hospital after my accident, I walked away from midwifery. I traveled for a while, and made a living at whatever odd jobs I could find. Finally I ended up in Four Winds."

"People tell me that I'm an excellent diagnostician, and I do rely on my instincts to help my patients. But that's a gift that only goes so far," Lucas explained. "You can't blame yourself for something you couldn't have known about."

He made no attempt to hold her, though the need to do so drummed through him with each beat of his heart. He was certain she'd see it as a form of pity, or worse, consolation. Guilt was a powerful emotion. He knew from experience that she would have to deal with it in her own way. Yet unless he allowed her to see the darkness in his own past, she would slowly draw away from him until he lost her forever.

"You said you see me as a man who stands for life. If by that you mean that I'll do my best for my patients, you're right. But if you think I haven't made mistakes, costly ones, you're very wrong." Lucas stood by the window, then turned to face her. "I served during the Gulf War. I was a Navy corpsman attached to a Marine recon unit. During a mission we got turned around, and my team walked right into an unmarked mine field. It took just a few unknowing steps to decimate our unit. I had my hands full. There were badly injured men that I couldn't get to right away without risking triggering another mine. Everyone was calling out to me for help, but I had to probe the sand with a bayonet, checking every step of the way to get to each one."

His body began to shake as he remembered, but he allowed her to see the way the memories still knifed at him. It was suddenly very important to him that she see him just as he was. When he made love to her, he wanted her to know that he was a man with a past, but one who would treasure all she had to give.

"One of the Marines with me was a Navajo who was a close friend. We'd even enlisted together. He stayed right by my side, helping me get to the injured men as quickly as possible, marking each mine he found. While I was working on the last wounded Marine, he tried to mark a lane out of the mine field so we could get everyone to safe ground. He brushed a trip wire. An antipersonnel mine went off right in front of him, and he and another Marine were hit by shrapnel. He called out to me, and I got to him as quickly as I could, but by then it was a triage situation. The other Marine hit would make it if I got the bleeding stopped right away, but my friend was already too far gone to save.'' Lucas turned away from Marlee for a moment, trying to get himself back under control. He didn't want to remember. It was like pouring salt into wounds that had never truly healed.

''You don't have to—''

He raised one hand. ''Let me finish. I need to do this—for me—for you.'' He took a long, deep breath, then continued. ''My friend needed something for the pain and needed it badly, but I couldn't seem to get the bleeding stopped on the man I knew had a chance. It seemed to take forever before I finally succeeded.'' He met her gaze, letting her see him for the flawed man he was. ''My friend died in agony that day. I will never forget the way he kept calling out to me, pleading, begging me to help him, and how his voice eventually grew weaker, then stopped.''

Marlee walked over and hugged him hard. ''We're two of a kind, you and I. We care too much. Somehow we both missed the part of our training that teaches us to distance ourselves from the pain.''

''We *are* two of a kind, two imperfect beings who have made mistakes. Yet in your eyes, I still see myself as the man I've always wanted to be.''

''What you see reflected in my eyes is the man you are,'' she murmured, burying her head against him.

''If you understand that, then why don't you believe how beautiful you are to me?'' He bent down and touched his lips to hers, then brushed a kiss against the scar on her cheek. He heard her gasp, but this time he knew she would not pull away. "Two people who need and care for each other more than they have a right to, that's what we are."

As Marlee's lips parted, Lucas savored the taste of her. Her body flowed into his, fitting into him as if they'd been created for each other. His tongue penetrated her lips, and stroked her mouth until it was more a possession than a kiss.

"Lucas," she sighed.

The way she called out his name made him reckless. He'd wanted it to be slow tonight, but he wasn't sure things would go that way now.

Marlee's hair was like silk in against his palm. He buried his hands in it, wanting to memorize the feel of this woman until it became a part of him forever. Emotions turned to substance as he felt her rubbing her hips against him, cradling his hardness.

His blood thundered; her breath seared his skin. He was aware of everything about her, but more than anything, he knew he needed more.

"Make love to me. Make me cry out until I beg you to stop, then just keep loving me," she whispered.

It was pure male instinct that drove him now. He wanted her wild in his arms, aching for him to fill her.

"I will love you—I do love you."

He hadn't meant to bind her with that admission, but the words had been said, and it was too late to take them back, even if he had wanted to.

Clothes fell to the floor around them. She was beautiful, all silk and softness. He fell to his knees before her and ravaged her with his hands and his mouth until she cried out, begging him to stop.

"It's just beginning. Know me. Feel me inside you. You're a part of me, a part of my heart."

She whimpered with desire, unable to manage anything but another passionate kiss as he lifted her into his arms and sat with her on his lap in the chair by the window.

A sliver of moonlight streaked through the blinds, playing over her skin. As his lips closed over her breast, she arched against him.

He lifted her up, then lowered her onto him, filling her in one smooth stroke.

Marlee's passion consumed him. His body was on fire. "Say it," he growled. "Tell me you love me." He thrust inside her, losing himself in the moist warmth of her body.

"I do love you," Marlee cried out in one ragged breath, then clung to his shoulders.

He wrapped one steadying hand around her waist, loving the way she clung to him. As she gave in to that sweet weakness of surrender, his strength enfolded her, keeping her safe.

He trembled as he looked at her, his body sheathed by hers. The hard walls that had protected him from love crumbled before the passion he saw in her eyes.

"No more holding back," she begged. "Take me over the edge."

It was too much, more than he'd expected. His tongue danced with hers, mating, as he drove into her and shudders racked his body.

He had no time to think, no time for anything except the raw sensations that heated his blood.

"It is as it was meant to be," Marlee whispered, desire burning in her eyes. She pressed down against him, meeting his thrusts.

It was the force of her passion that shattered him. He felt her muscles around the part of him that was within her, touching him, giving him more pleasure than he'd ever dreamed possible.

It was at that moment that the man who'd held himself in perfect control all his life, who'd lived his life bounded by a code of discipline, lost the final battle. He had found the love that could sustain him, and there was no turning back.

Lucas plunged deeper, mindless, driven by the need to give himself to her as she'd done with him. It was the only gift worthy of what she'd already given him. The night flashed with lightning and fire. Then, as a blinding flash of heat seared through his veins, he shuddered and, holding her tightly, surrendered.

As he held her through the last of the aftershocks, he realized that the only real freedom he'd ever known had come through the power of this love.

"This should have happened in a bed filled with rose petals, not here, not like this," he whispered in a raw voice.

"No, this is exactly the way it was meant to be," Marlee sighed. "No planned rituals, just our love, as strong and as wild as the wind."

And that was the way she made him feel. Nothing had ever touched him so deeply, and no matter what their future held, she'd remain in his heart forever.

HIS CELLULAR PHONE RANG early the next morning, but Marlee never even stirred. Lucas had carried her to her own bed halfway through the night. Now, with regret, he walked quietly out of her room so the call wouldn't wake her.

A new report had come in from the lab, but the technician there had been instructed to follow up the faxed report with a phone call.

"The water sample has shown minute traces of corn cockle. Despite the innocent-sounding name, that's a dangerous and poisonous herb. However, there wasn't enough of it in the water for anyone to have experienced adverse effects, and the symptoms you've reported aren't consistent with a toxic reaction caused by corn cockle. You've reported flulike symptoms, and corn-cockle poisoning would create nausea, severe stomach distress, sharp pains in the spine and so on."

"Could the herb have lost its potency after it had been in the water awhile?"

"The contamination level was so low that we don't believe that there's any way it's responsible for what you're facing there."

Lucas pondered the problem as he hung up. If anything, this new information raised more questions that it answered.

He went to his room, showered and got ready to go to the clinic. Hearing a knock at the front door, and hoping he could get there before it woke Marlee, he quickly went to answer it. Gabriel stood there, looking ashen and worried.

"You don't look so good, Fuzz. How are you feeling?"

"I'll live, but that's not why I'm here. You and I have to talk."

"Come in."

"Where's Marlee?"

"Asleep."

"Can you come over to my office now? I'd like to talk to you in private."

"Let me get a few things, and then we can be on our way."

As he headed down the hall, he saw Marlee come out of her room. "My brother's here. I'm going with him to take care of a few things."

"Okay. I'll see you later, then."

He knew by the noncommittal tone of her voice that Marlee was drawing into herself again, and pulling away from him. He understood, because he knew all about fear. She'd opened her heart and soul to him, and now the full import of what she'd done had hit her. She was vulnerable again, and that was the last thing she'd wanted. Most painful of all was the realization that he might not be able to help her through this. Four Winds needed him now more than ever, and he had a responsibility to the people here, a duty that went above and beyond anything in his personal life.

Lucas fought a stab of loneliness as he accepted the fact that he might lose the woman he loved because of that responsibility.

Not knowing what he could say, he turned without a word and joined his brother.

They arrived at the sheriff's office a short time later. "First the good news. I spoke to Jake last night. He's out of intensive, and he's going to be okay. But you were right, he doesn't have a clue as to who shot him."

"He was checking the water, right?"

"Yeah, he figured that it was worth testing it at the source, but he never expected to be ambushed and never saw what hit him." Gabriel stared at the file in front of him in pensive silence.

Lucas knew his brother well enough to realize that something else was eating at him. His guess was that Gabriel had uncovered bad news, and intuition told him that it was something he wouldn't want to hear at all.

Gabriel regarded Lucas thoughtfully. "Are you getting serious about Marlee, or am I misreading things?"

Lucas didn't answer right away. "It depends how you want to define *serious*. If you're asking me if I've made permanent plans for the future, then the answer is no."

Gabriel let out his breath in a slow hiss. "I've got something hard to tell you. If it turns out that you already know about this, then I'm going to wring you out good. But if you don't, then it's going to broadside you badly."

"Just spit it out."

"I was doing a background check on Earl Larrabee, as you know. I kept at it until I found out his real name, then I stumbled onto something else. It turns out that Marlee and Earl come from the same town, and neither is using the same name they had back then. Marlee Smith is her legal name now, but it used to be Marla Samuels."

The news hit Lucas hard. He'd thought there were no more secrets between him and Marlee—or was it Marla? He silently cursed the way Gabriel had to think everything through before speaking.

"Does she have a record or something?" Lucas pressed.

"No. What I found is an article that had come out in

their local paper. Earl had filed charges against Marla Samuels for wrongful death, but then the charges were thrown out of court.'' Gabriel pushed a computerized copy of the article that he'd downloaded across the table. "You can keep that one. I have another one for my files here."

Lucas studied the photo of Marlee before the accident. Her hair was longer back then, but to him, she looked nearly the same. In another frame was a photo of Earl Larrabee and his wife.

"It appears the mother had complications after delivering her first child. Marlee had been the midwife, and the father went off the deep end. He threatened her at first, then later charged her with negligence." Gabriel pulled out a bottle of water from a cardboard carton and fixed himself a cup of instant coffee in the microwave.

"She told me some of this recently, but she never mentioned Earl by name."

"Earl looked a lot different back then. Look at that photo. His hair was darker, and he had a beard and mustache. He also weighed about thirty pounds more. What I'm thinking is that he tracked her here, and he's the one responsible for the things that have been happening to her. The writing on the note, the one attached to the rock that smashed her window, is similar to Earl's."

The news of the note took him by surprise. Another secret. He was about to ask his brother about it, but it wasn't necessary.

"It was a simple note, just your basic get-out-of-town threat, and there were no prints on it, so it's pure conjecture. I'm certainly not qualified to make any kind of official handwriting comparison."

Lucas struggled to keep his expression neutral. "I can't tell you anything that you don't already know. But I don't believe that Marlee knows who Earl really is. She's not that good at hiding her emotions, and certainly knowing this guy was around would upset her."

Gabriel focused on his brother. After several long mo-

ments, he nodded. "I believe you didn't know about this."
Gabriel allowed the moment to stretch. "You care for that
woman—that's plain enough. And something really worries
you. Is it that she has secrets, or is it more? Are you worried
that with a woman in your life you won't be able to have
the freedom to pursue the job you've chosen? You've always prided yourself on being a loner, and giving everything to your duties here."

"There was a time in my life when everything was sim-
pler, when nothing was more important to me than my duties here," Lucas admitted. "But everything's changing.
No, I'm changing. I don't know if this is a good thing or
not. I'm not even sure what, if anything, I should do about
it. Whatever happens, I won't neglect my duties here.
That's the only thing I can say with complete conviction."
He felt as if a great weight were slowly crushing him. It
was disappointment, in himself and in Marlee for not fully
trusting him. But he couldn't get over what a gray and ugly
feeling disappointment was.

"I'm probably talking out of turn, but I need to say
something. For a long time, I've seen you hiding behind
that air of professionalism. Nothing touched you, even the
occasional death of a patient. You always quickly put it
into perspective and went on. That distancing enabled you
to do your job, but your way of coping with the demands
of your profession left you with no room for compassion.
Logic and reason alone don't allow for that, and it's a quality that's very much needed in the medical profession. I
realize it comes at a cost to you, but without compassion,
you can't reach the heart of the patient."

"Treating the whole, as the Navajo way teaches..." Lucas acknowledged. "Joshua does that."

"You're learning that there's a price to pay if you allow
yourself to become vulnerable," Gabriel observed. "But
what you now have to decide for yourself is whether the
cost is worth what you're trying to attain."

Gabriel stood up, swayed back and forth like a willow in a breeze and then fell back down into his seat.

Lucas was at his brother's side instantly. "It looks like your work day is over, Fuzz." He reached for his medical bag. "Just relax, and let me do what I do best."

AFTER TAKING GABRIEL back home, Lucas returned to the sheriff's office. Gabriel had assured him that he'd drunk only the coffee that had been made with bottled water, yet the symptoms had been ones Lucas had recognized. He hadn't said anything to Lanie or Gabriel, uncertain of his own theory, but he'd made sure he'd administered the necessary treatment for corn-cockle poisoning.

If he was right, Gabriel's throat would be raw for a long time, and the nausea would also persist until the poison was completely out of his system. There were other symptoms that they'd have to stay on the alert for, but Tree had come over to help. Gabriel would have round-the-clock care, and the best of both worlds—the Navajo Way and medical science.

He walked to the carton filled with water bottles and inspected each container. All were intact. Next he opened the can of instant coffee. Corn-cockle seeds were black and, ground up, would be undetectable in the coffee.

Without hesitation, he hurried out of his brother's office and went directly to the clinic. He would make arrangements for the private service that was coming into town to deliver emergency supplies to also pick up the coffee and take it to the lab for testing. It would mean another rush job for the lab, but he had to know if someone had deliberately poisoned his brother. After that was taken care of, he'd go see Marlee. Her lack of trust, even after the closeness they'd known, knifed at him.

He'd made the arrangements to have the coffee tested, and was hanging up the phone when Marlee came in the door.

"I need to talk to you," she said.

"What a coincidence. I need to talk to you, too," he said, his voice low and very controlled. He wanted to shout at her, or kiss her until she melted in his arms, and then demand that she tell him why she didn't, or perhaps couldn't, trust him.

"Me first. It's very important. I went by your brother's house, and I know he's been poisoned."

"He's going to be fine."

"I gathered that, but I don't understand how this happened. Gabriel wouldn't have drunk or eaten anything that wasn't prepackaged."

Lucas didn't look directly at her, not wanting her to see the pain raging inside him. Instead, he stared at the dust motes floating lazily in the faint rays of the sun that trickled in through the window. "I don't know how for sure yet, but I think it's corn-cockle poisoning. That's the same herb that showed up in the water."

"But how could that happen? Gabriel only drank bottled water."

"I suspect the instant coffee," he said.

"Corn cockle doesn't grow around here, you know. The flowers are quite attractive, but you can only get the seeds from specialty catalogs."

He sat up slowly, his eyes never leaving her face. "How do you know this?"

She hesitated. "I'd ordered some myself along with a dozen or so other packets from the mail-order company. It was that same shipment, by the way, that someone took from my mailbox and replaced with dead bugs." She shook her head slowly. "If those seeds were taken from an order I placed, and then used against Gabriel, I'll never be able to convince anyone that I had nothing to do with what's happening." Her voice broke, but she cleared her throat and turned around to face him. "What about you, Shadow. Do *you* still trust me?"

"If you're asking me whether I believe you poisoned my

brother, the answer is no. But do I completely trust you?'' He shook his head. "No more than you do me."

Her eyes widened as she turned around. "I don't understand.''

"I thought there were no more secrets between us." He took out the article Gabriel had given him. "My brother found this when he was looking into Earl Larrabee's past.''

She stared at the photo. "What has this got to do with Earl Larrabee?'' she asked, staring at the photo. As she saw the woman in the picture with Larrabee, the light of recognition and understanding changed her expression. "Now I know who my enemy is." She looked up and held Lucas's gaze. "But the real question is, can you believe me when I tell you that I didn't realize who he was?'' Her gaze stayed on him. Then, when he didn't answer right away, she looked away. "How much harm has this man done to my life this time?'' she added in a tortured whisper.

"My guess is that he's the one who marked up your mirrors and photos, and maybe did some of the other things that have been happening to you. He probably also wrote the note attached to that rock. The one you never told me about.''

Marlee never flinched. "I told your brother. He's the sheriff. I figured you had enough on your mind."

"The real problem is that you don't know how to trust. Until you can come to terms with that, we don't really have much we can give each other." He saw the hurt that flashed in her eyes, and knew that it went as deep as his own.

Marlee took a halting step back, then another, then turned and strode toward the door. "I'm going to confront Earl right now. He's destroyed enough in my life. It's got to stop.'' She ran out before he could catch her.

Lucas muttered an oath, then went after her, but she was already driving off in her car by the time he reached his Blazer.

Without hesitation, Lucas jumped behind the wheel of his vehicle and sped after her.

Chapter Seventeen

Catching up to her was more difficult than he'd expected. Although the roads were better today than yesterday, the Blazer skidded on the icy patches as he pressed down on the accelerator. Marlee was driving much too fast for the conditions of the road, and he hoped her old tires would still grip the surface.

Anger filled him as he thought of what had happened. He shouldn't have been so rough on her, but she'd hurt him far more than he'd ever dreamed anyone could. He finally reached her as she slid to a stop at one of the town's two stoplights. Lucas threw open his door and strode up to her car.

"This is crazy—you can't face Earl alone. There's no way you can predict his reaction. He may have been the one trying to kill you. As a matter of fact, it's a good bet. But you don't have any real proof against him, you know."

"So you're telling me to do nothing?"

"All I'm advising is that you postpone going to see him for a little while. We're going to need proof before we can make any public accusations. There's something else I think should be checked out first, and with Gabriel sick, I need your help to do it."

A HALF HOUR LATER, Marlee was riding with Lucas to the water tower. He was right. They'd all wanted to check out that place for a long time, but nobody had been able to get up there because of the weather. This was the first time the trip had seemed even remotely possible.

"If Earl *is* behind this, I'm going to do everything in my power to put him in jail or an institution. I won't allow him to run me out of this town. My life is here now—I don't want to start over again someplace new," Marlee said, her voice shaking with the strength of her conviction.

"You won't have to. My family and I will stand by you. We'll all do whatever is necessary to protect you."

"In honor of Flinthawk and his legacy?" she asked.

"Yes, but it's more than that. In this case, it's personal."

The implications of that took her breath away. "I don't know what to say. I never wanted to endanger anyone, nor did I ever expect to have such loyal allies."

"You don't see the good that is all around you because you're too intent on protecting yourself from the bad."

Marlee started to protest, but something else caught her attention as they approached the water facility. "Look over there," she said. "Jake may have broken the lock on that gate, but somehow I doubt it, since he has a key. My guess is that someone else came through here with a pair of bolt cutters, and this is exactly how Jake found it."

"Let's check out the water tower itself first. If someone tampered with things up there, we should be able to see evidence of it plainly enough."

When they reached the water tower, Lucas crouched down and began to carefully remove the layer of snow that had accumulated around the base of the ladder. "This is interesting," he said. "Right below the newly fallen snow there are tracks frozen in the mud. Help me brush aside more of the snow."

"These tracks may be Jake's."

"One set probably is, but there are two sets," Lucas said, continuing to work. "Jake's is the larger size boot, I'd be willing to bet on that, but this other person's foot-prints...there's something odd about them." Lucas brushed away more of the snow, finding more prints frozen into the earth. "This man has an unusual stride."

Marlee studied the footprints carefully, crouching beside Lucas. "How can you tell?"

"This person walks with a limp. See how one foot goes in deeper than the other?"

"I can't think of anyone around here who walks with a limp, can you?"

Lucas considered it. "There's Mrs. Carey, but she's in her nineties. I can't imagine her coming out here for a walk, much less anything as athletic as climbing the water-tower ladder." He stood up slowly. "And this isn't someone who walks with a cane, but rather someone with a disability that leaves one leg slightly weaker."

Marlee touched her scar. She'd left the small carving beneath her pillow, and for the first time since she'd started carrying it, her scar was now beginning to ache. Brushing the thought aside as coincidence, she continued. "Maybe it's not something that's a constant problem."

He nodded thoughtfully. "Good point. I know Alex hurt his foot a long time ago. He used to limp during the cold months, if I remember right. He never came to me with the problem, but maybe because of the damp weather, he's having problems again."

"I've never noticed him limping, but then again, it may be that it's only a problem in cases of extreme physical duress—which is how I'd qualify a trek up here. Interestingly enough, Earl doesn't have a limp. Maybe I was too quick to condemn him. It's possible he has nothing to do with any of the threats to me."

"The problem is, we could be dealing with two separate things here. What's happening to the town, and what has been done to you, might not be connected in any way."

They checked the water tower and, finding nothing out of the ordinary, proceeded to the pump house. Marlee and Lucas walked inside to look around. After looking under and around the machinery, Marlee saw something on the floor, and crouched down. "These *could* be corn-cockle seeds. But it would take an awful lot more than these to poison the town's entire water supply."

"Maybe this was only meant to mislead us right from the start. What got in the culprit's way was the weather, since no one could come here to check things out."

"You mean whoever was doing this wanted us to investigate and believe it was the water that was making people sick?"

"Yes, because then the real source of the illness would have remained hidden, and he could continue doing the harm he intended."

She stood up slowly. "We're dealing with a very sick person. To randomly poison the entire town, from infants to the very old, and to use wiles to lead people to the wrong conclusion... Who, or maybe I should ask *what* are we dealing with here?"

"Good question," Lucas answered thoughtfully, collecting some of the suspect seeds. "Let's go back to Four Winds. I need to check on Fuzz, and bring him up-to-date on what we just found."

THEY WERE HALFWAY into town when Lucas's cellular phone rang. Marlee could only hear his end, but it wasn't hard to figure out that Lanie was ill. The ramifications chilled her to the bone.

She waited when the call was over, wondering whether to ask him to explain. He now knew that she'd been a midwife. If anyone was capable of taking care of Lanie now, it was her. But whether or not Lucas would trust her to care for his brother's wife was another matter.

"My brother, believe it or not, is now up and back at the sheriff's office, taking care of a crisis there. There was a major problem at Rosa's. Supplies are dangerously low again, and although Fuzz made arrangements to have emergency supplies airlifted in, it won't be anywhere near what's really needed. People are running out of the basics, and the tension is getting to them. To make matters worse, the weather has caused a rock slide that has reblocked the lane out of town, and it's going to be a while before they can get it cleared again. I don't see things getting easier anytime soon.''

She noted that he hadn't mentioned Lanie. The knowledge stung her, but she remained quiet. She hadn't told him about the note on the rock, because at the time it had seemed pointless. Yet because she'd kept so many secrets, he wasn't sure of her anymore. She couldn't blame him, though his lack of faith in her now was breaking her heart.

"Lanie needs my help. I'm going to stop there first. Do you mind going with me? It would mean putting off dealing with Larrabee for a little longer.''

"He can wait.'' She still didn't ask for any particulars about Lanie, though she wanted to more than anything. If he wanted to share that information with her, she knew he would have. To ask, particularly under the circumstances, would have been an intrusion.

"I've got to tell you. I'm worried about my sister-in-law. She's in her last month now. I know she doesn't drink coffee, and I know my brother hasn't let her drink or eat anything that could have been contaminated. He takes far better care of her than he does of himself.''

"But you're thinking she may have been poisoned?''

Lucas nodded. "And I'm worried about what that might do to the child she's carrying.''

His voice was taut, and she longed to offer him comfort, to hold him, to let him know how much she cared. But their time had come and gone. Perhaps it was better this way.

They arrived at Gabriel's house a short time later. Marlee felt Lucas's fear as keenly as her own, but as they walked inside the house, they both masked it well. Lanie was at the kitchen table, sipping some carbonated mineral water.

Marlee noted with relief that Lanie's color was normal. As Lucas worked, checking vitals, she recorded what he needed on the charts. Finally Lucas stood up. "You don't have any symptoms that are out of line with a mother-to-be," he assured her. "Your baby's heart sounds strong, too."

Lanie placed one hand over her stomach protectively. "I was feeling really queasy earlier and I guess I panicked. I don't want this child to arrive early. I was afraid...."

Marlee crouched in front of her. "You're doing great, but you have to remember that the baby will make its own rules. From everything that Lucas determined from your condition and vital signs, you shouldn't be worried."

"Lucas is so busy right now, Gabriel's gone back to work and Nydia and Joshua rode out into the mountains to take care of a Navajo couple. I guess I got scared. I keep worrying that the baby will come unexpectedly, and nobody will be around to help."

Lucas looked at Marlee with raised eyebrows, then as she nodded, said, "I bet that if you ask, Marlee would stay with you. She's a licensed midwife."

Lanie looked at Marlee in surprise. "You never said anything!"

"I haven't worked in that profession for over three years, but believe me, you never forget what you learn."

Lanie asked a string of questions, barely giving Marlee a chance to answer one before she would fire off the next. Marlee answered everything, and was glad to see Lanie relax. Like so many new mothers-to-be, she was afraid and excited all at once.

Soothing Lanie's fears, and knowing that she could help Lanie make the wonderful transition to motherhood, filled Marlee with a sense of purpose and fulfillment she hadn't experienced in years.

At long last, Lucas took Marlee aside. "I don't think that she's in any trouble, and I highly doubt that she's ingested any of the poison. It would have had a more pronounced effect on her physically. I'm not worried about the child, either, at this point. Everything looks good on that score.

What I'm worried about is that we need to keep her calm, and with all that's going on, that's a tall order."

"I'll stay with her, then. Go find your brother and do whatever you have to." Marlee hadn't meant to volunteer. She'd wanted to be asked, but it was too late now. "That is, if you trust me to stay with her," she added quickly.

His expression grew intense, but an undeniable tenderness shone in his eyes, something she'd never thought to see there again. "I've already trusted you with everything that matters to me, with my very life. This is no different."

His words were like silk gliding over her naked flesh, but before she could respond, he hurried out. She watched the door for a second, gathering her thoughts. He was everything she'd ever wanted in a man, and more. But love often required sacrifice, and that was no different now. Lucas had made his commitment to Four Winds, and she would never tie him down and tear him in two by forcing him to divide that loyalty.

Hearing Lanie in the kitchen, Marlee went to join her.

Lanie was wadding up the newspaper with a fury.

"Here, let me do that. What's going on?"

Lanie sat back down. "I used a newspaper my neighbor wrapped a baby gift in to clean the window. Newspapers generally do a real good job, but the ink Alex is using now, not to mention the paper, is a disaster. It even smells funny. I used my window cleaner, wiped the pane, and now everything's streaked. I was going to throw it away, but I started feeling really queasy again."

Marlee looked at Lanie's fingertips. They were covered in blue-black ink that smelled vaguely like insecticide. "Wash your hands right now, okay? You may be allergic to that stuff."

Lanie washed off in the kitchen sink, and Marlee followed suit, a new thought forming in her mind. They'd been intent on looking for contaminated food or water, because the illness had been so widespread. But an awful lot of people in town took the newspaper, or had contact with it. She remembered the journalism class at the high school, and all the kids they'd treated, kids who had yet to completely recover.

"I'm really tired. I think I'm going to take a nap," Lanie said. "Do you mind terribly?"

"No, not at all. Get some rest, and don't worry about a thing." As Lanie went down the hall to the bedroom, Marlee picked up the phone and called Mrs. Burnham.

When Marlee identified herself, Mrs. Burnham's voice became instantly cautious. "I'm just calling about Muzzy," Marlee said, trying to set her at ease. "I was wondering how he's been feeling."

"He's just fine, but I don't dare let him out of the house unless I'm with him anymore. I just worry too much. He was really a pretty sick little dog for a bit."

"Did you or the vet ever figure out what happened?"

"No." Once again her voice grew hard.

She considered being more circumspect, maybe trying to make small talk, but she was too excited for patience. If she *had* found the missing piece of the puzzle, she wasn't going to wait one more second to warn people.

"Mrs. Burnham, tell me something. Do you buy the newspaper, by any chance?"

Mrs. Burnham didn't answer right away. Finally, after several long moments, she broke the silence. "If Mrs. Perez has been complaining, I've got to tell you, she just likes to make trouble. Muzzy likes to play. Sometimes he'll bring in my paper and get so excited he'll bring in every other paper on the street, too. But I always return them. And if Muzzy chews them up, I always replace them." There was another pause. "But why are you asking? Is there an article in the paper about my Muzzy? Is Mrs. Perez making trouble for us again?"

Marlee considered her answer carefully. She was getting more certain by the minute, but she didn't want Mrs. Burnham spreading an unsubstantiated theory at this point. "I've been thinking of adopting a dog," Marlee said lamely, unable to think of anything else, "and I was wondering if that's how you found Muzzy—through the want ads, that is."

"Oh, not at all. I went to a kennel in Santa Fe and picked him out myself," Mrs. Burnham continued talking so quickly, Marlee could barely get in a word edgewise.

Finally, as Mrs. Burnham paused a millisecond for breath, Marlee quickly jumped in and excused herself. As she hung up the phone, her mind was racing.

She had to contact Lucas and Gabriel. The Blackhorse family had trusted her with everything that mattered to them, and now, finally, she had found a way to repay their trust. If this new information proved true, perhaps they could finally solve the puzzle that had haunted Four Winds. But there was more than that at stake here, and she knew it.

She owed Lucas a debt of gratitude. He'd reminded her what it was like to feel desirable and wanted. He'd shown her how to start truly living again, and for that she owed him far more than she would ever be able to express in words.

No promises had been made between them, and she would not bind him to her in any way. She loved him, and for her, that was enough.

LUCAS WAS AT Gabriel's office when Marlee called and told them what she'd learned and suspected. There was no proof, but it did open an entirely new avenue of investigation none of them had considered before. Then, just about the time Gabriel and Lucas had decided to go have a talk with Alex, a call came in. The emergency airlift helicopter was scheduled to land within fifteen minutes. Gabriel had to meet it, deliver the sample of coffee and a copy of the newspaper that needed to go to the lab for analysis, then supervise the distribution of supplies that had been flown in. Their plans to confront Alex about the ink had to be postponed.

Lucas agreed not to confront Alex on his own and went to check on some patients, planning to meet up with his brother later. Lost in thought, he drummed his fingers on the steering wheel impatiently. The question of Larrabee's involvement still weighed heavily on his mind. Gabriel had spent quite a bit of time trying to locate the bank teller, but the man, so far, was making himself scarce. The thought that perhaps the man had escaped disturbed him.

As he drove past the newspaper office and saw Alex leaving, a new thought formed. Gabriel had made him promise that he wouldn't try to question Alex. In that respect, Lucas's hands were tied. He wouldn't break his word to his brother. But there was another way to get answers. It certainly couldn't hurt to take a look around the newspaper office. With Alex gone, there was no one to stop him.

The idea tempted him. He might be able to find out what, if anything, had been put in the ink, or the paper. Knowing that could make it a lot easier to treat those who had become ill. If everything was locked, he'd leave. And if he did get in, he'd wear his gloves so he'd be sure not to leave any fingerprints that might later jeopardize evidence in court.

He went to the back of the building and looked around. Nothing was open. He tried the back door, then the windows. They were locked tight. Then he spotted a small high window that probably led to a bathroom or janitorial closet. He stared at it for a second or two. If he had any chance of finding an open window, the inaccessibility of that one made it the logical choice. Whether he'd fit through it was another matter.

He pulled one of the trash cans closer to the window, hopped on it, then tried the window. It gave, but not much. Putting all his strength into it, he gave one merciless shove, and with a creak, it slid open.

He squeezed through, and ended up with bruised ribs and a scrape on his arm, but he was inside. He looked around the darkened janitorial closet, then tried the door. It was unlocked.

Lucas went down the hall to the room where he knew the presses were, and turned on the light switch. He walked around, studying everything, yet touching nothing, despite his gloves. A large metal cabinet stood alone against one wall, and had a new-looking hasp installed on the doors, equipped with a combination lock.

Instead of trying random numbers, Lucas considered human nature. He looked around the cabinet, then opened the top drawer of a nearby desk. On the side of the drawer, normally out of sight, was a piece of masking tape with the numbers ''36-4-18'' written on it. Lucas had the lock off in thirty seconds. Inside the cabinet were the supplies for the printing presses.

Next to the bottles of printer's ink, which were double-bagged in clear plastic, he found a heavy-duty painter's respiration mask and a set of thick rubber gloves. He wasn't sure if that was standard practice when dealing with newspaper ink, but somehow he doubted it. Most printers used a nontoxic soy-based ink, he'd read once in this very newspaper. As he searched behind the ink bottles, he found his answer.

Double-bagged in plastic were two bottles of Aldicarb, a highly toxic pesticide. One had been opened, and chemicals had stained the label to the point of unreadability. Lucas read the small print on the warning label on the other bottle, and learned that it was readily absorbed through the skin. The symptoms—poisoning, nausea and muscle weakness, dizziness and stomach cramps—matched the illnesses that had recently affected the residents of Four Winds.

Lucas looked over at a big worktable where newspapers lay in stacks. About half of the papers had been folded and placed inside plastic bags that would protect them from the snow. The bags were labeled, too, so maybe the poisonings hadn't been quite as random as he'd thought.

As he was pondering that question, he heard the floor

creak. Lucas turned around and caught a glimpse of Alex's face just before something hard impacted against the side of his head. Lights exploded in front of his eyes, then vanished, engulfed by all-consuming darkness.

Chapter Eighteen

Lucas woke up slowly and painfully, aware that someone was pulling him roughly up to a sitting position. His hands were tied behind his back. Before he could gather his wits, he was grabbed by his hair and something was jammed into his mouth. He tried to jerk his head aside to get rid of the spout of the big squeeze bottle, but the gritty liquid cascaded down his throat anyway.

He coughed, spitting out what he could, but he had a feeling it was already too late.

"Goodbye," Alex said quietly. "This wouldn't have been my choice, but you chose your own fate when you got nosy. Did you really think I hadn't seen you driving slowly by my office? You underestimated me, and that's going to cost you your life, and more. When they find your body, and learn you've been poisoned with corn cockle, your girlfriend will be blamed for your death. Think about what your curiosity has cost you—and her—while you're dying."

Lucas heard the door slam. His throat burned badly. He knew Alex had ground up the seeds and mixed them with water, then sprayed it down his throat. Tasting the bits that lay burning on his tongue, he tried to spit them out. It was a pointless gesture. Unless he got help soon, he would die.

It didn't seem long before sharp pains began in his stomach and spread to his spine. As he felt the poison work, he tried to hold on. Nobody knew he'd detoured to stop at the newspaper office. It would be some time before anyone even realized he was missing, and by then, it would be too late for him. He filled his mind with thoughts of the woman he loved.

"Marlee," he whispered her name in the dark, as if the sound alone would bring her to him. Navajo ways taught that names had power. Lucas wasn't sure if he believed that, but he believed in his love for Marlee.

He concentrated on her face, on her softness, on the sound of her voice. He clung to the images, knowing that they were his lifeline. His love for Marlee was the only thing that would help him find the strength to endure.

MARLEE STARED at the phone. She hadn't heard from either Gabriel or Lucas in hours, and Lucas wasn't answering his cellular phone. Lanie was asleep, and the house was quiet. Restless, she paced around the living room. The uneasiness she felt was like a poison that undermined everything she tried to do.

She paced around the room, then, catching a glimpse of herself in the mirror, stopped abruptly. Her scar was a dark, angry red, just like it had been right after the accident. She couldn't understand it. She ran her fingertips over it gingerly. Was she being punished? Was it her desire to return to midwifery that was exacting such a painful toll on her?

The more she studied her reflection, the darker her scar seemed to become. She tore her gaze away from the mirror, and renewed her pacing. She couldn't understand why she hadn't been able to reach Lucas. Every instinct she possessed was warning her that he was in grave danger.

Fear tightened its grip around her as she dialed his number again. He still wasn't answering his pager or his cellular phone. It didn't make sense, not unless he was... No. She pushed the thought back. She wouldn't give in to panic.

She'd just decided to try Gabriel's number when the

phone rang. Even as she picked up the receiver, she knew it wouldn't be Lucas.

She was right. She listened as Gabriel asked about his wife. "Lanie's okay, but I'm afraid Lucas might be in trouble," she said quickly. "I've been trying to reach him, and it's not like Lucas to be out of touch this long."

"Something might have gone haywire with his cell phone."

"Gabriel, listen to me. My feelings for your brother tie me to him in a way I can't really explain. It isn't anything magical. It's simply a gift women have. Believe me when I tell you it can be relied upon, and right now it's telling me Lucas is in trouble."

"Women's intuition," he acknowledged. "I'm not one to discount that easily. All right. I'll see if I can track him down and I'll keep you updated."

"After what we discussed earlier, I think you should probably check either at Earl's house, at the newspaper office or wherever Alex lives."

"Earl hasn't been seen for some time. I already told Shadow that. I also made Shadow give me his word that he wouldn't approach Alex. That's a tricky situation, and I didn't want him to muddy the waters."

"Lucas wouldn't break his word," she said thoughtfully, "but if he thought there was a way to get some evidence against Alex…"

"Oh, yeah. That sounds like Shadow, all right. I'll head over to the newspaper office right now."

Marlee glanced down the hall. She couldn't leave Lanie alone. Yet every fiber in her body told her Lucas was in danger. She desperately needed to do more than simply wait for Gabriel's call.

She telephoned Nydia, hoping against hope she and her husband had returned from the mountains. If Joshua or his wife could come and stay with Lanie, then Marlee would be free to help Gabriel search. As she dialed, Marlee heard Lucas call her name. The whisper touched her mind like a soft, warm summer breeze. Marlee held her breath as a feeling of love swept through her, then slowly gave way to a profound sense of loss.

Marlee gasped as horror and fear drove the air out of her lungs. Lucas needed her, and there wasn't much time.

NYDIA WALKED into Gabriel and Lanie's house a short time later. Her eyes widened as she looked at Marlee's face. "Are you okay?"

Marlee reached up and touched her scar. Nydia's gaze had unconsciously stopped there. "I'll be fine—it's Lucas I'm worried about. I need to go find him."

Nydia nodded once. "You're lucky you called when you did. We'd only just returned from the mountains." She tossed Marlee her keys. "Take my car, and go do whatever you have to. I'll stay with my sister-in-law."

Marlee was surprised that she'd asked for no explanations. "Lanie's sleeping right now, and should be fine. I still have Gabriel's extra cell phone. If there are any problems, call me. I'll be back here in a flash."

Marlee went to the boardinghouse to see if Lucas had left any message there. Not finding one, she retrieved her carving of the raven from her room before heading out the door. The moment her hand closed around the carving, her body seemed to relax. She knew she was reacting like someone given a placebo, but it didn't matter. She'd take all the help she could get now. A new sense of confidence filled her. She was halfway to the car when the cellular phone rang. Her heart froze as she heard Gabriel's somber voice.

"I just found my brother, and you were right. Shadow's in bad shape. I think he's been poisoned. He was tied up and dumped in the shed behind the newspaper office. Lanie says you've had some medical training. I could really use your help. I'm on my way to the first-aid station with him right now. The airlift helicopter can't get here because of high winds in the Santa Fe area, so I need to use the radio he has there to communicate with the doctors over at county hospital. The doctors will give us all the advice they can, but my medical training doesn't go beyond first aid.''

"Mine does," Marlee said. "I'll meet you there."

Marlee pressed down on the accelerator, knowing every minute was critical. The headlights would do little to reveal the glare ice on the darkened road, but if Lucas had been poisoned, there wasn't time for caution. The thought of losing him filled her with such anguish her body began to tremble.

She gripped the steering wheel tightly, forcing herself to focus only on the present. She hadn't lost him yet. This was the time to fight, not the time to grieve.

Using every bit of her driving skills, Marlee managed to keep the unfamiliar vehicle on the road. Then, just as she carefully negotiated a curve, she saw a brief flash of light in her rearview mirror.

In the darkness, she couldn't make out who was behind her, but the elevation of the headlights told her it was a pickup. She focused again on the road ahead, but the high-beam lights of the truck behind her were getting brighter in the mirror, distracting her and blinding her, as well. She reached up to adjust the rearview mirror to divert the light. Just then, the pickup accelerated to ram the rear bumper of her car.

The steering wheel jerked out of her hand, but she quickly grabbed it tightly again, fighting to stay on the road. She tried to get a look at the driver behind her, but it was impossible with the blinding light from the high beams. Using all her willpower, she concentrated on one thing only, staying on the road. She was fighting for Lucas's life now, not just her own. Her enemy would not win.

All she needed now was one break. She'd try something unexpected. Just as her attacker moved up to ram her vehicle again, she picked a spot that looked free of rocks and turned off the road.

Bouncing around like a pebble in a can, Marlee struggled

to keep her vehicle under control. Unless she slowed down, she'd crash into the big rock ahead, or worse, go over the cliff just beyond it. Marlee managed to swing the car sideways without rolling and slide to a stop about a foot away from the rock.

Still shaking, she saw the driver of the pickup rocket past her, the rear end of his truck fishtailing as he tried desperately to brake in the icy snow. The momentum of his heavy truck now worked against him, but still, he almost succeeded. A heartbeat later, she saw the ruby taillights slowly rise up into the air as the vehicle tipped over the rim of the canyon.

Marlee threw open her door. She didn't want to stop now, particularly not for someone who'd just tried to kill her, but she had no choice. There had been no sound of a crash, so maybe something had slowed the descent of the pickup.

As she made her way through the snow, she called in the accident using her cellular phone. She got no answer from Gabriel, and the dispatcher told her there was no one available to respond except for the volunteer fire department, and they were already pulling someone back onto the road who'd gone into a ditch. It would be a half hour before they could get to the scene. She knew it was her responsibility legally and ethically to help the crash victim, if she could without endangering herself any further.

Marlee stood at the top of the incline and looked down. The pickup had dropped about twenty feet, and was now sandwiched precariously between two slender trees growing out of the cliffside. The driver's-side window had shattered. The man inside was struggling to open his door, which was further blocked by a thick stand of scrub oak brush. The vehicle shifted as he pushed from the inside, and one of the trees crackled with the strain.

Marlee climbed carefully down toward the pickup, intent on learning the identity of the man who'd tried to kill her. She was not surprised to see Earl Larrabee inside the cab, his face covered with blood and embedded glass fragments. Again he tried to force the driver's door open.

"Don't move," Marlee yelled. "If you keep shifting your weight around, you'll shake the truck loose from the only thing holding it up here."

"I can't...won't...stay here," he managed to say, and leaned over, trying to go out the passenger's side. He hurried back as the truck began to swing dangerously. "Did you come to gloat?"

"I came to help you. But if you keep trying to get out of there, you'll rock the truck so much it'll fall. You'll die. Why don't you try crawling out the driver's-side window instead?"

"I can't, not without your help. Give me your hand."

Marlee fought against her common sense, which warned her clearly against getting within reach of this man. She should leave this would-be murderer to face the consequences of his own actions and hurry to Lucas's side.

"Please, give me a hand. I think the truck is about to go," he begged.

Marlee knew she'd never be able to live with herself if she just walked away from someone, anyone, in need. Overcoming her reluctance, she extended her hand, and braced herself as he tried to climb out of the car window to reach her.

"Ironic, isn't it? Here you are helping me stay alive when I just almost killed you." He reached out the window and took her hand, his grip tightening painfully. "Don't you know who I really am? I scarred up those photos in your house, and I broke your front window. I did everything I could to ruin your cozy life here in Four Winds. I even blackmailed Rosa, forcing her not to take credit from anyone to make things even more tense here in town while I spread rumors about you everywhere. I wanted people in this town to turn on you just as you made my wife turn on me."

"I know who you are. I'm really sorry that you've never

been able to accept the responsibility for your own actions. Your wife loved and trusted you. You were the one who refused to get medical care for her, and she paid for your negligence with her life."

"Your friendship with my wife is what changed her. She stopped listening to me after you came into our lives." He managed to get half his body through the window, but then, with a groan, settled back.

"What's wrong?"

"A piece of glass," he muttered. He broke the remaining fragments from the bottom of the shattered window then tried to crawl through again. "You ruined my life. You left me with a baby who had no mother to take care of her."

"Where's the baby now?"

"I gave her up for adoption. I had no way of taking care of her."

His grip on her hand was viselike now, and Marlee realized he wasn't trying to crawl out.

"I wanted you to pay for everything you stole from me—my family, my future. I tried to kill you and myself that night after you left the hospital, but you swerved and ran off the road. You survived the crash. But maybe it was better that way. The scar on your face marked you, like a leper. You had to live your life with something that made you as ugly on the outside as you were on the inside."

"You were in the car that almost hit me head-on?" she repeated dully. For so many years, she'd thought of it as divine retribution. Now she understood the crash that had scarred her had been no accident, but the work of a man crazed by guilt. The knowledge lifted a heavy burden she'd shouldered for far too long.

The truck began to slide as Earl deliberately started rocking back and forth. "But it all ends now," he said. "Judgment day is finally here, and we're going for that last ride together."

Marlee struggled to get free of him as the truck began to slip down the incline, but his fingers clasped her wrist in a death grip. As the truck gathered momentum, she was dragged alongside, slipping along the icy ground. "Let me go!"

He gave her a peaceful smile but said nothing. His grip never wavered.

Marlee leaned back and pushed off with her feet against the pickup. The sudden force knocked her free of Earl's grip.

She hit the ground rolling, and reached out with her hands to grab the brush to stop herself. Her arms were almost pulled out of their sockets, but she held on tight. As she clung to the brush, she saw Earl scrambling to get out of the pickup, without success. A second later, the vehicle carried the trapped man over the vertical drop, out of sight. Seconds went by, then there was a distant thump. An explosion followed, rocking the ground, and flames leaped out from the canyon below.

She approached the edge slowly. Fifty feet below, Earl's body, illuminated by the flames, lay twisted like a rag doll upon a pile of refrigerator-sized boulders. Turning away, she hurried back to her car, ignoring her own cuts and bruises. The man's death, the hatred he'd harbored, had all been so pointless. Freed of her past at long last, her thoughts turned to Lucas. It was time to concentrate on the living.

She managed to get Nydia's car back onto the road, and raced to the clinic. She prayed that she would reach Lucas in time and that there would be something that could save him. Breathless with fear and desperation, she wondered how she'd cope if he were to die. Shaking away momentary tears, Marlee tried not to think such thoughts. Fate couldn't be so cruel as to rob her of love after all she'd been through to find it.

When she arrived at the clinic, she found Gabriel by his brother's bedside. He glanced up at her, and then shook his head.

For a heart-stopping minute, she thought that Lucas was

dead. Everything began to spin, and her knees almost buckled.

"No, you misunderstand," Gabriel said, grabbing her by the shoulders. "The doctors say we have to wait it out. Shadow was lucid long enough to tell me he was poisoned by corn-cockle seeds. The doctors told me how to treat the symptoms, but that's all that can be done at this point."

Marlee felt Lucas's pulse. He was weak, and his breathing was shallow. Her knowledge of herbs told her that if he went into a coma, death would follow from respiratory arrest.

"He needs to be in a hospital," she said.

"There's no way to get him there. The road is completely blocked. It could be hours before weather permits a helicopter flight. And he'd be dead from exposure to the cold and climate in his condition before he could be carried over that rock slide to an ambulance on the other side," Gabriel answered. "His only chance is right here in Four Winds."

"Will you give me a moment alone with him?"

Gabriel looked at her, and with a heaviness of spirit she'd never seen in any of the Blackhorse brothers, he stood, and walked outside.

Marlee took out the raven carving from her pocket, then, taking Lucas's hand, pressed it between their palms. She'd never believed in magic, nor trusted in the power of love, but now they were her only hope.

She closed her eyes and concentrated. She remembered what the peddler had said about the wish, and pleaded with all the strength of her yearning heart for the life of the only man she'd ever loved.

When she opened her eyes, Lucas remained still. There was no sign of improvement. It hadn't worked. She chided herself for ever thinking it could. But she wouldn't give up, no matter what. Her gaze stayed on Lucas, tears streaming down her face. "Lucas, please find your way back to me. I can't come to you, my love. You'll have to find me.

I'm here.'' She pressed his hand to her heart and, as her tears moistened his fingertips, she felt him stir.

She watched him move again, afraid to even breathe. "It's Marlee, I'm here. Fight with all your strength and find your way home, Lucas," she whispered.

He opened his eyes slowly. "Hello, my heart," he managed to croak in a weak voice. "I heard your voice calling me, guiding me back." He squeezed her hand gently. "I'm here."

"I love you," she said past the enormous lump at her throat.

He smiled. "I know." He picked up the carving of the raven that had dropped onto the blanket covering him. "What's this doing here?"

She picked it up quickly. "It's my good-luck charm," she said. "I figured we needed all the help we could get."

Hearing footsteps behind her, Marlee turned her head and saw Gabriel had returned. Relief was etched clearly on his face. "Let me talk to my brother. When I'm finished, you and I will have to have a few words of our own. This isn't over. Someone out there has gone to a lot of trouble to make our lives miserable, and now it's our turn to return the favor."

Marlee stood up and glanced down at Lucas. His eyes were filled with tenderness as he gazed at her.

"You'll need to get some rest now," she said softly, then looked at Gabriel. "Take it easy with him."

"I'll transport him to my house, and Tree will watch over him there. He'll be safe. Nobody gets past my little brother."

Thinking of the huge, youngest Blackhorse brother, Marlee nodded. "I have no doubt of that."

As Gabriel sat down and began talking to Lucas, Marlee allowed herself one final glance. Lucas was getting stronger by the minute; she could see it. Knowing that he was going to be okay was all that really mattered to her now. She wasn't sure if the carving had made the difference, or if it had been the power of love, or if it had all just been a coincidence. But in her heart, she knew her actions had sealed her fate. Lucas had heard her words pleading for his return, and before long he'd figure out how she tried to use the carving. It had been an act of desperation, one she wasn't sure had worked, but it had also revealed the only secret she'd still kept from him. She wasn't at all sure how he'd react when he realized that still another secret had continued to exist between them until now.

Marlee could try to tell him the truth, that she'd never really taken the peddler's promise of one wish seriously until fear had forced her hand. Yet she wasn't sure he'd ever understand or forgive her for not telling him about it.

She touched the scar on her face gingerly. It was now raised and tender, and she didn't need a mirror to know that it was probably bloodred again. Marlee tilted down the rearview mirror and stared at her reflection, her eyes riveted on the scar. It wasn't red, as she'd thought. If anything, it was less noticeable than usual. Yet inside, she felt weary and scarred in a different way. Although she'd come to terms with her past, some experiences left permanent scars that went so deep they couldn't be seen with the naked eye.

Her biggest mistake had been to discount the power and the magic of love. Lucas had been right when he'd said that she'd forgotten how to trust. That would now cost her the love of the man she loved.

She regretted all the time she had spent protecting herself from the one emotion that could have healed her, in whose light scars disappeared as darkness gave way before the sun. Now it was too late. Her soul had been made whole through love, but it would shatter again as she lost what mattered most. And this time, she had only herself to blame.

MARLEE DROVE around town aimlessly, not knowing what to do next or where to go. Yet she knew she wouldn't leave Four Winds until she faced whatever happened now between Lucas and her. The thought of seeing him every day, and knowing their time had come and gone, made sadness swirl around her like a heavy cloud. She'd always known, in an intellectual way, that losing love could hurt, but she had never dreamed that the devastation could be so total.

She wanted to fight to keep Lucas, but she had no idea how. She could beg him to forgive her, and it was possible he would, but whether he'd be able to love her, to trust her again, was something else entirely. She didn't believe that was possible, after all the secrets she'd kept from him.

She stopped at Charley's gas station and filled up the five-dollar maximum allowed during this crisis. A few people glanced in her direction, but it was late, and in the darkness no one saw her crying. A sign on the self-serve pump said the lane in the highway had just been cleared again. She could leave, it seemed, but why should she? She had no place else to go. Marlee paid for the gas by leaving five one-dollar bills on the counter for Charley, who was in the bay underneath somebody's pickup.

She slipped back behind the wheel, and was reaching for the ignition key when someone threw open the passenger's door and slipped inside.

Marlee jumped and stared at Alex. "What the heck do you think—?"

"Shut up. No more games, Marlee. I know the peddler gave you something. I've know since the day I saw him at your house. I want it *now!*"

"The carving? It's nothing, just a pretty raven. It's not worth anything."

"Yeah? Well, I'll be the one to decide that. Hand it over."

When Marlee hesitated, Alex pulled a small pistol from his jacket pocket. "I know how to shoot this. Ask Jake if you don't believe me," he said with a cruel smile. "Don't make me do it again. I've already burned all my bridges in this stinking town. I'm sure Lucas told you I'm the one responsible for the illnesses here. After shooting Jake and poisoning Lucas, killing you wouldn't be that big a deal. Don't push your luck.''

"I wouldn't dream of it,'' Marlee snapped. Reaching into her purse, she pulled out the raven carving. "Here. It won't do you any good, you know. It has no powers. It isn't like the bowl or the rug.''

"I heard what the peddler said." He glanced around. "I bugged your house. I bought the bugs to get better stories, but this was the best of all. I heard the peddler say the carving grants one wish. If it turns out to work only for you, then it'll be your job to make my wish for me—if you want to stay alive, that is," he said, pressing the gun to her side.

"What makes you think I haven't used that one wish already?"

"Your lifestyle hasn't changed, and you still have that scar," he countered. "That does puzzle me, though. Why didn't you use it before and get out of this nowhere town? It can't be much fun looking at yourself in the mirror.''

"I probably have an easier time of it than you do," she retorted.

Alex shrugged. "I'm reaching out for what I want in life. You've spent so much time hiding, you've forgotten how to live.''

The truth in his words stung. She wasn't sure if she'd get out of this alive, but if she did, she meant to rebuild her life, not just mark an endless parade of days. If her love for Lucas was not to be, she still owed it to herself to go back to the work she loved, to embrace life and build a future.

"I've had it with this town, personally," Alex continued. "I came here hoping that a miracle would happen and I'd finally find a way to make something out of my life. But all I've found here is frustration and more broken dreams. Four Winds owes me big time, and you're the one who's going to help me get paid."

"Give me back the carving. I'll make the wish for you. Then you can get out of my car, and out of my life."

"No way. We're leaving town together right now, while the road is still open. I know the sheriff found his brother, and that the medic is going to live to squeal on me, so it's only a matter of time before the law comes gunning for me. But any roadblocks he sets up won't be on the lookout for your car, so you're my ticket out of here. Get going." Alex shifted nervously in the seat, his eyes darting all around.

Marlee saw Charley inside the garage moving around, but she couldn't cry out. She had no doubt that Alex was desperate enough to shoot her at the slightest provocation.

She pushed down on the accelerator pedal several times, trying to flood the engine. It worked. The smell of gasoline filled the car, and although the engine turned over, it wouldn't start. "Look, this is a very old car. You could do better for yourself by stealing another vehicle. I'm not sure how far this bucket of mine is going to take us."

"Try the engine again."

"Why are you doing this? You can't really hope to get away. Where could you hide, now that the sheriff knows what you did to the newspaper ink?"

Alex just laughed. "It's too bad my plot to frame you failed. I was rather hoping the town would go after you a lot harder. Then it would have been easier to trick you into giving me the carving willingly in exchange for my help getting out of town. I'm not sure if my forcing you to give it to me will make a difference, but *you* better hope not."

"You scattered the seeds around the pump house?"

"Sure. I did anything I could to shift suspicion to you."

She said nothing, but continued to try to flood the engine.

"Stop that," he said. "Keep your foot off the gas pedal. Just turn the key."

Marlee felt sick to her stomach. This man had almost killed Lucas, and now he was going to use her to make his escape. She couldn't let that happen.

He pressed the barrel of his gun against her face. "I know you've always been bothered by that scar. You know what? Unless you get this car started, you'll never have to worry about it again."

She heard the click as he pulled back the hammer. "Get that thing out of my face," she said, keeping her voice steady.

He drew the gun back and laughed. "You have more courage than I gave you credit for. But don't push me. Get this car going now, or I'll go shoot Charley. Would you like that?"

Marlee's car spluttered and then started. She wouldn't let this maniac get away. Though Alex didn't know it, she was about to give the Four Winds legacy a helping hand.

Chapter Nineteen

Lucas felt his strength returning with each breath he took. Although Gabriel wanted him to stay in bed, he knew he had to get going. He'd heard Marlee making her wish, pleading that he be restored to health. Her love had bathed him in a warm light filled with promise, and it was the strength of her feelings for him that had shown him the way back.

He wasn't sure what part the carving she'd brought along had played in restoring his health, if any. Maybe it had all been part of the blessing Flinthawk had bestowed on their town so many years ago, promising that no evil would ever prevail here.

The only thing he knew for sure was that Marlee loved him. Though she had kept yet another secret from him, the love he felt for her was so strong, so binding, that nothing else seemed important in comparison. If anything, through her actions she'd tested the strength of their feelings. If she had truly believed that the carving had power, the one shining truth that had come out of that moment was that she'd used the wish to help him, not herself.

"I've got the state police manning a roadblock on the only open road out of town. If Alex tries to drive out of Four Winds, we'll catch him. Now, let me get you over to my house. Tree will keep an eye on you there."

Lucas sat up slowly, surprised by how quickly his

strength was returning. "What if Alex doesn't try to leave town?"

"Why would he stay?"

"Think about this. Earl Larrabee wouldn't have had any reason to bug Marlee's home, he already knew who she was. He'd tracked her here. That means Alex must have been the one to plant the bug. That man must have hated Four Winds with everything he had. Look at his life here. He wanted to be the one who ran the paper. He wanted respect. Then, when he finally gets his chance during Ralph Montoya's absence, there's no real news except Bradford the buffalo and the early storm.

"But he spots the peddler's van in Marlee's driveway, or followed it there, more likely. He thinks this is his big chance to make a name for himself. He bugs Marlee's home, and figures that the real story will lie in whatever the peddler gives Marlee. But she refuses to tell him or anyone else what that is, or even admit a gift exists. What he wants most of all is a once-in-a-lifetime news story. He may have been waiting for the peddler's return all this time, and kept an eye on me, knowing I'm the only Blackhorse brother who hadn't been affected yet by the old man's visits. Why else would he have purchased an electronic bug and a tracking device beforehand, unless it was for something like this?

"But the peddler thing turns out to be no news because this time nothing happens, so he decides to punish Four Winds and come up with a big story all at the same time. This 'epidemic' sold a lot of papers, and he must have gained perverse pleasure knowing he was spreading an illness with his very words, at least in the ink. He could even select who got sick by how he distributed the papers. Some had the poison, some didn't. That explains the labels on the newspaper bags, which he'd never used before. He knew it would point suspicion toward those who didn't get sick. But ultimately his style of reporting gets him even less respect than before. Alex is still Alex, and he hated the lack of attention people paid him.

"At that point, he's still got one chance. The peddler's gift to Marlee—and that one magic wish. It's the only thing that Four Winds can give him now, and he figures it's his just dues. But Marlee's standing in his way."

Gabriel stood. "I'll go find her right now."

"We both will," Lucas said, getting to his feet.

"Alex is not your responsibility."

Lucas stepped around his brother, surprised that he felt as strong as he did after being so ill. "You're right, Alex is *your* problem. I'm not concerned about him. I'm going after Marlee."

Lucas went to the boardinghouse first, but neither Marlee nor her car were there. He drove around, determined to find her. As he came within sight of the police roadblock at the rock slide, he was surprised to see her parked by the side of the road. Then he noticed Alex was with her. Unfortunately Alex saw him, too.

Lucas turned abruptly, but it was the wrong move on the icy road, and he nearly spun completely around. By the time he was back in control and headed in the right direction, Marlee's car was racing back toward town.

Lucas didn't dare take his eyes off Marlee. Determination and fear filled him. If Alex harmed Marlee, no hole on earth would be deep enough for him to crawl into.

Marlee was blood of his blood and bone of his bone now. No one, not even his brothers, had ever been so close, so much a part of him. "Hang on, my heart. You're not in this fight alone."

Ahead Marlee turned off onto a dirt road that led into the mountains. Lucas raced the Blazer down to the turnoff. He had just reached the road when he saw Gabriel's vehicle approaching.

Lucas stuck his head out the window and in a few sentences filled his brother in.

"I'll call Tree. You try to keep them in sight, and I'll see if I can cut them off," Gabriel said.

Lucas nodded and roared off, his eyes focused on the forest road ahead. He'd have help now. Lucas knew there were few things that could stand against the Blackhorse brothers, and nothing had the power to keep him from the woman he loved.

Less than five minutes later, his cellular phone rang, and Lucas heard his youngest brother's voice.

"I'm in this with you," Joshua said, letting Lucas know he'd joined the chase. "My guess is that Alex will try to go through the south pass. It's the only unblocked road, and though it might take hours, a car could possibly get through."

"They won't make it that far," Lucas said. "I can see her car up ahead."

To his surprise, Lucas saw Marlee's sedan slowing down. It didn't make any sense until he noticed the peddler's old van ahead, blocking the road. Marlee skidded to a stop.

Alex hauled Marlee out of the car, keeping her in front of him and his back to the sedan. "Old peddler," Alex shouted. "I want you to look into that bag of tricks of yours, and find something that will make it possible for me to get out of town."

Alex tied Marlee's hands to the car door handle with his belt. Then he glanced back at Lucas, who had stepped out after blocking the road behind Marlee's car.

"If you come any closer, I'll shoot her. Clear?" he said, stroking Marlee's cheek with the barrel of his gun.

Lucas stopped cold. "You can't get away, Alex. Give it up."

"The game's not over yet, Blackhorse, not by a long shot."

The peddler waved for Alex to approach. "I'm an old man. I won't fight you. If you want my wares, then come over here and pick something out for yourself."

As Alex turned and hurried toward the van, Lucas met the peddler's gaze. The old man smiled. Suddenly a thick cloud of dark gray smoke billowed from the van, obscuring everything around them. Three shots rang out, then all they could hear was Alex cursing.

Lucas ran toward Marlee blindly, more afraid of the peddler's magic and the cost it exacted than of Alex and his gun. The air shimmered around him. He wasn't sure what was real and what was illusion.

Lucas reached out, sensing Marlee wasn't far. Then he felt the warmth of her body near him, and his hands tangled in her hair, skimming its softness. She was here, with him. He untied her quickly. For that one brief eternity, nothing else mattered to him except that she was okay. He wanted this woman in his life, to love, to take care of, to share the things that mattered and the things that didn't. And he needed to tell her so.

"I won't let you go without fighting for you, my heart," he whispered as he guided her to the safety of his vehicle, hoping to reach it before the smoke cleared. "You're mine. It's as it was meant to be."

Instinct guided him through the worst areas where he couldn't even see his own hands, much less the car tracks. Feeling for the door handle, he helped her inside, then followed her.

Alex suddenly stopped cursing, and was deathly silent for a moment. Then Lucas heard a curious crackle in the air, and the sound of a siren rose up around him like the cry of an angry war god. As the smoke cleared, Lucas saw that the peddler and his van were gone. Alex was standing alone in the middle of the road. He was looking around fearfully, waving his pistol, yet he didn't make a sound. Then Gabriel's Jeep came into view, and Joshua's truck appeared from the other side, locking him in.

As Gabriel stepped out of the Jeep, Alex made a run for the woods, his bad leg slowing him down. Joshua cut him off before Alex could get far. Picking him off the ground by the collar, Joshua carried him back to Gabriel.

Lucas and Marlee went to join Gabriel as he handcuffed Alex to the back seat of the Jeep.

Gabriel grinned at his middle brother. "Looks like you finally caught her. The question is, now what are you going to do with her?" He gave Marlee a wink.

"I'm sure I'll think of something," Lucas said, smiling down at Marlee, his arm draped over her shoulders possessively.

"Where did the peddler go?" Marlee asked. "I'd like to talk to him about that magic trick of his."

"Wouldn't we all?" Joshua said. "He's a part of Four Winds. I expect he'll be back someday. If we're lucky, we may get to talk to him then."

As Gabriel took Alex off to jail, and Joshua drove away to rejoin Nydia and Lanie, Lucas pulled Marlee into his arms. "It was thoughts of you that kept me alive, kept me fighting, when I was locked up in that shed."

Marlee leaned against him, savoring his touch. "Then we're even, because you've given me back my life. For the first time in years, I want to do more than just mark the passage of days. You don't have to trust me again—I don't expect that—but I hope that someday you will forgive me."

Lucas continued to hold Marlee. He had no idea how, but he had to find a way to make Marlee believe he had faith in their love. When a heart was filled with love, there was no room for fear or the need for caution, or room for doubt.

Lucas groaned as his cellular phone rang, but ethically knew he couldn't ignore it. Hearing the news on the other end, he smiled. It was definitely a time for miracles.

Lucas closed up the phone and smiled at Marlee. "It seems our presence is required right away."

"*Our* presence? What are you talking about?"

"Four Winds is about to get a new resident, and Lanie wants you to handle the delivery. Do you suppose you'll want an extra pair of hands to help out, or maybe even a cheering section, 'cause I'd sure like to be there when my new niece or nephew is born.''

SIX HOURS LATER, Marlee took the small blanket-wrapped bundle and presented it to Gabriel. The look on the baby's father's face made a piece of her heart melt away.

Lucas stood close beside Marlee as his brother and sister-in-law celebrated their new daughter's arrival. ''You were magnificent, my heart,'' Lucas whispered in her ear. ''This work is a hard-earned gift that's rightfully yours, and you obviously love it. It also insures you'll always be needed here in Four Winds.''

Holding her tiny daughter, Lanie looked up, her eyes weary but filled with joy. ''Shadow is a great medic, but having a midwife around would be wonderful. I hope you're planning to set up an office here in town.''

Marlee smiled. ''Already planning on the next baby, are you?''

Lanie laughed. ''Well, my daughter will need brothers and sisters.''

''Have you settled on a name for her?'' Marlee asked.

''Hope. It's what Four Winds offers everyone whose motives are right.''

Marlee nodded. ''It's a good name.'' Giving the child a kiss, Marlee walked outside, leaving the family to celebrate their new addition.

Lucas followed her a moment later. ''Listen to what your heart is telling you.'' He turned her to face him. ''We belong to each other. Four Winds has offered us a gift, but we both have to accept it.''

Marlee fought the tears that stung her eyes. ''I do believe in your love for me. We've come too far for me to doubt you.'' Deliberately she moved her hair aside and touched her scar. ''But are you really ready to live with this reminder of my past, waking to it every morning, seeing it every night?''

He pulled something out of his pocket, then took one step back. "If my face was scarred like yours, is that all you'd see when you looked at me?" In a flash, Lucas flicked open the blade of his knife, then pressed the steel to his face. A trickle of blood began where the tip dug into his skin.

With an anguished cry, Marlee pulled his hand away, then sighed with relief, seeing the wound wasn't deep. "Maybe it's time to stop thinking and just let our love guide us," she said, stepping into his arms.

He held her tightly against him. "I couldn't have put it better myself, my heart."

Lucas heard his brother inside the house laughing and celebrating with his wife and new daughter. It was a time for healing and new beginnings in Four Winds. Most important of all, it was a time for love.